HIGHROAD TO ADVENTURE

"*Turistas?*" he asked. "The road is closed to traffic, señor."

HIGHROAD
TO
ADVENTURE

WHAT HAPPENED TO TOD MORAN
WHEN HE TRAVELED SOUTH
INTO OLD MEXICO

BY

HOWARD PEASE

Illustrated by FRANK DOBIAS

JUNIOR LITERARY GUILD
and
DOUBLEDAY, DORAN & CO., INC.
NEW YORK

PRINTED AT THE *Country Life Press*, GARDEN CITY, N. Y., U. S. A.

Contents

CONTENTS

HIGHROAD TO ADVENTURE

CHAPTER I

A Call from Captain Jarvis

Whenever the tramp steamer *Araby* arrived in her home port of San Francisco, young Tod Moran, third mate, always put up at his brother's home, where a room awaited him. Neil Moran, tied to a desk in a shipping office, liked to listen to his younger brother's tales of far ports of the world; and Sheila, Neil's wife, liked to fuss over Tod's health and his diet and his clothes.

Sheila was fussing over him as usual this morning as she helped him pack. "This will be your first vacation in years," she said, "so enjoy yourself. But I do hope you'll be careful on the road. You've never driven much, you know. Don't think that a highway is as free of traffic as a sea lane."

"No need to worry about me, Sheila." Tod turned

from his leather bag, open on the dining-room table. "I've practiced driving that Ford for two full days and already I'm an expert. Off for the open road—that's me. For years, don't forget, I've wanted a real vacation— away from the sea. I'm tired of ships and sailors and foreign ports."

"Really?" Sheila glanced up from Tod's suit case, her delicate eyebrows raised in disbelief.

Tod nodded firmly. "It's true. I want to see inland country for a change—not just seaports, all of them alike. This time I'm heading east on the highway. No salt air at all." His voice dropped lower and his gray eyes took on a dreamy look of anticipation. "I'll be breathing mountain air when I drive over the Sierras—and desert air all through Colorado."

"Aren't you a trifle mixed in your geography, Tod?" Sheila's charming smile flashed for an instant as she looked at her young brother-in-law. "I should think you'd be breathing mountain air in Colorado, too."

Tod flung out his hands in a gesture of resignation. "You see? I don't even know my own country. Why, I'm more familiar with Shanghai and Marseilles and Havana than I am with Denver or St. Louis or Chicago. Well, this time I'm out to explore these United States —and nothing is going to stop me."

The sharp ringing of the telephone from the hall interrupted his impassioned speech. Sheila said quickly, "I'll answer. It's probably Neil."

A Call From Captain Jarvis

Tod crossed to a window and glanced out. His brother's small home, built on the side of one of San Francisco's steepest hills, boasted a fine view of the bay. As Tod's gaze swept along the curving line of docks he frowned. For a whole month he'd get away from water fronts like this. There was nothing to hold him here, now that his ship was in dry dock for overhauling and his ship's master, Captain Tom Jarvis, visiting friends in Detroit.

His pulse beat faster as his thoughts turned to the Ford which his savings had bought from a used-car dealer. At the very first glance, his heart had gone out to that car. For it was a convertible coupé recently turned in by a college student who had owned it less than two years, and it still retained a certain air of smartness. Although obviously not new, its dark red body was marred only slightly by a few scratches on one rear fender. Furthermore, its motor was running with a quiet purring sound and its radio was playing entrancing music. Instantly Tod had seen himself in imagination rolling along a country road with the top lowered and the sunshine beating warmly down upon his head, while the latest dance hit made an undertone to his own voice raised in song. It was an attractive picture. He had bought the car at once.

Neil had dampened his enthusiasm by saying, "University students are usually rather hard on cars, don't you think, Tod? It would have been wiser to have had an expert look it over before you bought it. Suppose it turns out to be a lemon?"

Although Tod's knowledge of automobiles was hazy, he was sure that Neil knew even less. Why, this car would go places. Just wait and see. "It has a radio, too," he pointed out.

"Oh, so that's it." His brother's tone was caustic. "It was a radio you were buying, not a car."

Even now, as he remembered that remark, Tod's face reddened. For there was some truth in Neil's remark. That radio had been the deciding factor.

"Oh, Tod!" Sheila's voice came to him from the hall. "The Blakemore Steamship office is on the phone. It's for you."

Puzzled, Tod turned from the window. His brows drew together in a frown as he went toward the hall. "I don't like this one bit," he said to Sheila. "The boss told me good-by yesterday."

Sheila smiled. "Probably he wants to warn you about speed laws on land."

Tod grinned and picked up the telephone. "Hello."

"Mr. Tod Moran? One moment, please." It was a girl speaking. "Mr. Blakemore wishes to talk to you."

Tod flung an amused glance through the doorway to Sheila. "It's Mr. Blakemore," he whispered hoarsely. "Maybe you're right."

Over the wire came a low deep voice. "Moran? Jim Blakemore. I was afraid you might have left already.

A Call From Captain Jarvis

Could you run down to the office right away? Yes, it's extremely important. Sorry to interrupt your vacation."

"Interrupt?" Tod's voice rose while his spirits fell. "You mean, Mr. Blakemore, that——"

"Yes, something very urgent has come up. I've another job for you. No, I can't tell you over the wire. Could you be here at the office within fifteen minutes?"

Tod gulped. His tone was dead. "I'll be right down."

"Good. In fifteen minutes, then."

Slowly Tod put down the instrument. With laggard steps he went back to the dining room where his sister-in-law was folding socks into one corner of his suit case.

"Don't bother to pack any more, Sheila. My vacation's off."

For a moment Sheila regarded him in dismay. It distressed her to see Tod's well-built figure droop like this and his gray eyes fill with resentment. In spite of her former words of warning she as well as Neil had been eager to have Tod spend a full month on the highways that stretched east—if that was Tod's idea of a vacation. "You mean," she asked, "Mr. Blakemore is ordering you aboard ship right away?"

"I don't know yet. It can't be the *Araby*. Maybe it's some other ship." Tod sighed, then a wan smile touched his lips. "I had a hunch my plans were too good to be true."

Sheila frowned. "But, Tod, this isn't fair! If I were

you I simply wouldn't stand for it. Tell Mr. Blakemore it's too late to change your plans now."

"Oh, sure." Tod reached for his hat—a new hat he would probably never use again. "I'll enter the office leaning on a stick. I'll tell him the doctor is afraid I'm about to have a nervous breakdown. Then I'll put in a call for an ambulance to bring me home."

Sheila threw back her head and laughed. "Oh, Tod, you're the limit. You make me laugh when, in fact, I'm terribly sorry." She came toward him, her face sober. "Just the same, I'd be firm. And anyway, I intend to finish your packing while you're gone."

"That's the stuff, Sheila." Tod's head lifted. His eyes flashed and his wide mouth stiffened into lines of determination. "I'll be back here inside an hour and I'll go ahead with my plan. Nothing that Mr. Blakemore can say will change my mind."

"Exactly." Sheila nodded. "I'll have your lunch ready, too, so you can start right out. If you intend to spend the night with Gregg Richards at his aunt's in Sacramento you'll have to get going. You may have a puncture or two on the way."

Tod clapped his hat on his sandy hair. "Those tires will take me to Timbuctoo and back—and you know it."

"I hope so." Sheila's tone was doubtful. "Just the same, I wish you had bought a new car instead. Neil says the upkeep on an old motor will eat up the difference in price."

A Call From Captain Jarvis

"That sounds just like Neil." Tod stamped toward the door, then paused. "You know how he is—a good business man and all that rot, but too careful. Too full of fears for the future. Nobody needs to worry about me. Well, I'm off to navigate San Francisco traffic. See you in half an hour."

In the garage underneath the house Tod stepped into his dark red car, settled himself behind the wheel, and glanced with fond approval at the instrument panel with its elaborate line of gadgets. Let Neil call her a lemon if he wanted; she sure was a beauty. Why, just look at her helm! And her long bow was polished till it shone. With a happy sigh he started the motor and slowly backed the car out into the street. The top was down and the sun shining. A moment later he was plunging in low gear down the hill toward the water front.

All the way along the docks and up through the traffic of California Street he mulled over what he would say to Mr. Blakemore. Sympathetic but firm—that must be his attitude. As third officer of the steamer *Araby* he had certain rights. A horn shrilled close by. He jerked the wheel, missed another car by inches. It was a confounded shame he admired the president of his company so much. If he only disliked the man, and disliked his ship as well, then this whole affair would be quite simple.

At the Marine Tower he swung his car down the grade into the basement garage, turned it over to an attendant and went quickly over to the elevator. On the nineteenth floor he stepped out a few seconds later directly into the reception room of the Blakemore Steamship Company.

The girl at the telephone switchboard looked up as he paused at the counter. "Go right in, Mr. Moran. Mr. Blakemore is expecting you."

With his hat in his hand Tod pushed back the gate and swung across the office past several typists who glanced his way while their fingers continued to dance over the keys. He knocked on a door marked President and entered.

"Good morning, Moran." Mr. Blakemore spoke from across his wide flat desk. He was a tall handsome man with white hair. He got to his feet, extended his hand in greeting, then drew up a chair beside his desk. "It was a great relief to find you hadn't yet left town. Sit down. Your bags all packed?"

"Yes, sir. All ready to take to the highway. I planned to shove off right after lunch."

Mr. Blakemore dropped into his swivel chair and leaned back, his thoughtful eyes fixed upon the young third mate. "I'm sorry to disrupt your plans. But you see, Captain Jarvis got me on the telephone half an hour ago."

"Captain Tom? Did he call from Detroit?"

"No—New York. I might as well admit to you that I threw a monkey wrench into his vacation two days

A Call From Captain Jarvis

ago. He's sailing today for Vera Cruz—as a passenger."

Tod sat up with a start. For Captain Tom Jarvis to sail on any ship as a passenger was so incredible that he could scarcely believe his ears.

"Surprised?" Mr. Blakemore asked with a smile. "Captain Jarvis is going to Mexico City on business for me. He's helped us out on some rather intricate affairs before, you know, and I saw at once that he was the very man for this case. When he arrives in Mexico City he'll need a few letters of introduction and copies of certain business negotiations. I'd like you to take them to him. A passenger liner sails in the morning for West coast ports. I've already booked your passage. You can get off at Acapulco and go overland to Mexico City."

Tod shifted his weight in his chair. His new second-hand car with its shining red body and its convertible top was vanishing in a cloud of mist. He was ordered out to sea again—and to make the pill more bitter, he was ordered to go as a passenger. By thunder, it was just too much! The moment had come to be sympathetic but firm.

Before he could speak, Mr. Blakemore leaned forward and said, "I told Tom Jarvis of your plans. All the necessary papers were nearly ready to go by mail. But Tom wouldn't listen. He said he had a mighty good idea he could use you, that he would need your help."

Sudden interest glowed on Tod's blunt features. "It's that kind of job?"

Highroad To Adventure

Mr. Blakemore nodded his white head. "Yes, it's that kind of job. Of course, I don't intend to insist, Moran. I realize you've been planning this cross-country trip for some time, though how you figure to get back here inside of a month is beyond me. I wouldn't have been surprised if you'd ended up in jail for speeding."

The ghost of a smile touched Tod's lips, but his voice was steady. "I've made plans to stay tonight with Gregg Richards in Sacramento. I've written Stuart Ormsby that I'll see him in Washington, D.C. And Bruce Denton is expecting me in New York in ten days."

"I understand." Mr. Blakemore spoke slowly. "Suppose I simply wire Tom that you can't go?"

A feeling of uncertainty swept through Tod. Never yet had he failed Captain Tom, but—hang it all—a vacation was supposed to be a vacation. He wanted to see something of his own country just now—not Mexico. While he wavered and his eyes followed a gull swooping close to the windows of the Tower, a buzzer sounded.

Mr. Blakemore picked up the phone on his desk. "Yes? Captain Jarvis? Connect him at once."

He looked up. "Your skipper has just put in a call." He waited, sitting back in his chair, the instrument in his hand. "Hello. Tom? Yes, he's here now. Yes, right in this office. All right." He held out the phone. "Captain Jarvis wants to talk to you."

Tod drew up his chair and his hand closed round the telephone. "Hello."

A Call From Captain Jarvis

"Joe Macaroni?" Across three thousand miles came the well-known voice, deep, strong, friendly. "It was lucky we caught you."

On the instant Tod felt himself under the spell of that forceful personality. "Hello, Captain Tom." He swallowed. "How's everything?"

Again came the well-known voice. "Joe Macaroni, I'm sailing in the morning for Vera Cruz, then going by train to Mexico City. I want you to meet me there on the fifteenth of the month."

"Sure thing." Tod's tone was eager. "I'll be glad to. If you can put up with going as a passenger, I guess I can, too."

"Good. Did you buy a car yet?"

"Yes. I got it yesterday—a secondhand Ford. She's a beauty."

"Now, listen, Third. I know how you're feeling—disappointed and all that. But there's no great rush. You have a whole week to get to Mexico City. Why don't you drive down in your car?"

"All the way?"

"Why not? I've been looking up the details about the Pan-American Highway. It's in first-class shape. Only twenty-six hundred miles from San Francisco to Mexico City. Surely you could navigate that distance in seven or eight days?"

"Why, it'd be a cinch. This Ford can go places."

"I hope so. Remember, though, that I want a well and

strong third mate to meet me there. No excuses for broken bones. So take your time. I'd appreciate it, too, if that car of yours is still running when you get there. We could use it. I'll be at the Hotel Geneve on May fifteenth."

"The Hotel Geneve? I'll be there, Captain Tom."

"I knew you wouldn't fail me. Has Jim Blakemore told you what it's all about?"

"Not yet."

"The affair may not be as simple as Blakemore thinks. It has certain possibilities—interesting possibilities. Don't come directly to the Geneve. Register at some other hotel, then phone me."

"Careful is the word?"

"Exactly. Until the fifteenth, then. Good-by—and enjoy your trip."

"You bet. Good-by, Captain Tom."

A click sounded on the wire. Tod put back the phone and looked up to meet the smiling gaze of Mr. Blakemore.

"So you'll go, Moran?"

"Yes, I'll go. Captain Tom suggests I drive down. He says we could use the car."

"He's right. There's a silver mine south of Mexico City where he must go. It's near a little town called Tasco." Mr. Blakemore's eyes glowed with warmth. "It will be a sort of vacation, with all your expenses paid. Even so, I appreciate your giving up your own plans to help me out like this."

A Call From Captain Jarvis

"But I'm not giving up my plans entirely," Tod pointed out. "If I can drive all the way there in my car I'll have a motor trip away from the sea—and, after all, that's what I wanted. Maybe some other time I'll have a chance to see Chicago and Washington." His glance swept out a window, then came back. "Where will I enter Mexico?"

"At the border town of Laredo, in Texas. I made the trip myself about eighteen months ago. You'll enjoy it, though you'll have to be careful to plan each day's run so you'll find accommodations for overnight stops. But I'll send a clerk to the automobile association for maps and information." Mr. Blakemore leaned forward. "Listen, Moran. It's only fair that you should know something about this job that Captain Jarvis has taken on. It revolves around a silver mine in which I have invested rather heavily. The mine manager, Martin Welch, is now in the States. In fact he was here in San Francisco yesterday and will remain on the Coast for a visit of several weeks. He reported to me that things are going badly with American business interests in Mexico. The Mexican government, he says, is about to take over—to expropriate —all industries owned by foreigners, and the mining people are alarmed. They see a situation similar to the one that occurred when the oil properties were expropriated —the American and British oil companies apparently lose all their wells, all their equipment, and in return are given promises to pay small amounts of money that the government hasn't got. Welch strongly advises me to sell before this happens—and to sell at a great loss. Probably he's right, but I thought it would be well to investigate before taking such drastic action. That's why I got in touch with Captain Jarvis. I can trust him absolutely."

"Much money involved?" Tod asked.

"Nearly a hundred thousand."

"That's plenty." Tod nodded. "When will your letters of introduction be ready?"

"Within two hours."

"These other papers concerning the mine are valuable, Mr. Blakemore? What if they got lost?"

"They are not valuable in that sense at all, Moran. Merely copies that could be replaced if necessary, though of course it would take some time to send you others—and the time element is extremely important. The letters of introduction are to certain people high in political circles in Mexico, people who can put Captain Jarvis on the track of political developments down there. Without these letters and papers Tom wouldn't get very far. And you must both be back here to take out the *Araby* four weeks from now. That means you will have to work fast down there in Mexico. So you see the necessity of your arriving there safely and on time. When can you leave?"

"Right after lunch."

"Call back at one o'clock. I won't be here, but I'll see that everything is ready for you. The letters and papers will be in a brief case. Road maps and information, too. Draw expense money from the cashier. Better put most of it in traveler's checks." He held out his hand. "I trust you'll enjoy this trip so much that you'll forget we disrupted your plans."

"Oh, this trip will be fun, Mr. Blakemore. When Captain Tom is on a job like this, something interesting always happens."

Mr. Blakemore smiled. "Not on this job, I hope." He accompanied Tod to the door, flung it open, and walked with him across to the counter. "Will this be your first trip to Mexico?"

"I've put in at Acapulco, but that's only another port."

"You'll like Mexico City. It always reminds me of Paris. And Tasco, where the mine is located, is a little town that you might find perched on a hillside in southern Spain. A charming place—Tasco."

Mr. Blakemore paused as his glance crossed the counter to a man seated in a chair, waiting. "Ah, Welch! I thought you'd already left for Seattle. Come in."

Tod felt a momentary start of surprise as he went through the swinging gate. Welch! Could this be the Martin Welch who managed the mine in Mexico? He looked at the man with interest.

Mr. Welch rose and threw Tod a quick, searching glance. "My motor needed some work on it. Not surprising after that long trip from Tasco. So I'm waiting over for a couple of days."

Highroad To Adventure

Martin Welch, Tod saw, was a short, heavily built man nattily dressed in brown. His face was florid and his dark hair gray at the temples.

"Good-by," said Mr. Blakemore to Tod. "Come in, Welch."

Tod crossed to the elevator and pushed the button. Behind this sudden assignment, he knew, lay more than met the eye. Obviously Captain Jarvis was to carry out his investigation while Martin Welch was away. Was it possible the mine manager had heard the name Tasco mentioned?

CHAPTER II

Across the Border

I T WAS a tired but very contented Tod Moran who drove his convertible coupé four days later into the border town of Laredo, Texas.

His trip through the Southwest had been the sort of vacation he had wanted, though he seldom traveled with the top lowered as he had planned. For sea air and mild sunshine were things of the past. It was desert air now, hot and stifling under a sun that burned and blistered. Yet so fully was he enjoying every minute, nothing so far had dampened his spirits. When a rear tire blew out with a bang and the wheel of the car almost jerked out of his hands he was not even annoyed, though it meant changing the tire on a lonely road outside Phoenix with the blinding sun beating down without pity. And when late one night he made an unfortunate choice of an auto court he only grinned and fell into his bed with a thankful sigh. Live and learn, he told himself. He'd pick his lodgings with more care, especially after he crossed the border.

Now that he had reached Laredo, he drove through the narrow bustling streets with the feeling that more days of carefree travel lay ahead. Behind his dark sun glasses his gray eyes were keen and eager. His shirt sleeves were rolled above his elbows. On the seat beside him lay his coat and tie and new Panama hat. He threw the gear into second and slowly turned a corner. From information given him by the Blakemore office he knew exactly where to go—to a glorified service station which furnished travelers with the necessary papers for entering Mexico.

When he drove into the large corner station he found two other cars already parked, their passengers making ready to cross the border. In a little office an agent of the Mexican government met him with a smile of welcome. "How long do you expect to stay in Mexico, señor?"

"About a month. Not longer, I'm sure."

The man's typewriter clicked as he filled out the answers. With his black eyes on his work he asked, "Would you care to join the Mexican Automobile Association? In case of trouble on the road it would be of great assistance."

Across The Border

Tod shook his head. Always independent and perhaps too sure of himself, he saw no reason now why he should expect to ask for aid. "Oh, my car's in good shape," he replied.

"To have a good car for such a trip, señor, is exceedingly wise. The road, you see, is lonely most of the way. For miles you will not even see a thatched hut. A few words of caution, señor. Do not drink water unless it is bottled."

"I'm all prepared," Tod answered. "A couple of gallon bottles are in the trunk. I'll fill 'em here."

The olive-skinned official nodded with approval. "Eat sparingly of fresh foods, señor. Until you are certain of your cook, it would be better if you did not eat salads or butter—and of course do not touch fresh milk. Be certain that all food is well cooked."

"I'll remember."

"And do not stop between towns, though you will see soldiers now and then along the highway. They act as guards." The man jerked a card from his typewriter and handed it to Tod. "Would you like to change any money to Mexican currency?"

"If you will, please." Tod took out his bill fold, tore out a traveler's check and signed with a pen on the desk.

"Fifty American dollars, señor? That is really too much. It is only two and a half days between here and Mexico City and it is wise not to carry too many pesos on the trip."

"I'm sorry," Tod said, "but that's the smallest check I have."

The man turned to a safe and counted out so much paper money that Tod felt suddenly wealthy. "The rate of exchange is down, señor, so you will find food and lodging quite cheap. Will you be able to speak Spanish on the road?"

"Only a little I've picked up in California."

"Then take this booklet. Some maps, too. They may help you." He rose. "Good luck, señor. We are proud to have you travel down the Pan-American Highway. It is part of the new Mexico we are building."

Tod left the office with the feeling that the world was a friendly place. If this was a sample of Mexican courtesy, he was going to like this country south of the border.

The young American who was servicing the red coupé looked up from the battery at his approach. "She'll be ready in another half hour."

"Good. Then I'll eat lunch."

"First time across the border?" asked the youth.

"Yes. I'm going to Mexico City."

"Driving alone?"

"Sure."

"Well, take my advice and don't stop on the road for anyone who isn't in uniform. If anyone tries to stop you, run him down rather than slow up."

Tod looked down in astonishment. "You mean that?"

Across The Border

"Yes, sir. I sure do. And don't drive after dark."

Thoughtfully Tod crossed to a coffee shop. It was evident that this land south of the border was not the United States. And then he recalled that strange things happened too on lonely roads across New Mexico and Texas. Well, he'd watch his step. He was nobody's fool.

In the cool dim coffee shop he was soothed by the lunch he ordered—a tuna sandwich, a salad and a thick chocolate malt. If this was the last of such lunches for a month, he'd enjoy it to the final mouthful. When he came out again into the blinding sunlight his car was ready.

"Did you see your friend?" the young man asked as Tod paid him.

Surprise flashed across Tod's face. "What do you mean?"

"Why, Señor Gomez came out of his office with a man who was asking for you. I told them you were eating in the coffee shop. Didn't he join you there?"

"No."

"That's mighty funny. Maybe you better ask Gomez. He'll know."

Tod turned to the little office. The agent rose to greet him. "Something else, señor?"

"I just wanted to find out if anyone asked for me."

"Yes, certainly, señor. Surely you saw him."

"No." Puzzled, Tod shook his head.

"But he inquired for you, señor. He came into this

office not twenty minutes ago and said, 'Has Señor Moran from San Francisco crossed the border yet?' and I said, 'What bad luck! I fear he has just left.' But I went outside with him and there was your Ford being filled with oil. The boy told us you were eating. You did not see him?"

"No."

"But, señor, he went toward the coffee shop."

"Did you see him enter?"

The man shook his head. "It was rather warm and I had no hat, so I hurried back inside. Strange."

Tod glanced out the door. A sudden stir of hope went through him. Maybe Captain Jarvis had changed his mind about sailing to Vera Cruz as a passenger. Maybe instead he had taken a plane to Laredo to join him here. Expectant, Tod moved to the doorway. No tall familiar figure met his gaze.

His glance came back to the man behind the desk. "Was it a Captain Jarvis who asked for me?"

"No, señor. This was a Mexican."

Tod stared in astonishment. "But I don't know anyone here."

"This was a gentleman from Mexico City, señor."

A perplexed frown settled upon Tod's brows. "He told you? What did he say?"

"He told me nothing, señor. But I knew by his voice, by his choice of Spanish words, by the clothes he wore that he was from Mexico City."

Across The Border

Tod shrugged. "He must have made a mistake. Forget it."

The agent's black eyebrows rose. "Would there be another Señor Moran from San Francisco crossing the border just now? But you will reach Monterrey before dark. Perhaps he, too, is traveling south and you will meet there."

"Perhaps." Tod thanked the man and left.

As he climbed into his car he pondered over the puzzle. There was no getting round the fact that someone was interested in his movements. Yet who could this unknown person be? And why, if this man was a friend, had he not come into the coffee shop and introduced himself? Tod threw in the clutch and headed the car across the sidewalk to the street. Of one thing he could be sure. This unknown person was no casual acquaintance. *Has Señor Moran of San Francisco crossed the border yet?* Who could be interested in knowing when he entered Mexico? The answer to that was simple—and disconcerting, too. The stranger must be someone connected with Mr. Blakemore's silver mine.

Tod's thoughts flew back to the Blakemore office in San Francisco. He recalled that farewell scene which had been pushed from his mind by the four days of travel through the Southwest. Martin Welch, mine manager, must have heard the name Tasco mentioned. Martin Welch must have known at once that something was up. Did he suspect that Tod Moran was being sent to Tasco to investigate? Tod grinned. Welch was a fool if he thought for one minute that Mr. Blakemore would send so young a man on such a mission alone. Lucky that Captain Jarvis' name had not been mentioned. For Jarvis would soon be arriving at Mexico City without anyone at the mine knowing.

Tod put his foot on the brake. The parade of traffic ahead of him was slowing up. He must be within a few blocks of the border. Was there perhaps a car close behind with a driver who kept his eyes on the convertible coupé? He sighed. It looked as though his pleasure jaunt had ended. His job had already started, and Mexico City was still eight hundred miles away.

The Ford drew near to a side street. Tod turned the corner to the right and headed down the street away from the traffic. Before he crossed the border he'd send a wire to the Hotel Geneve to be held for Jarvis' arrival. If anything happened on the road it was just as well for Jarvis to know the itinerary he had planned. He had it all written down in his notebook.

At the telegraph office he leaned on the counter and penciled a message.

Laredo, May 12
Entering Mexico 2 P.M. Think someone is on my trail. Suspect Welch knows. Plan to stop at Regina Courts in Monterrey tonight. Should be at Casa Grande at Valles tomorrow and reach Mexico City day later.

Across The Border

Tod read the message over and then crossed out a word here and there. As he started to fill in the address he paused. A doubt crept into his mind. Was he acting like a silly nitwit? Here he was about to spend good American money merely because someone had inquired for him at the service station. His nerves must be jangled by the days of driving over desert roads. A wire to Jarvis was all nonsense. He'd throw the thing in the waste basket.

"The Señor is finished with the pencil?"

With a start Tod looked up. At his elbow stood a young Mexican, well dressed in a light suit and hat. The man's dark eyes were friendly, expectant.

"I also would like to send a telegram, señor."

Tod dropped his hand over the message. "Sorry," he said shortly. "I haven't yet finished."

The man gave a courteous nod and turned away toward the other end of the counter. Tod's glance followed him until he saw him pick up another pencil. Funny. It was just a little incident, of course, but maybe it had a meaning, too. Maybe this stranger was the same person who had made those inquiries at the service station. And but for a bit of luck this fellow would have seen Captain Jarvis' address in Mexico City already written on the message.

Tod looked down with thoughtful eyes. He'd send the wire all right, but not to Jarvis. He'd let the Blakemore office know how his trip was progressing, and the office could get in touch with Jarvis if anything went wrong.

Back in his car three minutes later he settled himself behind the wheel, satisfied that for once he had been prudent. He sat there until the dark-skinned man who had asked for the pencil came out of the telegraph office. Intent, Tod watched. To his surprise the man did not even glance toward the car but turned up the sidewalk in the opposite direction.

Tod pressed his foot violently against the starter. Were his nerves so jangled that he was already imagining things?

After driving a few blocks he found himself back in the slow parade of traffic that was nearing the international bridge. When his coupé swung across the Rio Grande he scarcely gave the river a glance. Ahead, a Mexican in uniform was directing the cars to a halt before the customs shed. Tod drove in, shut off the motor, showed his tourist card, and then got out to unlock the trunk. His bags and brief case were carried inside for inspection. Tod lingered when he saw one of the officials peering with suspicion at the carton holding the two bottles of water.

The man unscrewed the cap of one bottle and sniffed. "*Agua*," he announced in scorn.

With a grin Tod turned away to the building. Inside, his bags lay open upon a counter. An inspector was examining their contents with hands that were careful not to disarrange the folded clothing. When the leather straps of the brief case were unfastened the man took out the large envelopes, pressed them against the counter and, apparently satisfied, put them back. Tod caught the phrase, "Nothing important here."

Nothing important? Tod's gray eyes grew thoughtful. He had almost forgotten this brief case. Yet its contents meant that Captain Jarvis could not begin his investigation until it reached the Hotel Geneve in Mexico City.

"Finished, señor."

Tod picked up the brief case and went outside. He'd trust no one but himself to see that it was locked in the trunk.

The two bags followed in the hands of a uniformed assistant who placed them beside the bottles of water. Tod stowed the brief case next to them, closed the trunk and locked it.

The man raised a hand in salute. "*Adios*, señor."

Tod waved good-by, sprang up behind the wheel and stepped on the starter. A moment later he was heading down the street through the Mexican town of Nuevo Laredo. He peered up into the mirror of the windshield. The cars in his rear were turning off into side streets.

The adobe houses of the town soon fell away behind. The paved road climbed a short distance until it reached flat desert country. Under the blazing sun the Pan-American Highway stretched white and glistening to the south. No car was visible ahead. No car was following.

Highroad To Adventure

He picked up his dark glasses from the seat beside him and put them on. His trip down into Mexico had started. And he was alone.

A white post at the side of the road announced that it was 1228 kilometers to Mexico City—nearly eight hundred miles. He pressed his foot on the throttle. The speedometer climbed to forty, to forty-five, to fifty. The purr of the motor blended with the faint hum of the tires. With a smile of satisfaction he realized he was no longer an amateur driver who must concentrate his mind upon the wheel and clutch and gear shift. He was now a part of the machine itself.

Comforted by the thought, he let his gaze rove ahead toward a horizon obscured by haze. Monterrey must be reached before dark.

CHAPTER III

The Trailer

Twice during his afternoon run from the border
to Monterrey Tod was again stopped for federal inspection. The first time was just thirteen miles south of
Nuevo Laredo at a station set down in the blazing heat
of the desert. While cicadas hummed from the cactus
alongside the highway, a man in uniform looked over
his tourist card and then motioned him on without asking to look inside the trunk.

The second time was after he had passed through the
town of Sabinas Hidalgo and climbed two thousand feet
through mountains sparsely covered with shrub. Again
the inspector merely glanced at his card.

"How far to Monterrey?" Tod asked.

"Fifty kilometers, señor."

Highroad To Adventure

Tod drove on, pleased with his progress. It was just five o'clock, his motor was working perfectly, and he had only about thirty more miles to go. The wind that whistled past the car was now cooler. The road was descending and the bleak landscape showing spots of green. As he rounded a hill an auto trailer loomed up just ahead. Quickly he pulled his wheel to the left and overtook a blue house on wheels being towed by a blue Chevrolet coach. In the front seats an elderly couple smiled and waved at him. He waved back and sped on ahead.

These trailers, he decided, were getting as thick as trucks on the highway—though not in Mexico. With surprise he realized that he had passed only three or four cars going north toward the border. Not a single bus or truck had he seen, and this was the first trailer he had overtaken.

Twenty minutes later, just when he had glimpsed a grove of filmy green trees ahead and had pushed down the throttle to speed up as the road straightened out, he was almost thrown from his seat as a blow-out sounded. His hands tightened on the wheel until his knuckles grew white. His right front tire! The car bumped clumsily along while he guided it with the utmost care to the edge of the road and stopped. For a moment he sat still, relieved to find the car right side up. Whew! That was a close call.

He changed the wheel quite cheerfully, however, and

The Trailer

was putting the ruined tire into the trunk when he heard an automobile approaching. He looked up. The blue Chevrolet with its trailer in tow pulled up beside him. It carried a Nebraska license plate.

"Need any help?" asked the driver.

Tod flashed the elderly couple a smile of appreciation. "About finished, thanks. I've decided to buy a new set of tires in Monterrey."

"You ought to have done that back in the States, young man." The driver was perhaps sixty, with gray hair and sharp brown eyes. "I hear as how it ain't so easy to get tires down here. And mechanics who can fix an engine jest ain't to be found till you hit Mexico City."

"That so?"

The man's plump wife clicked her teeth. "Don't you mind what Paw says, young man. If you want to get somewheres you can always get there if you try hard enough. Why, me and Paw wouldn't be here at all if we'd listened to what folks said at home."

Her husband nodded. "You ought to have bought yourself a trailer, then it wouldn't matter where you had to stop."

"Now, Paw." The gray-haired woman in her light calico dress threw her husband a look of protest. "Everybody can't take their home along with them like a turtle. Everybody hasn't got the time."

Tod, gazing quickly back at the blue trailer, saw with approval that each window was painted white and draped with neat white curtains. "It looks mighty homelike," he commented.

"Young man, you look kind of hot and sweaty," said the woman. "How about some ice water?"

"Ice water—here?"

"Of course. This is our home. Paw'll get you a drink."

The man reached behind the seat and brought up a large thermos jug. With a smile of satisfaction he unscrewed the top, took off two extra cups, poured out a drink and passed it to Tod.

The old couple's tongues wagged on in kindly fashion until Tod had locked the trunk. "I feel like a new person after that drink," he said as he thanked them. "If we meet again I'll stop and ask for ice water."

"If you don't," said the woman, "Paw and me will be put out with you. Where you stopping tonight?"

"At the Regina Courts in Monterrey. I've my whole trip laid out. So many miles each day."

"Well, that ain't the way we travel. We jest stop when we feel like it. Maybe we'll see you again." Slowly the Chevrolet with its trailer got under way.

Tod passed them a few moments later with another shout of thanks and sped on. Presently he could make out far ahead the red-tiled roofs of a city with mountains rising abruptly beyond. Good. He would make Monterrey before dark.

A sign announcing the Regina Motor Courts met his eyes as he entered the suburbs of the city. He turned into broad gardens thick with palms that slanted over groups of Spanish buildings. His information gained in far-away San Francisco, he thought, was certainly dependable. Even the California auto camps and motor courts and luxurious motels were no more inviting than this tile-roofed tourist court on the Pan-American Highway.

He drew up his car under the portico of the office and went inside. A room with a shower? The clerk behind the counter inclined his dark head and suggested apartment number eight at a price amazingly low.

"I need some new tires," Tod said. "Can I buy them around here?"

"Yes, señor. A service station is just beyond our trailer camp. Anything you desire will be found there. Will you register, please?"

As Tod wrote his name and home address, he asked, "Has anyone inquired for me today?"

The man glanced at the name and his eyes narrowed. "Señor Moran of San Francisco?" All at once he became exceedingly talkative. "No, señor. No one has inquired for you. This is between seasons, you know. The winter traffic has ended and the rainy season is about to begin. You will find few cars on the highway these days." He lifted his voice. "Pedro! Show the Señor to number eight."

The sun was low in the sky as Tod drove slowly after the Mexican youth to number eight. The cabin boasted a large bedroom with tiled floor, a shower bath and a kitchen with gas and electricity. He glanced around with approval. Every window looked out upon a wide lawn bordered with flowers and palms. The air was cool and scented with a fragrance new to him. While the boy carried in his luggage, Tod drove the Ford into the narrow garage that separated his cabin from the next.

Back once more in his room, with the screen door hooked, he put his leather brief case into a dresser drawer and took a cold shower. Then he shaved, combed his unruly hair and slipped into a Palm Beach suit that was somewhat in need of pressing.

A knock sounded. "Oh, señor!" called a voice.

Tod turned, his hands straightening his tie. In the gathering dusk outside the screen door stood a man in white. "Señor, I am the manager. I have come to apologize."

Tod switched on the light, went to the door and opened it. "Won't you come in?"

The man stepped inside and bowed slightly. "Señor, I have sent home my clerk. Such service I will not have."

Tod buttoned his coat. "But I'm afraid I don't quite understand."

"Ah, señor, you asked if anyone had inquired for you. I was in the inner office at my desk and I heard what Roberto told you. Señor, he spoke not the truth. But it shall not happen again. In the morning a new clerk will be on duty."

The Trailer

"You mean someone did ask for me?"

"Yes, señor. At five o'clock—perhaps an hour before you arrive—I am working on my books in the inner office when I hear inquiries made about you. Oh, I listened! I always listen so I know what is going on. And then later, when you arrive, I hear Roberto tell you no one had made inquiries. Oh, I knew he lied. So when the boy brought you here I asked Roberto to explain to me why he did not tell the truth. It was five pesos that did it, señor. The man gave him five pesos not to tell you. And now he loses his fine position as my assistant."

"I see. Was it a Mexican who asked for me?"

"No, señor. I only heard the voice, but it was the voice of an American who speaks bad Spanish."

"So you did not see this man?"

The manager spread out his hands in a gesture of exasperation. "I am sorry, señor."

"Is this man who inquired for me a guest here?"

"No, señor. He must be at one of the hotels. Perhaps the Ancira."

Tod moved uneasily toward the dresser, then turned. "I'm deeply grateful for your telling me this. If I have a friend in Monterrey, I'd like to meet him, of course."

"But this man did not wish you to know, señor! Else why pay my assistant to keep his inquiries secret? Unless he wishes to surprise you. Ah, that must be it! He will surprise you."

"You may be right. Maybe he'll surprise me."

Highroad To Adventure

"Anything else, señor? I am at your service."

"Nothing, thank you. But don't let your assistant go because of this little misunderstanding. It was hardly his fault."

A wide smile of relief spread over the dark, anxious face. "Ah, señor, you are a gentleman. I shall tell Roberto it is your wish that he has another chance. *Buenas noches*, señor. Our restaurant across the courts is open until midnight."

When the manager had gone, Tod locked his windows and door securely and then strolled across to the restaurant for dinner. All through his meal of well-done steak and hot vegetables he turned over in his mind the meaning of this occurrence. In Laredo it had been a Mexican who had asked for him. In Monterrey it was now an American who spoke bad Spanish. Could there be some mistake? Tod ordered a bottle of chilled spring water, made sure that the seal had not been broken, and sat back deep in thought. Whoever had inquired for him certainly had no intention of making his presence known. Perhaps, after all, it was only one person who was interested in his movements. The voice heard by the manager might be the voice of a Mexican born and reared in the States. That might account for the poor Spanish the man spoke. Tod drank a glass of water and stood up. He'd better stroll across to the service station and ask about tires.

The attendant there had no tires in stock but he

The Trailer

promised to have them first thing in the morning. "Bring your car around by seven o'clock, señor. It will not take long to change them."

"But I wanted to leave by seven," Tod protested.

The man shrugged. "It is the best I can do."

Tod thought it over. His itinerary called only for a three-hundred-and-twenty-mile drive on the morrow, so there was plenty of time. "Very well," he agreed. "If you're on hand by seven o'clock with those tires I'll make you a present of the old ones."

"Ah, the señor is kind. I shall be here before seven."

On his way back to the tourist court Tod glanced in at the trailer camp where three trailers were parked, electric lights burning, camp chairs set up, radios blaring. A blue house on wheels caught his eye. Why not say hello to his trailer friends? It was too early to turn in just yet.

As he approached, he heard a high but still strong voice ring out. "Ma, here comes our young Californian! Put on another plate for supper."

From the front end of the trailer the old man appeared. "I was uncoupling the car when I saw you coming. You're just in time."

"But I've already eaten," Tod said quickly.

"Shucks, a husky young feller like you can always eat home-cooked food."

Tod laughed. The unaffected warmth of the old man's greeting was too rare a thing to be tossed aside; and, furthermore, the chance of getting inside one of these trailers was not to be missed.

At that moment a stout apron-clad figure appeared in the doorway. "If you don't set right down with us, Mr. San Francisco," said the woman, "we'll be terrible disappointed. We got three sons at home, and the youngest reminds us of you—only maybe he isn't quite so sunburnt and cheery, being worried, as he says, because his parents have become gadabouts. But surely you'll have dessert, anyway. Chocolate cake. I baked it in Laredo this morning."

"Home-made chocolate cake? I'll stay." Tod walked over to the steps and looked up at the woman. "Maybe I'd better introduce myself. My name's Moran—Tod Moran."

"Pleased to know you, Mr. Moran. Our name is Whipple. We come from a town near Omaha."

It was a merry, homelike meal that Tod sat down to inside the trailer. Built like the cabin of a ship, neat and compact, it was filled at the same time with womanly touches that a ship's cabin always lacked—ruffled white curtains at the windows, a red-and-white cloth for the folding table, a woven rug on the floor. The two-burner gasoline stove boasted an oven that could bake a cake, Tod admitted, that melted in your mouth. Above the table an electric light shone brightly. Tod's interest made the old couple beam with pleasure. When they weren't stopping in a trailer camp, they informed him, they used kerosene lanterns.

The Trailer

Ben Whipple, tall and thin and amazingly spry, had retired several years before from his business of house building. Then he realized with a sense of shock that their five grown children, most of them married and with children of their own, were now beginning to boss him. Old Ben puttered sadly round the house while Ma Whipple took to tatting. But one year of that was enough. On the second anniversary of his retirement the old man started building himself a trailer. All his children laughed indulgently, but they hadn't laughed when the trailer was finished and loaded and attached to the Chevrolet, for the old couple headed straight for Florida.

"Do you know what they said?" Ma Whipple's plump face broke into a smile and her blue eyes twinkled. "They said we were out of our minds. Well, maybe we were. Maybe we still are."

"That's right," agreed her husband. "Another slice of cake? Shucks, you ain't even started yet. Yes, sir, we was on our way home from Miami when Ma gets the idea we might as well roll up a few more miles and go down into ·Mexico. We mailed a letter at Laredo telling the folks what we was doing. We wanted to get across the border before they put the police on our trail."

Tod's face sobered as he looked across the table at his host. "What time did you leave Laredo today?"

"Oh, about eleven o'clock."

"Paw, it was eleven-thirty. I looked at my watch."

"Many cars overtake you on the road?" Tod asked.

"About four."

"Now, Paw, it was only three." Again Mrs. Whipple cut in. "Remember? A little coupé overtook us at the first inspection station. Then later a black sedan came up behind us when we were climbing through that pass. And the third car overtook us just before we met Mr. Moran."

"That's right." Mr. Whipple nodded his gray head.

Tod leaned forward, intent. "Do you happen to remember anything about those cars, Mr. Whipple?"

Ben Whipple raised a thin, toughened hand to his chin. "Well, you see, I was driving. You better ask Ma. She always looks."

Mrs. Whipple's blue eyes were serious. "I never miss the license plates. I like to see how many cars from different states we see in one day, and I'm always watching out for cars from home—from Nebraska." Her voice grew low, meditative. "The coupé was from Ohio, the black sedan from Mexico, and the last one before you overtook us was from Massachusetts."

Tod's mind was working rapidly. The Massachusetts and Ohio cars were probably out, but he'd better make sure. "Remember who was in the Ohio car, Mrs. Whipple?"

"Yes, I do. They drew up alongside us at the inspection station. A young couple. Both of them smoking. Cigarettes!"

The Trailer

"And the Massachusetts car?"

"It was a big limousine. It whizzed by mighty fast. I think it had a whole family of young people just growing up. And a chauffeur."

"And the car with the Mexican license?"

"The black sedan? Let me think a minute." The old lady's eyes took on a far-away look, then she suddenly nodded her head with vigor. "Two men in it. Yes, Paw, I remember perfectly. A Mexican was driving and an American wearing a straw hat was sitting beside him. The back seat was empty."

Tod sat up with a start. He felt his pulse quicken. Two men! One an American and the other a Mexican. Now he was getting down to facts. "Was it a good-looking car?"

"A Buick."

"Now, Ma, how can you be sure? Maybe it was a Chrysler."

A slight flush of indignation touched Mrs. Whipple's plump cheeks. "I'm better at naming cars than my own grandchildren, Ben Whipple, and you know it! That car was a Buick, a new one and a beauty."

Ben Whipple grinned. "When Ma speaks like that you can be sure she knows what she's talking about. A Buick it is. That's settled." All at once he leaned forward and a shrewd look crept into his eyes. "Would it be polite to ask why you're so interested, Mr. Moran?"

Tod smiled. "Of course. Only please don't call me Mr.

Moran. My name's Tod. I'm interested because someone has been inquiring for me secretly along the road—first in Laredo and now here in Monterrey."

"You don't say?" Mr. Whipple sat back in surprise.

Tod glanced out the door. A few yards away a silver trailer was parked, but its windows were dark and it apparently was deserted. Nevertheless, when his glance came back to the old couple opposite him, he lowered his voice. "I'm carrying some letters and business papers to a friend in Mexico City. I've got to get them there by the fifteenth—three days from now. And I'm afraid that somebody I don't know is trailing me."

"Land sakes!" Mrs. Whipple's eyes were round. "They wouldn't do you no harm, would they?"

"Of course not." Tod grinned. "They probably only intend to watch my movements so they can see what I do when I reach Mexico City."

Ben Whipple said quickly, "But this country ain't like the States, young man. You jest watch your step."

"I intend to."

Mrs. Whipple's practical mind was evidently less concerned than her husband's. She took up a knife and cut into the swiftly disappearing cake. "Have another slice?"

"Filled to the brim." Tod shook his head. "I never expected to eat such cake south of the border."

With a knowing smile Mrs. Whipple picked up the slice of cake on her knife and passed it across to Tod's plate. "All my boys eat three pieces of my chocolate

The Trailer

cake. I'd feel I'd forgotten how to bake if they didn't."

Ben Whipple leaned forward. "What say if I finish unhooking the car and we go for a ride round the city? Monterrey might be right well worth seeing."

Tod nodded, his mouth full, and Mr. Whipple got to his feet. His wife said at once, "It won't take me two minutes to clean up this mess." She looked intently at Tod. "Young man, what about those letters and business papers you're carrying south? Are they in your pocket?"

"No. In a brief case."

"And is the brief case in your car?"

"No. It's in my cabin. Number eight."

"Land sakes, if I was you I wouldn't trust no doors or windows down here. I'd carry that brief case around with me—and at night I'd sleep on it."

Tod got to his feet. "You're right. I'll take the brief case with me. I don't know what I was thinking about, Mrs. Whipple. You've got sense."

Ma Whipple sighed as she smoothed her iron-gray hair. "I haven't heard anyone say that to me for a long time. No, not since Paw built this trailer."

CHAPTER IV

After Midnight

Tod OPENED HIS EYES, aware on the instant that something had roused him. He lay still while he tried to recall to his sleepy mind just where he was. Now he remembered. He was in apartment number eight where he had tumbled into bed about ten-thirty, after returning with the Whipples from a brief tour of the city. What, he wondered, had awakened him? Maybe it was the heat. But it wasn't really hot, and he was wearing thin pajamas and covered only with a sheet thinner still. He listened. Outside the screen door a breeze stirred the palm trees. Their sharp fronds scraped against the stucco walls of his cabin.

A furtive sound close at hand struck his ears. Suddenly alert, he tried to pierce the darkness of his room with his gaze, but only the oblong of pale light at the door was visible and the square to one side—an open screened window. All at once the shadow of a man moved across the window. Somebody had passed without a sound on the grass outside.

Outside? He blinked once, twice, and cautiously raised his head. Near the foot of his bed a small cone of light leaped out toward the dresser against the wall. He caught his breath sharply. Someone with a flash light was in his room.

With an effort he downed an impulse to spring up and throw himself upon this unknown intruder. In the darkness the man might be holding a gun poised for action. Tod lowered his head with care to his pillow. Better to wait and see what happened.

Through narrowed lids he saw the beam of light grow smaller as the man approached the dresser. The top drawer was pulled open inch by inch, then the light was flashed into its empty interior. When it was pushed shut again a faint thud was audible. At once the flash light swung round the room toward the bed. Tod closed his eyes. A second later he was aware of light against his eyelids. After a moment of intolerable suspense it moved away and darkness settled down once more.

Not until he heard the whisper of another drawer being opened did he look again. The man, whoever he was, was going methodically through the dresser. But there was nothing there. With satisfaction Tod remembered that when he had come to bed he had placed his brief case beside his pillow and covered it with a folded blanket. But for Mrs. Whipple's warning he might have left the thing in that top drawer, and the man by this time would probably have been gone, and Mr. Blakemore's letters and papers with him. Or was it possible that this man was merely a thief after money? Tod tossed the thought aside. The fact that someone had inquired for him first at Laredo and then here in Monterrey must mean that this was no common thief. Instead, it must be someone who knew what he carried south, someone who wanted to hold up that investigation in Mexico City and Tasco.

And who could it be except Martin Welch? The mine manager, he recalled, was a short, heavily built man. Undoubtedly he had followed the little coupé all during that trip down through the Southwest. In a car newer than the Ford, the man would be able to draw ahead or skulk behind as he desired. Slow anger surged up within Tod. Lifting his hand he pulled the sheet aside and made ready to leap. Under his pajama coat he could hear his heart beating rapidly. Was it loud enough for the intruder to hear, too?

Slowly he drew his husky young body taut, then he leaped up and landed with bare feet on the tiled floor. The cone of light winked out, but Tod knew the location of the dresser. Without pausing he threw himself forward through the darkness.

After Midnight

His arms closed round the thin form of a man as they both went down with a thud. In vain Tod tried to hold his antagonist. The man, spare and lithe and muscular, was underneath for only a moment. With the quickness of an eel he struggled to free himself. Tod felt a knee pressed against the pit of his stomach, he heard a grunt of exertion, and the knee shot forward. Tod's hands relaxed. There was a ringing in his ears and a blinding flash before his eyes. A stabbing pain shot through his body.

In dismay and resentment he lay still, gasping for breath, while to his ears came a sudden rush of feet, the slam of the screen door, and silence. When he pulled himself erect a minute later he told himself bitterly that it served him right. He had taken it for granted that this unknown person was Martin Welch, middle-aged and heavy, certainly too soft to be much of an opponent. And instead, he had flung himself upon a man who was at least his equal. His equal? In the darkness Tod grinned wryly. Maybe the fellow was even better. Certainly he was a slender athletic type who knew how to fight back. Why, this unknown visitor must be twenty years younger than Martin Welch.

Tod crossed to the door and listened. A sibilant whisper came from the palms outside the screen. Otherwise the night was still, the dark sky thick with stars. Pushing open the screen, he stepped down to the walk and on bare feet went to the open garage. The shadowy rear of the Ford was vaguely visible. There was little chance that the intruder had stopped in there to hide. By this time he could have gained a car parked down the road and be lost already in the city streets.

Back in his room once more he switched on the light and sat down on the edge of the bed beside his brief case. Should he throw on some clothes, go over to the office, ring the night bell, and make a report? If he did, what would happen? Most likely the police would be called. It might mean that in the morning the chief of police would demand his presence downtown. No, he mustn't chance any delay. This was the morning of the thirteenth. By carrying out his schedule he should reach Valles by evening and Mexico City on the next night—one full day before the fifteenth which Jarvis had specified.

Tod got up and glanced toward the door. Without surprise he saw that the screen had been cut near the hook that fastened it. Well, he must have been sleeping mighty sound not to have wakened when a knife slit that wire screen. He closed the wooden door, turned the key in the lock, and came back toward the bed. Abruptly he stopped and looked down. A bare foot had stepped upon something that hurt. He kicked it aside, then stared. A button lay there on the tiled floor.

Stooping, he picked it up. It was a light brown coat button, still carrying a slender bit of cloth. Deep in thought, he turned it over on his palm. It did not belong to any of his own suits, and surely he would have noticed if it had been there on the floor all evening. It must have been torn from his opponent's coat in the struggle.

He glanced round the room. How clean had this place really been? Maybe the little apartment, as the clerk called it, was never brushed up thoroughly more than once a week—perhaps a Mexican habit. And yet this motor court was new and catered to American tourists who demanded cleanliness as the first requisite for a lodging. He ran his fingers across the top of the table against the wall. No dust there. He went into the kitchen, switched on the light and inspected the place with care. It was spotless. No, the chances were that this button belonged to the unknown visitor. And this visitor must be one of the two men who had driven south from Laredo in that black Buick sedan—either the American or the Mexican. Mrs. Whipple had only glimpsed them; it was expecting too much for her to notice the clothes they wore. But it was possible that the clerk Roberto might remember the man, for hadn't he made inquiries for Tod Moran at the desk and paid five pesos for silence?

Quickly Tod slipped into his clothes and, with his brief case held securely under one arm, went out and locked the wooden door. The motor court was dark, the air redolent with the damp smell of a semi-tropical garden where the flowers themselves lacked perfume. An electric light burned under the portico before the office.

Highroad To Adventure

He pressed a finger on the night bell. Somewhere behind the outer office a buzzer sounded. After waiting for several minutes he heard the scuff of slippers on the tiled floor, a light inside flashed on, and the olive-skinned clerk swung open the door.

"You're on duty all night, Roberto?"

"Yes, señor. I sleep here. Will you come in?"

"I just wanted to ask you a question or two," Tod said quickly, not yet sure how much he should divulge to this man.

Roberto stepped behind his counter. "Anything I can do to help? You see, I was grateful for what the Señor said to the *propietario*."

"Forget it." Tod grinned. "How often do you have these apartments cleaned up? Once a week?"

A horrified look came into the man's dark eyes. "But, no, señor! Every day. Was your apartment not clean? Every day it is inspected."

"I picked up something on the floor." Tod put his hand into his pants' pocket and brought forth the button. "Do you suppose this could have been overlooked when the woman cleaned up?"

Roberto shook his dark head. "Only perhaps if it was under the bed. You found it there?"

"No, it was near the center of the floor."

"And it is not the Señor's—come loose perhaps?"

"Come loose? Take a good look at this. It was torn off someone's coat."

After Midnight

"Strange, señor. I do not understand."

"Never mind. I had a visitor a short while ago. I thought he probably lost it in the scuffle, and I wanted to make sure."

"Scuffle, señor?"

"A little fight." Tod's eyes kindled. "He got the best of me—and ran away."

"Señor, I shall telephone the proprietor. I shall call the police. Never have we had thieves at this motor court."

"Forget it." Tod put both hands on the counter and spoke with emphasis. "Roberto, you asked what you could do to help me. Very well. Then don't say anything about what happened tonight. I do not wish to be questioned or delayed by the police. I must leave in a few hours for Valles."

"Certainly, señor. It is already forgotten. And the Señor lost nothing at all?"

"Nothing at all. Now, listen. I want you to try to remember that man who asked about me late this afternoon. Was he an American?"

"*Si.*" Roberto inclined his head, his brows puckered in a frown. "He was an American, but he spoke Spanish."

"Poor Spanish?"

"*Si.*"

"What did he look like? Remember?"

Roberto stood silent for a moment. Outside on the highway a car whizzed by with tires humming. Roberto frowned. "I cannot remember exact."

"Was he a heavy-set fellow, sort of big in the stomach?"

"Ah, he stood right where you stand now, señor, behind this counter. I could not see."

"Was he tall?"

"Perhaps not any taller than you, señor. I am not sure."

"Did he wear a light suit?"

"I cannot be sure, señor." The man threw out his hands in a gesture of despair. "I did not notice."

Disappointed, Tod shifted his weight and looked down.

Roberto spoke in an ingratiating tone. "You see, the man did not come back into the office again."

"Of course not." Tod sighed. "Why should he?"

"But he is stopping here, señor. He took apartment number ten—close to yours. It has two bedrooms. One was for his friend."

"Here?" Tod's head jerked up. "Why didn't you tell me this before?"

"Ah, I did not wish to let the *propietario* know. I thought perhaps he might see this man and tell him I had not kept my promise—for the five pesos."

Tod leaned over the counter, speaking hurriedly. "But your boss told me the man did not register as a guest here."

Roberto glanced round. "He did not ask for an apartment when he first came in. His friend came back and registered."

"And this friend?"

After Midnight

"A young man, señor—perhaps twenty years old. He was a Mexican—of very good class."

"Well, now we're getting somewhere." Tod regarded the clerk sharply. "You saw their car? What kind was it?"

"I do not remember. So many automobiles stop here. But you may see the registry card. It is all written down."

"Please. And hurry, will you?"

The man turned, pulled open a small file drawer and fingered the cards inside. Then he took one out and laid it before Tod. "This is it. Two gentlemen in a Buick."

Tod's eyes rested eagerly upon the written words. Evidently the Mexican who had filled it out was a youth of some education, for the writing was clear and firm. Two names were there—Richard Brown and Enricques Lopez, both of Vera Cruz. Tod's lips came together tightly. Both names most likely thought up on the moment. He looked up at the clerk. "Take me over to number ten. I'd like to see those two gentlemen."

"You would wake them—at this hour?" Roberto hung back.

Tod nodded grimly. "They won't be asleep. You can be sure of that."

With laggard footsteps the clerk led the way outside and across the gardens toward Tod's own room. On the graveled drive, the man stopped short and said in a low voice, "It is that one, señor. Two doors past your own."

Tod's glance swept along the line of dark windows,

each apartment separated by an open garage. Except for Tod's Ford, no other car was visible.

He put his hand on Roberto's arm. "Their Buick? They parked it in their garage?"

"*Si*."

"Well, it's gone. I suppose they had it parked outside on the road in case they had to make a quick getaway. Come on. Let's look inside."

The screen of number ten was unhooked, the wooden door open. Tod reached in and switched on the light. Without surprise he saw that the place was empty, the occupants gone.

Roberto seemed vastly relieved. "They said they would be off early this morning."

"This early? Why, it isn't two o'clock yet."

"Our guests come and go as they please," the clerk explained. "I always collect in advance."

Tod said good night, went back alone to his room and locked himself in. At least from now on he knew what to expect. From now on he would be prepared. A black Buick sedan with a Mexican driver and an American passenger—probably Martin Welch of Tasco and an employee who acted as chauffeur. Well, the leather brief case was still safe. Martin Welch without a doubt would go ahead with his deviltry under the impression that Tod Moran did not know who was on his trail. Welch would think that his quarry believed he had merely been wakened by a petty thief.

After Midnight

Tod undressed, turned out the light and slid into bed. Although from now on it would be a battle of wits, he had no fear of not winning out. For Mexico City and the Hotel Geneve and Jarvis were less than six hundred miles away. Why, that was only two more days of travel. He closed his eyes. Two more days. Nothing to it. No . . . nothing at all.

CHAPTER V

The Hare and the Tortoise

AT SEVEN O'CLOCK that morning Tod drove his Ford past the trailer camp to the service station just beyond. The operator was waiting for him.

"*Buenos días*, señor. The new tires are here—four of them. I change them at once."

"Good." Tod stepped down and slammed the door. "The old casings are yours."

"*Gracias*." The man rolled a jack under the rear axle. "This left tire is low. Look, señor. It has a nail in it!"

"Are you sure?" Tod bent over to inspect the tire. "You're right. I wouldn't have got far with that today. Maybe you'd better not use this inner tube. Put in a new one." He straightened up. "If you need me, I'll be over at the trailer camp."

"*Si*, señor. The car will be ready in an hour."

The Hare And The Tortoise

One of the trailers, Tod noticed as he crossed the grounds, had already pulled out. Two were left—one silver and the other deep blue.

"Morning, Frisco." Ben Whipple greeted him from the doorway. "Ma's got coffee on. Just in time for breakfast."

"I had breakfast at the restaurant, Mr. Whipple. But if you insist, I might take a cup of coffee."

"Only a cup of coffee? Rats! You gotta have some bacon and eggs, too."

The stout little figure of Ma Whipple appeared beside her husband. Her blue eyes shone with welcome and her voice was warm and friendly. "I hear as how the coffee they serve south of the border is pretty poor stuff."

"It wasn't as bad as I expected," Tod said.

"Paw grinds our coffee fresh every morning. Always has. Always will. Step right in. Cabin's all made up. Have to do it before we get breakfast."

Tod went up the step and looked around in admiration. "Seven o'clock in the morning and beds already out of sight! This trailer is certainly slick. No wonder you and Paw like it."

Ben Whipple's lined face broke into a grin of delight. "Now, I sure like to hear you call me Paw, young man. It sounds jest like home." He waved Tod to a settee along the wall.

"Land sakes, Ben, you ain't getting homesick, are you?" Ma placed another cup and saucer on the small folding table, took the coffeepot off the stove and filled the cups with the dark steaming liquid. "Maybe we better turn right round and travel north this morning."

"I ain't homesick," Paw protested. "Anyway, it wa'n't me who suggested this Mexican trip. It was you."

"Why, Ben Whipple, how can you say that!"

Tod chuckled as he slid along the settee to the table. The good-humored banter that went on while he drank his coffee and the old couple ate their bacon and eggs and buttered toast made him almost forget the occurrence of the night. Finally he said, "I slept with my brief case right next to my pillow, Mrs. Whipple. It was lucky I did. I had a visitor sometime after midnight."

"No!" said Ma Whipple.

"Yes," said Tod.

"Land sakes!" Her plump face showed concern. "Not —not a thief?"

Tod nodded. "He cut the wire screen on the door. He was going through the dresser when I woke up. Yes, he got away, but he didn't take anything."

Ben Whipple reached for a can of condensed milk and poured some into his coffee. "And I thought Ma was jest imagining things when she told you to be careful. Did you call the police?"

"No. I can't afford to be held up here, even for a few hours."

"Any idea who your visitor was?"

Tod's glance turned to Mrs. Whipple. "That's what I

wanted to speak about. I've a hunch it was one of those men you saw on the road yesterday in the black Buick sedan. Do you happen to remember what they looked like?"

"They whizzed by too fast." Ma Whipple sighed. "I only seen a Mexican driving and an American sitting beside him."

Tod thrust a hand into his pants' pocket, brought it out again, and tossed a button onto the table. "The fellow left that behind. It must have been torn from his coat. You can see a bit of cloth that came away with it."

Ma Whipple picked up the button and held it in the palm of her hand. "It's from a linen coat. I'm sorry, but I jest can't seem to remember what those two men wore." Her glance met Tod's. "What makes you think it was one of them who broke into your cabin?"

"The clerk at the Regina Courts said they asked for me. They put up for the night at apartment number ten, but they disappeared before I could get a look at them." Tod took the button and put it back into his pocket. "Anyway, now I know enough to look out for that black sedan. They won't take me unawares again."

"Paw," said Ma Whipple with emphasis, "no matter how homesick you are, we're going south so we can keep an eye on Tod Moran. Suppose our George was making a trip like this all alone in a foreign country? We'd appreciate having someone kinda look out for him, wouldn't we?"

"You're right, Ma." Ben Whipple cocked an amused eye at Tod. "How far you plan to drive today?"

"To Valles. Only about three hundred and twenty miles."

"Well, we usually don't go quite that far, but we can do it if we hurry. Young man, that black sedan ain't going to be the only car trailing you on the road."

Tod's lips twisted in a grin. "It wouldn't make me feel bad at all to know I've a couple of friends following. How about you two having dinner with me tonight in Valles? My schedule calls for a stop at a new motor hotel there. The Casa Grande, I think." He reached into the inside coat pocket of his Palm Beach suit and took out a notebook. "Yes, that's it. Right on the highway. I'll be waiting for you there."

"Now, that's real nice." Ma Whipple's smile revealed how pleased she was. "If Ben'll jest get a move on we can get going in no time. We ought to be at this Valles place by six o'clock."

"By five o'clock," Ben Whipple declared. "No bad grades to make today."

"I'll be expecting you for dinner," Tod told them when he left. "But you probably won't get as good a meal as the ones you serve here."

Upon his return to the service station he found the operator checking the oil.

"She took ten gallons of gas, señor. And one quart of oil will do." The man paused, and his voice became troubled. "Señor, it is queer, but all those old tires had nails in them."

Tod's head jerked erect. "Nails—in all of them?"

"Yes, señor. You watch where you drive next time. Nails are not good, even for new tires."

Tod walked across to the shed where the old casings lay on the ground. "How many nails in each tire?" he asked.

"Only one in each. But one is enough, yes?"

"Too much." Thoughtfully Tod drew out his bill fold and signed one of the traveler's checks. As he got into his car he asked, "Do you find many nails in tires around here?"

"Almost never, señor. That is what is so very queer. And all those nails are new."

Tod's hands gripped the wheel as his glance roved out along the highway. At the moment he wouldn't have been surprised to see a black sedan drawn up near by with its occupants laughing at him. But only a huge brewery truck was rumbling toward the center of the city. With a foreboding sigh he turned the key in the ignition, stepped upon the starter and shifted the gear into low. The car moved forward to the highway.

Those nails, of course, had been hammered into his tires sometime around midnight in the hope that on a lonely road far beyond Monterrey they would begin to take effect. Delay—that was what these unknown persons wanted. They were trying to keep him from reaching Mexico City by the fifteenth. Or could they know about his meeting with Captain Jarvis scheduled for that date? Probably not. Well, anyway, he'd show them. Everything pointed to the fact that something was vitally wrong with the management of Mr. Blakemore's mine in Tasco. There was no doubt now of the importance of Jarvis' investigation. There was no doubt, either, of the importance of getting that brief case to the Hotel Geneve. Tod shifted the gear into second, into high. For the present he'd better keep his mind on the traffic. Some of these Mexican drivers were rather wild.

All the way along Madero Boulevard and down Zaragoza to the heart of the city he fancied that black sedans were waiting for him at every corner. Once near the plaza he passed a black Buick, but it carried Utah license plates and its occupants were a family of three, obviously tourists. Yet even when he had left the city and was spinning along the highway past villas set in gardens of tropical luxuriance, he was still made uneasy by a feeling that furtive eyes were watching him. They were all around—in the orange trees growing off to the right, in the open doorways of adobe houses that pressed against the road, in the overcrowded bus that thundered up from the south and roared past with a rush of wind.

As he speeded up after crossing Arroyo Seco Bridge he tried to shrug aside the uncanny feeling of still being under observation. This morning's drive promised to be more interesting than that of the day before. The air was clear and not too warm. To his right the Sierra Madres loomed against a cloudless sky of blue. To his left, bare peaks rose closer at hand. And cutting the valley between, the paved highway led through verdant land that was cool and inviting under the sun.

By nine o'clock he had discarded his coat and hat and tie, had put on his dark glasses and was enjoying himself. By ten o'clock he was worried.

This time he had something tangible to worry about. For his motor sputtered and gasped. The car jerked, threatened to stop any moment, then moved on again for a few yards. He put one foot on the clutch and the other on the gas. The motor back-fired with the noise of a pistol shot. His face became grim. By thunder, something was wrong. The gas line wasn't feeding properly.

For another mile he nursed it along. When the motor again took up its regular beat he smiled in satisfaction and settled back. This was hardly the place to be stalled. The town of Linares was at least fifteen miles behind; and according to his map the next place would be Hidalgo, thirty miles ahead. The highway led through a country seemingly uninhabited except for an occasional thatched hut set back amid low trees. Maybe the carburetor needed adjustment. He'd see about it when he came to a garage—if such a thing as a garage was to be found in this country south of the border.

All at once the motor gasped and died again. He pressed his foot on the gas. The car jerked, rolled forward, lost headway. Hurriedly he pulled the wheel and steered to the right side of the road. He tried to start her without result. Maybe it was flooded, he thought. Better wait a minute or two. He waited and tried again. Not even a sputter came this time from the motor.

Annoyed, he put on his Panama hat, stepped out to the paved road, walked around to the other side and lifted the hood. He knew where the carburetor was, but that was about all. "I'd better not try to adjust her myself," he thought. "I might only make her worse."

He glanced to the south. Under the sun the empty highway gave forth little whorls of heat. He looked toward the north. No one coming there, either.

He pushed back his hat and sat down on the running board to think it over. Here he was, stalled at a lonely spot on the Pan-American Highway with no help in sight. With a grin he recalled what the station attendant in Laredo had said. He was not to stop for anybody on the highway unless for a man in uniform. Run the fellow down rather than slow up! Well, anyone would be a mighty welcome sight right now, uniformed or not.

Every moment the sun was getting hotter. Under his thin shirt his shoulders burned. Sweat trickled down from his hatband. A bird flew across the road and disappeared over the low green shrubs that extended far back toward the distant mountains. A profound silence brooded over the landscape.

Far down the highway to the south a shadow moved.

The Hare And The Tortoise

Something was coming. He stood up. As the minutes passed, he made out a peón walking beside an ox loaded with produce. Not much help there, he thought, but maybe he could learn something about the road ahead.

Soon he could hear the steady footfalls of the approaching animal. "Hello," Tod called when the man was in earshot. "Any town ahead before you reach Hidalgo?"

The peón, dressed in white baggy trousers and a large straw hat, stared at him dumbly.

Tod tried again. "How far from a town?"

The man came on with a tread as slow and even as that of his ox, but still he did not answer.

Tod sighed. The fellow of course didn't understand English and, alas, Tod himself didn't understand much Spanish. His mind turned to the booklets given to him at Laredo. At the thought, he threw open the car door and reached into the pigeonhole in the instrument panel. Here it was—*Spanish in One Lesson*. He couldn't repress a grin as he read the title. If Spanish were only as easy as that!

Flicking the pages of the booklet, he turned back toward the road. The peón and his ox were already passing. He hurried toward them, his eyes scanning the pages for a phrase that would make the fellow understand.

Ah, here was one that would do: Please tell me where to find a gasoline station. With the utmost care he read the Spanish that followed, pronouncing each word in a manner which he suspected was far from correct.

[65]

Highroad To Adventure

"¿Sírvase decirme donde esta un expendio de gasolina?"

The peón did not even glance his way. As far as the man was concerned, it was evident that his questioner might as well have spoken in Hindustani.

In despair Tod touched the man's arm. *"¿Gasolina?"* he cried. "Garage?"

The peón shook off the grasp. Slowly his glance came to Tod and his black eyes flashed in anger. *"¡Americano!"* He spat out the word in scorn.

Tod came to a halt. It was apparent there was nothing to be gained in questioning this fellow, even in correct Spanish. It was apparent, too, that Americans were not what you'd call popular around here. Well, he'd just have to wait for another passer-by.

Fifteen minutes later he sighted another moving shadow on the highway, this time to the north. This was no ox, either. It was coming too fast. He stood up and riveted his gaze in fierce concentration upon the distant object. As it grew larger he felt a swift upsurge of hope. A car! At once he ran to the rear of the Ford and held up his hand for help. The approaching machine soon revealed itself as a Lincoln Zephyr carrying a Texas license. It was slowing down, too.

"Friendly people, Texans," Tod told himself. "Here's where I get help."

Instead of coming to halt, however, the car suddenly leaped forward with increased speed and, to Tod's astonishment, whizzed by with a soft purring sound. He

The Hare And The Tortoise

stared after it in dismay. The man and woman in the front seat had looked out at him with suspicion.

Tod took off his Panama hat and almost threw it to the ground. Why in thunder hadn't they stopped? He looked down. In chagrin he realized he was standing directly before his own license plate, so that it could not be seen. A wry smile moved on his lips. The occupants of that car must also have been warned against stopping for anyone not in uniform. Well, that warning worked two ways—to a traveler's disadvantage as well.

Again he went back to his coupé and seated himself on the running board. Half an hour later, far to the north, there hove into view what at first appeared to be a huge covered truck; then, as it gradually came nearer, he caught a flash of blue in the sunlight. His heart expanded. The Whipples' trailer!

After a few minutes he could make out Ma Whipple leaning out the side of the Chevrolet and waving to him. The hum of tires grew louder. He heard the murmur of Ben Whipple's voice and Ma's reply: "It's him, all right."

Tod stepped forward. "The hare and the tortoise," he called.

Ben Whipple slowly brought his caravan to a halt. "What's wrong, Frisco? Another tire?"

"No. I think it's the carburetor this time."

Ma Whipple surveyed the Ford with disapproval. "Seems to me you have too much bad luck. Your Ford ain't very new, is it? But maybe Paw can help you fix it. If he can't, he's always good with advice."

"Now, Ma!" Her husband's eager glance crossed to the open hood. "Jest give me my specs, will you? I gotta go to work." He adjusted a pair of gold-rimmed glasses over his long nose, blinked twice, smiled, and then got down. "Let me take a look. I'll soon tell you what's wrong."

Ma Whipple's placid gaze settled upon Tod. "You might as well get over here out of the sun, young man. When Paw says it won't take no time at all, it generally means about two hours. But he'll enjoy himself. He likes to tinker with engines."

Tod put his hand on the door of the Chevrolet, suddenly aware that his throat was dry and parched. "How about a drink of ice water, Mrs. Whipple?" he asked.

She bestowed upon him a pleased smile. "It's here, right handy."

When Tod turned back to his own car, Ben Whipple was in the seat behind the wheel. "Seems like a clogged gas line to me," he announced. All at once he peered across at Tod. "Do you figure you might have some dirt in the gas tank?"

Tod gave a start. He looked around. Again the eyes were watching. Yet no black Buick, he knew, needed to be near to bring results like this. A handful of earth tossed into the gas tank the night before might be the cause of all this trouble. "Maybe you're right," he said at last. "Could we blow out the gas line? I haven't an air pump."

The Hare And The Tortoise

Ben Whipple climbed out of the Ford. "I got any tool you ever need. But what you ought to do, maybe, is to drain that tank and put in clean gas."

"And where am I going to get the gas? The next town on the map is about thirty miles ahead."

"Shucks. I always carry an extra ten gallons. We'll jest be sure what's wrong, drain that tank, blow out the line, and put in new gas. Let's git busy."

Both of them were hot and dripping with sweat by the time the tank was drained. "Look," said the old man. "A handful of dirt is right. Jest cast your eyes over that stuff coming out. Frisco, you sure got some nice friends on this road."

Tod, crouched by the rear tire while the gasoline drained out onto the gravel, spoke in a tone that conveyed his feeling of appreciation. "You and Ma are certainly the kind of friends to find."

"Shucks, I didn't mean us. I mean your other friends in that black sedan. Seems like they don't want you to travel south."

Tod's lips came together tightly. His gray eyes took on a look of determination. "And that's why I'm on my way. I intend to be in Valles tonight. We'll be having dinner there, don't forget."

"I hope so," said Ma Whipple from her seat in the Chevrolet. "Though I don't figure to be disappointed if I have to get dinner for all three of us somewhere along the road."

Highroad To Adventure

When Tod presently climbed into his seat, pressed a foot upon the starter and heard the motor cough and then take up its regular throb, he threw out a hand in triumph. "That dinner still holds! I'll go slow from now on and keep right ahead of you."

"You're real sensible, Tod." Ma Whipple nodded her gray head in approval. "I'll feel lots better if we keep your Ford in sight." She paused and looked round. "There's a car coming, Ben. You ought to have driven off the road."

"Aw, there's plenty of room to pass," Ben Whipple retorted.

Tod turned off the motor and got out. "One more cup of that ice water before we move on, Mrs. Whipple. I need it badly."

But Ma Whipple made no move to bring out the thermos jug. She was still gazing back along the road as though fascinated. "This car that's coming," she said. "It looks like—— Yes, it is. A black sedan!"

Tod stopped short. His startled gaze swept back up the highway. "Is it a Buick?" he whispered.

"Ma knows 'em all. It's coming purty fast. What is it, Ma?"

"She isn't close enough yet. Wait a minute."

Tod's fingers tightened in his palms. Motionless, intent, he watched the approaching car grow larger every second. He noted the headlights, the line of the hood, the windshield. The distant whine of the tires on the pavement became audible.

The Hare And The Tortoise

Ma Whipple said with conviction, "She's a Buick!"

On the instant Tod ran to the end of the trailer and held up his hand. Behind him came Ma Whipple's horrified voice. "Tod, don't stop them! You don't know what they might do."

But there was no danger of the approaching car coming to a halt. With a hum of tires and a low throb of a powerful motor the black sedan shot past the trailer at seventy miles an hour. Tod had time only to glimpse a white-clad figure at the wheel. No one else was there. He made out one thing, though. The car bore a Mexico license—1283.

"Well, they wasn't friends," Ben Whipple said consolingly. "Ma's happy, anyway."

Tod hurried back to the side of the Chevrolet. "I didn't see anyone but the driver, and not much of him. Was he an American?"

"I didn't get a chance to look." Ma's tone revealed her disappointment.

Ben Whipple declared heatedly, "A Mexican was driving. I saw him. He was wearing a white cap pulled low over his face, but I could tell. He was dark."

"Young or old?" Tod asked.

"Young. Maybe your American was hiding in the back seat."

"Maybe." A look of determination spread over Tod's face. He opened the door of the Ford. "I'm going after that car."

Highroad To Adventure

Ma Whipple's voice rose in protest. "No—don't! You stay right here with us, Tod Moran!"

"But I've got to get a good look at those two men."

"It ain't safe. You'll get into trouble."

"Now, Ma, don't try to tell Frisco what to do."

"But I don't like it," Ma Whipple wailed.

Tod, with a thrill of satisfaction, felt the throb of his motor. "I'll see you both at Valles," he cried. "Thanks a million for all your help. I'm off."

"Good luck!" called Ben Whipple.

"We're coming, too," shouted Ma.

Tod leaned close to the wheel, his foot on the accelerator. The coupé plunged ahead like a new car. The speedometer climbed to forty, to fifty, to fifty-five. His gaze was riveted upon the paved white highway extending straight ahead. The black sedan was still visible.

CHAPTER VI

The Black Sedan

UNDER THE SPEEDING WHEELS the road fell away behind. Tod pressed his foot harder still upon the accelerator. The Ford swept on in swift pursuit. The motor roared. Wind rushed past the open windows. Yet far ahead, the Buick was steadily growing smaller.

Disappointed, Tod plunged into reflection. If he'd only bought a new car, he would have had some chance of overtaking that fleeing sedan. Neil had been right. A newer Ford would have leaped ahead at sixty-five without a murmur. He glanced down at the speedometer. The dial pointed to fifty-nine.

By thunder, the old car wasn't doing bad at all! In the distance the Buick sank from sight for a moment, then came into view again. The highway was beginning to dip and rise. Ignoring the warning road sign which read *vado*—dip—he heard the car's springs squeak in protest as he almost bounced from his seat. Stubble fields of corn flashed by on his right. When he presently saw the Buick vanish round a rolling hillside, he leaned forward, intent and anxious.

The Ford sped on, swept across a concrete culvert and rounded the curve with whining tires. The highway extended straight ahead for a half mile before it again curved out of sight. The road was empty, the Buick gone.

Tod lessened the pressure of his foot. The thought struck him that he must take care not to run into a trap. Suppose the other car stopped round a turn and waited for his approach? The driver might be armed, and in a lonely spot it would be simple to block the highway and demand the brief case at the point of a pistol. He glanced off to his right. In a sugar-cane field several natives leaned on their hoes to watch him pass. Well, this country wasn't so lonely. And the Whipples with their trailer were not so many miles behind. No, for the present at least, he was safe.

With a shrug he settled back in his seat and let the car roll along at forty-five. Once he reached over and turned on the radio, but the static-filled music of a Spanish orchestra did not fit into his mood. He switched it off. The conviction seized him that he had not seen the last of the Buick for that day.

Just before one o'clock he drove into Ciudad Victoria, a small city apparently untouched by the American civilization to the north. This, he told himself as he passed the shaded plaza, was the real Mexico. On a building at the corner a yellow arrow pointed to the left with the notation: Hotel Hidalgo. Suddenly aware that he was hungry, he followed the arrow and entered a narrow cobbled street flanked by adobe houses with iron-barred windows.

The Hotel Hidalgo was an old whitewashed building of Spanish colonial design. Opposite its simple and attractive entrance Tod parked his car, rolled up the windows and locked the doors. As he turned away he found himself abruptly surrounded by several dirty-faced urchins who shouted all at once, "Wash car? Wash car?"

Tod shook them off with a smile. In the hotel entrance he was met by a Mexican woman of middle age. She was thin and sharp featured and wore her black hair tightly wound in a knot at the back of her head. "It might pay you," she said in excellent English, "to let one of those boys keep an eye on your car."

Tod laughed. "I thought they wanted to wash it. But why should a car have to be watched?"

The woman shrugged. "This is your first trip into Mexico? Then you should know that things have a way of disappearing when your back is turned. A few centavos will assure you of its safety. I know these boys. You can trust them."

Tod's glance roved over the five breathless urchins. Choosing the one with the dirtiest face and the fewest clothes—no simple task—he nodded. "All right. Watch that car."

With a shout of glee the boy waved the others away, walked proudly to the Ford and seated himself with an air of importance upon the running board. The four other boys gazed at him with envy.

"Am I too late for lunch?" Tod asked.

"Not at all, señor. Come in."

The high-ceilinged dining room was dim and cool. Near his small round table, French windows opened upon a patio where an ancient fountain leaked water across the flagstones. The woman, evidently the proprietress, clapped her hands. A servant appeared and took his order.

Tod, unfolding his napkin, glanced round the deserted room. "Many tourists going south these days?" he asked.

The proprietress shook her head. "Not many, señor."

"Did a black Buick sedan stop here for lunch?"

"No. You are the first American today." She sighed. "It is too bad, señor, but Americans are not popular in Mexico now. The people show their dislike and that scares the tourists away. It is the oil that has done it—the oil!"

Tod rose and pulled out a chair. "Won't you sit down? You see, I am new to this country. I'd like to hear about it."

Pleased, the woman seated herself across the table. "The government is improving things, señor, trying to make the new highway attractive to travelers, trying to make it safe, even bringing English-speaking Mexicans here along the highway so they can cater to the tourist trade. But it is difficult with this oil question still unsettled. We are in the midst of the Reforma, a great movement to give Mexico back to the Mexicans. Our President desires the Indians to own a bit of land, to be educated in public schools, to raise themselves from poverty. It is a noble undertaking, señor, but difficult to carry out."

"It sounds," Tod said, "like a New Deal."

"It is an era of reform. For generations foreign capital has come into Mexico, milked the country dry, and sent its earnings out of the country. That is what the President desires to stop. Oil and minerals that lie under the soil of Mexico should belong to the Mexican people, yes?"

"That seems fair," Tod admitted.

The woman smiled. "The President"—and when she said the word, her voice revealed admiration and affection—"ah, he leaves his home in Mexico and travels through the country so he can see for himself."

Tod's brow creased in a frown of perplexity. "Mexico? But isn't all this country Mexico?"

"Ah, señor," explained the woman, "to us Mexico means simply Mexico City, our capital in the Federal District. You are now in the state of Tamaulipas."

The arrival of the servant with enchiladas and tortillas interrupted the conversation, but the woman soon went on with her account of the glorious Reforma, which was bringing hope to the people of Mexico and cries of rage from the wealthy class as well as from the foreigner. In the midst of her narration she stopped and suddenly looked up. From outside came shrill voices raised in anger.

"Those boys! They are up to something. Sit still, señor. I shall look."

Before she was out of her chair, the door flew open and into the dining room rushed the urchin whom Tod had last seen seated on the running board of his car. The boy's face was filled with distress as he halted beside the woman. From his trembling lips came a torrent of words that Tod could not understand.

"Señor!" The woman's voice was sharp. "This *muchacho* says someone offered him two pesos to leave your car and go home, and when he refused, he was knocked down. Come. Quick!"

It took Tod only a moment to reach the sidewalk. The hood of his Ford was raised on the far side, but no one was near. His glance swept up to the near-by corner. The four other urchins were there, shouting and pointing down a side street.

"Señor, they say the man stepped into a black car and sped away."

"An American?"

"No, señor. I am sorry to say—a Mexican. What can it mean?"

Tod said bitterly, "I think I know, all right." He

[78]

stepped round his car and looked down under the open hood. One glance was enough to tell him what had happened. The electric wiring had been ruthlessly pulled and broken.

Quickly he unlocked his car, climbed in behind the wheel and stepped upon the starter. It was dead.

His face was grim as he regarded the woman. "Any garage near here where I can get a good electrician?"

"Perhaps." She threw out her hands in a gesture of resignation. "I would not advise you to let them work on your car. They are very inexperienced."

"But I can help them. Maybe I'll need wire and tools."

The proprietress turned with a puzzled frown to the boy beside her. She spoke quickly and pointed down toward the plaza. The boy nodded, shot a swift glance at Tod, then left at a run. The woman followed him with her glance. "He will go for help to the garage. I also ordered him to tell the police."

"Good." Tod got out. "Is there a highway patrol around here?"

"Yes, señor. One cruises this road on a motor cycle. The chief will know where he is."

Tod looked down again at the mess of disarranged wires. Delay—that was what this meant.

"Come," said the woman. "You may as well finish your lunch. If you don't try to hurry the mechanic, it will be repaired all the sooner. By four o'clock you may be on the road again."

"Four o'clock?" Tod was aghast. "But I wanted to reach Valles before dark."

"It would be wiser, señor, to stay here for the night."

"But I can't! I've an appointment in Valles for this evening."

The woman shrugged. "Finish your lunch, señor. You will need it."

It was exactly four-thirty before the car was repaired. By that time Tod was in a fury of impatience. The little coupé had been hauled by a rickety tow car to a garage several blocks away where two mechanics worked over it with such a palaver that Tod suspected the men repaired electric wires by a process of experimentation. The chief of police arrived, astounded at the occurrence, and promised to notify the highway patrolman when he came through sometime toward evening. Tod paid his bill, got into the car, and drove back to the Hotel Hidalgo.

In the lobby he asked the proprietress, "Is there any chance of my buying a pistol around here?"

She regarded him in surprise. "Have you a license to carry firearms?"

"No."

"Then I'm afraid there is no chance at all. The government is very strict about weapons. No one is allowed to carry guns."

Tod's face fell. "But I need a pistol badly—for protection."

The Black Sedan

"One minute." She stepped to the entrance, swung the two heavy wooden doors in place, and dropped a bar across them. Then she came back to the desk, opened a drawer, and selected a large key. "Come with me." She led the way into the patio and back to a door at one side. "My husband's room. He has a pistol which he might part with if he were here. But he isn't here and he wouldn't be allowed to sell it, anyway." She turned the key in the old-fashioned lock and threw open the door.

Tod caught the implication behind her words. "Would he present it to me—for a certain remuneration?"

The woman's black eyes gleamed shrewdly. "How much would it be worth?" She opened a drawer and brought forth a dark revolver.

Tod took it eagerly. "Ten dollars—American."

"You accept it at your own risk," she pointed out. "Don't show it to anyone until you obtain a license."

"And how long would it take for me to get a license?"

"Perhaps a day or so."

"I'll take the pistol, anyway. It's riskier not to have one. Don't worry. I won't use it unless I have to."

The woman nodded. "If you insist upon going on to Valles today, it is well to carry this. Wait. I'll get you a dozen shells."

It was nearly five o'clock when Tod passed the plaza and again headed south on the highway. At a service station on the edge of town he learned that a blue trailer pulled by a Chevrolet had passed several hours earlier.

His lips were compressed tightly together as he drove on. No friendly Whipples would pick him up if anything happened this time.

When he was safely outside the city, he stopped the car, took the revolver from his pocket, loaded it, locked the safety catch, then laid the weapon beside him on the seat, under his coat. With a new sense of security he drove on again. The black sedan would no longer find him such easy prey.

A short time later he passed kilometer 670, the point at which the road map announced he would cross the Tropic of Cancer. Now that he was really in the tropics, he looked about to see if any change was noticeable. The landscape, however, appeared the same. The same high mountains rose far to his right, and occasional cane fields were passed just as before, though perhaps the streams were more plentiful and the air more oppressive. But when he glimpsed in the passing trees several dry clumps of twigs not unlike bird nests, he knew he had reached the tropics at last. For he recognized those air plants as orchids, dry now, but only waiting the coming of the rains to spring into bloom.

The paved road climbed through hills, descended again, climbed once more, and then slid down into a great tropical valley that extended far to the south. Palms and banana trees dotted the countryside in profusion. Bits of jungle crept up to the roadside. A large green bird winged its way across the darkening sky. A parrot?

The Black Sedan

Night was near. And straight ahead the sky was thick with clouds that were black and threatening. The air grew sultry and still more oppressive. Soon after he switched on his headlights he came into Villa Juarez, but he drove through the little town without stopping. Valles was still sixty miles away. Luck holding, he should be ordering dinner for the Whipples by eight o'clock.

His thoughts flew ahead to his lodging for the night. The Casa Grande, he knew, was a modern motor hotel built especially to accommodate travelers on the road. One of the booklets given him at Laredo had shown pictures of a flowered courtyard with wide screened verandas, and a tiled dining room with white-clad waiters in attendance. French cuisine was advertised. Well, he'd order a dinner that would at least partly make up for the Whipples' waiting so long—thick juicy steaks, French-fried potatoes, and every delicacy he could find on the menu.

A sudden clap of thunder broke in upon his thoughts. He looked up at the sky. Not a star was shining. The headlights showed the road stretching ahead through flat country with palms and vegetation pressing toward it on both sides. At least no curves or hills were visible. He'd hold her at fifty.

Rain began falling. Soon it increased in volume until the drumming on the car top drowned out even the throb of the motor. Huge drops splashed upon his thin shirt,

[83]

upon the worn upholstery. Quickly he rolled up both windows part way. The windshield wiper, rubbing from side to side, was no longer able to keep his vision clear. The glass streamed with water. Well, if he didn't want to find himself in a ditch beside the road, he'd better stop until this tropical shower was over.

Carefully he steered the car off the pavement to the gravel and put on the brakes. A sense of caution warned him not to stop the motor in this flooding downpour, but the drumming sound on the car top was so loud he could not be sure that the engine had not already died. Pressing his foot upon the accelerator, he was relieved to catch the unmistakable vibration of the motor. Good. He'd keep her going for the present. How near, he wondered, had he driven to the ditch? At the thought he reached into the pocket in the instrument panel and took out his flash light, pressed the button and, leaning over, pointed it out the window. Only a dense waterfall met his gaze. He sighed. It was a good thing he'd stopped.

Twenty minutes later the rain lessened. He turned on the windshield wiper and, as the glass cleared, he peered out. The headlights brought into relief the gentle slope of a ditch and a wall of green jungle, wet and shining. The sight brought home to him with the force of a blow the utter loneliness of this highway. He reached into the watch pocket of his trousers for his thin gold Hamilton and held it up to the instrument panel. Why, it was nearly seven-thirty. He'd never make Valles by eight.

The Black Sedan

He threw in the clutch, pulled the wheel to the left, and guided the car to the middle of the road. Only a few drops of rain were now falling. The treads on the new tires took hold of the pavement. He could hear the wet splash of water as he gained momentum. A sense of well-being flowed through him. He only needed to spin along to feel like his old self again.

All at once something flashed in the mirror above his windshield. He stared at it. In the blackness of the night far behind, a pair of headlights was visible. A car was creeping up in the rear. Well, that was good. He wouldn't be alone on this road.

Carefully he pulled the coupé toward the right, for every moment the headlights were drawing nearer. On each side of him the green growth of jungle took form. He could see the shadow of his own car on the pavement. By thunder, whoever was driving that other car was certainly eating up the road with no regard for the wet pavement. His ears caught the swish of tires overtaking him. The headlight beams were piercing the night to his left.

Suddenly the sound changed. Why, the other car was slowing up! Its powerful motor was audible. Surprised, he looked out the window. The shadowy shape of a large black sedan was slowly drawing abreast.

His hands tightened on the wheel. A shiver of dread went through him. The Buick!

Without thinking, he pressed his foot down hard

upon the gas. His car shot forward. Gazing down at the speedometer, he saw that it was climbing swiftly. Here, he told himself, this wouldn't do. He must keep to an even speed so that perhaps in the darkness the driver of the Buick would pass without recognizing him. One glance to his left, however, informed him that the sedan was almost abreast again. Its front wheels were even with his window.

With a quick movement he reached over to the instrument panel, found the middle button, and pressed. The lights on the gauges winked out. The driver of that other car would not now be able to glimpse his figure crouched over the wheel. The driver? He peered out as the black sedan crept past. Maybe there was a second man seated beside the driver. Maybe that unknown American was even now looking his way.

All at once he pulled the wheel to the right, for the sedan was edging slowly ahead and getting directly in the way of the Ford's left front wheel. He caught his breath sharply. He was being forced off the road.

Frantic, he took one foot off the gas and pressed the other on the brake. He felt the coupé leave the pavement and touch gravel. The brake screeched. In despair he realized that the rear wheels were skidding. His seat tipped. He almost lost his balance as the car slid quietly, softly into the ditch.

Reaching for the key, he turned off the ignition. Lucky he hadn't tipped over. He looked out. The black sedan

The Black Sedan

had stopped a short distance ahead. Under the beams of the Ford's headlights its black paint shone wet and dripping.

With an effort Tod tried to collect his thoughts. He must act quickly, he knew. No use now to think of getting his coupé back on the road again. He must first get rid of that black sedan. With a sudden movement he switched off his headlights. Darkness closed down around him. He felt along the seat, flung his coat aside. His fingers touched the cold barrel of the revolver. With satisfaction he picked it up, flung open the right-hand door and stepped down into the ditch.

His feet sank into slime. Water lapped softly round his ankles. Unmindful of both, he released the safety catch on the revolver and slowly raised his arm. He could see the two red tail lights gleaming and the dim outline of the sedan standing up against its own headlight beams. Aiming as close as he dared to the sedan roof, he pulled the trigger. A loud report sounded.

At once the lights on the other car winked out. He was lost in a black tunnel of darkness with only the soft purr of the Buick's motor audible. Then to his ears came the low murmur of excited voices. The motor roared. Tires hummed with a swishing sound. The road ahead took form as the Buick's headlights flashed on again. Rapidly the black car gained speed. The roar of its motor receded into the distance.

Motionless, exultant, Tod watched the two red lights

grow smaller and smaller. Not until they dimmed and finally vanished did he remember to lower his pistol.

For the first time, then, he became aware of the water about his feet. With an anxious step he moved to the rear of his coupé. He put out a hand to the fender and felt it quiver under his touch. Every moment the right wheel was sinking deeper into the mud.

CHAPTER VII

To Valles

As HE PROWLED ABOUT THE CAR, flash light in hand, Tod saw with relief that no damage had been done. Yet his predicament loomed large, just the same. Even though the slope of the ditch was gentle, the right rear wheel was so deep in the mud that the Ford tipped precariously. To think of getting her out without aid seemed a forlorn hope.

Straightening up, he released the button on his torch and looked around. In the sky to the south a few stars were visible. Otherwise, only the deep shadows of the night met his gaze. From the wall of vegetation rising beyond the ditch came the faint drip of water falling from vines to the ground. Well, there was no help at hand. There was not even an ax or a shovel to assist in such an emergency as this. But there were numberless dead palm fronds in that tropical growth and plenty of gravel alongside the road. Furthermore, he had two hands. Time to get to work, Tod Moran!

During the next hour he became so weary and depressed that he was often ready to call a halt to his efforts. The uncertainty, however, of finding any help within miles kept him doggedly at work. His face and chest streamed with sweat; his hands were scratched and bleeding from pulling with all his weight at the fronds hanging dry and sharp from the palm trunks; and his trousers were wet to his thighs from kneeling in the ditch while he dug around the wheel. Whenever he started the motor, threw in the clutch and felt the tires spin without catching hold, he would tell himself he'd try just once more to get those palm fronds under the wheel. And when he tried once more and the wheel continued to churn water, he would set his teeth, straighten his shoulders and get out of the car and start all over again. For there was nothing else to do. The one alternative was to spend the night in the little coupé and wait for possible help when someone passed along the highway in the morning. Yet delay was the one thing he would not accept without a fight. He must keep to his schedule if he was to meet Captain Jarvis in Mexico.

He was still trying to build a roadbed up the slope when all at once he stopped and listened. An automobile was coming—and coming from the direction of Monterrey. At least this could not be the black sedan. He sprinted up to the road and gazed north. Two headlights grew in size until he was blinded by the glare. Raising a weary arm, he waved. The hum of tires grew louder, and a small sedan swept by without stopping. Although he stared after it, disheartened, he was not really surprised. For he knew that with his hair tousled, his face dirty, and his clothes clinging wetly to his body, he must have presented an unfavorable picture—more like a ruffian than a traveler in distress.

With a shrug he turned back to the ditch. Just one more try!

When he finally climbed in again behind the wheel, threw in the clutch and felt the rear wheels grip his roadbed of palms, he leaned forward with a swift upsurge of hope. By slow degrees the Ford bumped jerkily up the incline. The front tires touched gravel. In another breathless moment they had reached the smooth level pavement of the highway. He straightened out the car, put on the brake and stopped. Before he went on, he'd have a good long drink from one of those bottles in the trunk. What did he care if the water was warm and stale! He was in luck at last. Luck? He grinned happily. Downright hard work was a better explanation.

Three minutes later he was spinning along the highway toward Valles. He reached over and switched on the radio, but the reception was still so poor that he turned it off. Anyway, he told himself, he didn't need music to make him feel light-hearted. For the road, though still damp, was straight and deserted, and the Casa Grande with a hot bath and food was not so many miles away.

He had gone nearly half the distance before he met any other travelers on the road. Then a pair of headlights came into view from the direction of Valles. He slowed down to thirty while his right hand made sure that his pistol lay beside him on the seat. If this was the black sedan returning with the driver, perhaps armed this time, he'd be ready.

The approaching car was slowing down, too. Putting his foot gently on the brake, he went on with more caution. The glare of the light in his eyes permitted no view of the other car. All at once he gave a start. The glare vanished as the strange car turned off its lights and stopped. Under the beams of his own headlights a blue Chevrolet took form. A voice called, "Is that you, Frisco?"

"Paw Whipple!" He leaned out the window and brought his car to a halt beside the Chevrolet. "I didn't expect to see you around here."

"Why not?" Ma Whipple's voice came from beside her husband. "We got so worried I had Paw unhook the trailer so we could come back and look for you. The service-station man in Valles said we wasn't supposed to drive at night, but I told him he couldn't give me orders. Need help?"

"Not now. That black sedan put me in the ditch. Had dinner yet?"

To Valles

Ben Whipple chuckled. "We're still a-waiting."

"That's right," Ma Whipple agreed. "We aimed to eat with you tonight, so I told Paw the longer we wait for that slow poke the bigger dinner he'll have to order. We better hurry back before that dining room closes up. Wait a minute. I'm going to ride with you, Tod. We got things to tell you. Paw, you turn around and keep right behind us. And don't let the Ford out of your sight."

Tod got down and held open the door of his car while Mrs. Whipple climbed in. "It'll be good to have someone to talk to," he said.

"Go ahead," called Ben Whipple. "I'll follow."

As Tod slid in behind the wheel Ma Whipple said, "My, what a sight you are! Your clothes look all wet. You might catch cold."

"In this heat?" Tod threw in the clutch. "No chance."

Ma Whipple heaved her stout little form toward the door. "Gracious, I been setting on something. What in the world is it?"

"I guess it's my pistol. Bought it back in Victoria. I already fired one shot at that black sedan."

"Land sakes alive! I'll just hold it. If that Buick comes along again I'll show 'em I can shoot, too."

Tod chuckled. "I bet you could, at that."

Ma Whipple nodded vigorously. "I don't trust these foreigners. This is the first time Paw and I have been out of the States and it makes me feel kinda scary."

"But it isn't these natives I'm afraid of," Tod said as

the dark jungle growth slid by on both sides. "It's the American who owns that black sedan."

"We saw it," said Ma Whipple, raising her voice above the throb of the motor. "That's why I was mighty sure something had happened to you."

"You saw the black Buick?"

"Yes. When it pulled into Valles this evening."

"Did it put up at the Casa Grande?"

"No. Paw and I took a walk to the corner and we saw the black sedan come down the highway from the north and turn off toward another hotel. That was when I made Paw start out to look for you."

"Did you see who was in it?"

"Only two men, that's all."

"Two men! Are you sure?"

"Yes, I'm right certain there were two in that car. We waited while they drove up to the Hotel Condesa, then we decided to get out the Chevrolet and go back for you." She paused and glanced his way. "You don't aim to go looking for those two men, do you?"

Tod smiled at her. "Not till I have a shower and a change of clothes and dinner. Maybe I'll ask the chief of police to go along, too."

Ma Whipple sighed. "It seems like our plans don't work out so well. I wish you wouldn't go looking for trouble, Tod. Tomorrow you'll have a long drive over those mountains before you reach the Valley of Mexico. You better get a good rest tonight and follow us in the morning."

To Valles

Tod glanced up into the little mirror where the Chevrolet lights were showing. "You and Paw don't plan to pull that trailer all the way to Mexico in one day, do you?"

"No. We couldn't go that fast through the mountains. But tomorrow is only the fourteenth of the month. You told me yourself you didn't have to be in Mexico City until the day after tomorrow."

"I know, but I'd like to make Mexico City tomorrow night so I can get in touch with my friend on the morning of the fifteenth."

"It's important?" Ma Whipple asked softly.

"Very important."

Ma Whipple's next words came in low, troubled tones. "If those men in that Buick done all this to you, Tod Moran, they'll do worse yet before they're through. They won't never be satisfied until they get that brief case." There was a slight quiver in her voice. "This foreign country sort of worries me, I guess. I'm scared."

"Why, Ma Whipple, I'm surprised at you!" Tod frowned at her in mock disparagement. "I'd have said that nothing on earth could put a scare into you."

"Maybe some things do," she admitted with a tremulous laugh. "Hungry? Why don't you speed up? The Chevvy isn't pulling the trailer now."

When they came to Valles, Ma Whipple pointed with interest to the bamboo houses with their huge thatched roofs. "Cozy, aren't they? Smell the wood smoke." She peered ahead. "You can see the electric sign on top of the Casa Grande. We're almost there."

But Tod's eyes were contemplating something else. The highway, now that it was passing through the little town, was dimly lighted by electric bulbs; and beneath one of these cross-street lights two men stood in the middle of the pavement.

"Let me have that pistol," he said quietly. "See those two men ahead? I don't like their looks."

Ma Whipple thrust the cold steel into his hand. "They're soldiers, Tod. They've got rifles. It looks like they want us to stop."

Tod threw the gear shift into neutral and let the car roll on. "Since they're in uniform, we'll obey. But we never stop for civilians."

"You don't say!" Ma Whipple's tone held a hint of laughter. "You only stop for civilians when they run you into a ditch, eh?" She leaned forward intently and her voice became worried. "Isn't this kind of funny? Nobody stopped me and Paw when we came through."

Tod shoved the pistol out of sight beneath his thigh while he pressed gently on the brake. In the glare of his headlights one of the soldiers raised a peremptory hand. As the car drew to a halt, the man lowered his arm and stepped up to the open window. Without a word, he inspected the inside of the coupé. His dark glance took in Tod's bedraggled appearance, then his gaze moved on as if in surprise to the stout little figure of Ma Whipple.

To Valles

Puzzled and annoyed, Tod asked, "You wanted something?"

The man shifted the rifle strap on his shoulder, stepped back and spoke in a low tone to his companion. The other man nodded somberly to Tod and motioned him to drive on.

Relieved, Tod stepped on the gas and the car shot ahead.

"Now what did they mean by that?" whispered Ma Whipple.

"Oh, they must have been looking for somebody else."

Ma Whipple twisted round until she could look back through the rear window. "They're stopping Paw, too. I hope he doesn't get smart with them."

Tod raised his eyes to the huge motor hotel they were approaching. "Here we are, Mrs. Whipple. Let's hope the dining room is open."

Ma Whipple was still gazing out the rear window. "Paw's got through, all right. When I ain't there to back him up, he'd most likely be real polite."

The Casa Grande, ablaze with lights, was a large white stucco building with a red-tiled roof. An arched passage-way in the center of the hotel revealed an open court-yard beyond. As Tod drew up the car beneath the covered passage, the thought struck him that this wayside hotel was not unlike the old stagecoach inns he'd seen in Europe, and he wondered if modern motor hotels like this, built for the convenience of guests with cars, would not soon displace the old-fashioned hotels of the city.

"Welcome to the Gran Hotel Valles," said a formal voice. A white-clad bell boy opened the car door for Mrs. Whipple.

While Ma Whipple stepped out with dignity, Tod reached for his coat on the ledge behind the seat and, shielded by his companion's ample form, put his pistol carefully into the inside pocket. Then with the coat over his arm, he stepped out and moved to the rear of the car to unlock the trunk.

Another white-clad bell boy rushed down the steps and picked up the luggage. Tod firmly took the brief case from his grasp and followed Ma Whipple up to the lobby. He was registering at the desk when Ben Whipple joined them.

"Dining room still open?" Tod asked the clerk.

"Just ready to close, señor. But I shall hold one of the cooks."

"Good." Tod turned to the Whipples. "Suppose you order our dinner while I'm cleaning up. I'll be with you in ten minutes. What about a juicy steak and French-fried potatoes?"

Ben Whipple's brown eyes glowed with interest. "You leave it to me, Frisco. We'll order plenty." He moved off with his wife across the tiled floor toward the dining room.

Tod gave his car keys to one of the boys, then followed the other along a wide inner veranda that encircled the courtyard where a fountain spouted water up into the luminous tropical night. In his room, he tipped the boy, locked the door, and started to pull off his damp shoes. All at once he paused. The boy had said that the Ford would be parked in the garage at the rear of the hotel. Yet to leave it there perhaps unprotected while the owner of the Buick was in town, was something he did not relish. Hurriedly he went out, locked his door behind him, and walked toward the lobby.

Voices came to him from lighted rooms off the screened veranda. In the lobby a radio was playing "*La Cucaracha*"—probably an orchestra in Mexico City. He glanced into the dining room as he passed and saw with satisfaction that the Whipples were seated at a table and a waiter was taking their order. Unmindful of his appearance, he crossed the lobby where several American tourists looked his way with smiles of amusement. With a shrug he went out the door and down the tiled steps to the entrance passage.

Lounging in a chair there was a Mexican who wore a sombrero on the back of his dark head and a poncho over one shoulder. Tod stopped. "Want to earn a few pesos?" he asked the man.

"*Si*, señor."

"You understand English?"

"Oh, yes, señor. I studied English in a school."

"Come with me. I'd like someone to guard my car."

"Yes, señor."

Highroad To Adventure

Tod glanced closely at his companion as they crossed the flagstones of the courtyard. The fellow was a young Mexican, probably in his early twenties, olive-skinned and almost handsome. There was intelligence in the dark flash of his eyes.

Across the courtyard another passage led out into an open yard, surrounded on all sides by sheds. Perhaps six or seven cars were parked there in the dim light. One glance around the unguarded spot told Tod he had made no mistake in seeking out this young man.

He led the stranger across to his Ford. "I'd like you to watch my car all night," he said. "Could you possibly sleep in it?"

"All night?" The deep dark eyes turned his way in surprise.

"I'll pay you well. How much for the job?"

The young man hesitated. "Is one dollar, American, too much, señor?"

"No. That'll do fine. Here's the car." He threw open the door, extracted the key from the lock and put it in his pocket. "Shall I get you a rug?"

"Oh, no, señor. It is never cold here at night. Toward morning it will rain, but the rain is warm, too."

"What's your name?" Tod asked.

"Rico, señor. You need not worry about your car. I shall not leave it one minute."

"I'll depend on you. Good night."

"Good night, señor."

To Valles

With a lighter heart Tod turned back to the hotel. In the passageway into the courtyard a rear door opened onto the veranda and he entered this. When he reached his room again he locked the door and flung off his clothes. When, after a quick shave, he stepped into the shower and the warm water was falling over his tired body, he felt almost a new person again. He had made Valles in spite of everything intended to delay him, his brief case was safe, and a dinner was awaiting him with the Whipples' homely conversation to cheer him up. Rubbing his body with soap, he raised his voice in an ear-splitting version of "*La Cucaracha*."

All at once he stopped in the middle of a bar. Someone was knocking at his door. He put his head out of the shower and called, "Who's there?"

It was the clerk who answered. "Señor, the police are here."

"The police?" Sudden foreboding gripped him with a clammy hand. "What do they want?"

"They wish to speak with you, señor. I told them to wait, but they insist."

"Give me two minutes. I'm taking a shower."

"Yes, señor."

Tod washed the soap from his body, his thoughts awhirl. Why should the police want to talk to him? Could there be any connection between this visit and those two uniformed men who had stopped him at the edge of town? Maybe those two men had not been soldiers, after all. Maybe they were members of the police force.

He turned off the shower and grabbed a towel. To his ears came the sound of a key in a lock, then footsteps entered the room. Frowning, he put his head out the door and saw the clerk entering with two armed men in uniform. With a sinking heart he realized they were the same two who had halted him at the edge of town.

"What's the big idea?" he asked angrily. "Can't they wait?"

"Señor, I'm desolate." The clerk's face wore an expression of despair. "They make me unlock your door. A thousand apologies. Señor, I am helpless."

The two men were down on their knees before the luggage. Silently they went through the bag and the suit case. Tod's voice rose in protest. "What are they doing?"

"Looking for something, señor."

"That's quite evident." Tod's tone was sarcastic. "And what do they expect to find?"

The clerk approached, his hands raised in a gesture of apology. "They say they believe you have a pistol. There was trouble on the highway this evening. Travelers have lodged a complaint against you with the chief of police."

"So that's it." Tod rubbed himself dry and stepped into the room. His eyes went unconsciously toward his coat hanging on a chair by the bed. "Tell these men there is no pistol in my bags."

To Valles

The clerk spoke quietly in Spanish, but the two search-ers did not even pause to look his way. The clerk's throat moved convulsively. "Señor, they have orders. I can do nothing. Please forgive me, señor. I do not wish the other guests to know that the police are here. It would never do. Please let these two men satisfy themselves you have no gun, and they will leave by a rear door. I am desolated that such a thing should happen at my hotel."

"Forget it." Tod reached for his shorts and hurriedly dressed. All he could do, he realized, was to attempt to carry this off with an air of outraged innocence. His eyes narrowed, however, when he saw one of the men open the brief case and glance at the thick envelopes inside. He breathed easier when the man fastened it again, but his whole body grew rigid a second later when the other man got to his feet and crossed to the chair.

The man picked up the coat and at once a muttered exclamation came from his lips. He held up in triumph a dark pistol.

In silence Tod fastened his belt, took a comb and brush from his bag, and stepped to a mirror on the wall. As unconcernedly as possible he combed his hair, his eyes directed upon the three men in the glass. They stood close together, conversing in excited tones.

At last the clerk swung about and announced, "They wish to see your permit."

"My permit?" With an effort Tod held his voice steady. "I have none."

"But, señor, you cannot carry firearms without permission. The government is exceedingly strict. It is not allowed. Never!"

"Tell them I'll see about getting permission in the morning."

Again a rapid exchange of words took place in tones more excited still. The clerk coughed, with an inquiring lift of his brows in Tod's direction. "Señor," he finally said, "you must go with them to the police station. I am sure the chief will not hold you in jail when you explain."

Tod gave him a long searching look. "You are sure?"

The clerk's glance shifted. "It is out of my hands entirely, señor. The men also insist that the elderly lady who rode with you must come with them, too, from the dining room. When you arrived in town with her they were puzzled, because they were informed you drove alone. That is why you were not taken directly to the *Inspección de Policia*."

"I see." Tod's eyes gleamed feverishly bright. "The Whipples are chance acquaintances I met in Monterrey. Mrs. Whipple rode only a few miles with me. She has nothing at all to do with this affair."

"But they insist, señor."

"Very well. If they keep insisting, I'll yell to high heaven until every guest in your hotel comes running."

"Señor, not so loud! Please."

"Well, how'd you like me to yell at the top of my voice?"

The clerk's mouth dropped open. "The manager is not here this evening," he stammered. "What will he say when he returns—if I allow this to happen!"

"He'll say plenty, don't worry. My voice is pretty strong. It wouldn't take more than a minute to bring all your guests on the run."

The clerk stared, aghast. "But surely the Señor would not do that!"

Tod nodded grimly. "The Señor certainly would. Now, listen to me. I'll agree to go without a fuss if you leave my friends out of this. Otherwise, take the consequences."

Cold sweat broke out upon the man's dark features. He stepped to the foot of the bed, put one hand on it for support, and turned pleadingly to the police. His voice sounded low, urgent, passionate. Clearly he was both threatening and begging for mercy. The other two men, gazing appraisingly at Tod's stalwart young form, gave in at last with reluctance.

The clerk's face cleared. "They agree, señor. The chief ordered them to lodge only you in jail. Please go quietly by the rear door." He paused and moistened his lips with his tongue. "I will inform the Señor's friends he may be a trifle late for dinner."

"All right." Helpless, Tod nodded. "See that my door

is locked. No one must enter this room. Tell these men they needn't unswing their rifles. There's no chance of my escaping out of their country, even if I tried. And tell them, too, that I'm ready to go."

"Ah, the Señor understands!"

"Yes," Tod said, "the Señor understands only too well."

CHAPTER VIII

Behind Bars

Hungry and depressed, Tod sat on a bench in a boxlike cell which had only one narrow barred window to let in the starlight. His thoughts were as black as the walls about him. To find himself locked in a jail with no immediate prospect of freedom was enough to make him fret in impotent rage. And to make matters worse, he had to admit to himself that the chief of police was not overstepping his duty.

In despair his mind ran back over the scene in the jail's little front office. An interpreter, summoned from a cantina on the highway, had explained the situation in careful and precise English.

"Señor Moran, the chief says you are charged with carrying a gun without a permit—a very serious offense under the present government of Mexico."

"I know it. I'm sorry. Let me pay my fine and go back to the hotel."

"But it will be necessary for you to appear before the judge."

"And when will that be?"

"This is Saturday. Tomorrow is Sunday. Perhaps the judge will be back by Monday or the day after."

"He's away?"

"Yes, señor. He has gone to Tampico. The chief is not certain when he returns."

"But I can't afford to stay shut up here for days! I must get over the mountains to Mexico City by tomorrow night."

"Impossible, señor."

"Then I'll have to get in touch with the American consul. Is there one here?"

"In Valles? Oh, no, señor. The nearest consul is in the capital. But you will be allowed to send word to him in the morning."

With firmness and courtesy—that was the way they had treated him. And he had protested, "But I haven't committed a crime, have I? Surely if I pay a suitable fine I won't be held."

"But, señor, there will be a second charge placed against you. You fired at a traveler on the highway."

That had been the blow that left him speechless. A sense of defeat swept up in a wave and overwhelmed him with bitterness and despair. Oh, he knew now what he was up against. He knew, too, how clever were his unknown opponents. It was useless to berate himself for playing directly into the hands of those men, useless to regret having bought that pistol. He had bought the gun, knowing the risk it entailed; he had fired instinctively because he'd been in danger; and he must now accept the consequences. But the consequences involved not himself alone, but Captain Jarvis and Mr. Blakemore as well.

At the thought he had felt the blood drain swiftly from his face. What would Tom Jarvis and Mr. Blakemore say when they learned how his carelessness had brought failure to their plans? He raised his head. Failure? No, he hadn't failed yet. Somehow he must manage to get that brief case to Mexico City.

His eyes were sharp as he faced the interpreter. "But that man deliberately crowded me off the highway with his Buick!"

"Señor, he admitted to the chief he drove a little too close to your car. It was because the highway was slippery. When he saw what had happened, he stopped to render aid. But you fired upon him without warning. This is indeed a most serious matter, señor."

Yes, Tod had realized at once the seriousness of this second charge. Yet he had gone doggedly on. "Who is the man who lodged this complaint against me?"

"His name is Lopez."

"And he must appear also before the judge with his complaint?"

"*Si.*"

"He lives around here?"

"No. His address is Mexico City. The chief will send word when it is time for him to return."

Days stretching ahead without end! Tod had thrust the unwelcome thought aside. "And does this Señor Lopez own the car he was driving?"

"No. Señor Lopez is only the chauffeur."

"The chauffeur? I see. And was not this man's employer in the car, too?"

"Yes."

"Please ask the chief the name of this man."

"Ah, señor, the chief regrets that he does not know. The chauffeur said he was a wealthy American."

"But doesn't the owner of that car have to sign the complaint? Isn't he more important than the chauffeur?"

"Yes, señor. The chauffeur reported that his employer's nerves were so shattered by the experience that immediately upon his arrival at the Hotel Condesa he went to bed. The chief realizes now that the judge might ask for the owner to sign the complaint. The chief says to tell you he will send word to the hotel for this American to come to the office first thing in the morning."

"Good. That's something. Will the chief allow me to see this man?"

"If the señor desires to confront both men, it shall be done. Perhaps it has all been a mistake. Perhaps you two Americans can settle this second charge between you.

Behind Bars

The chief says he will be very much relieved if you do. For the government has given strict orders to protect all tourists on the Pan-American Highway. So the chief will be pleased if the American owner of the Buick fails to press this charge. With that matter out of the way, a fine not too large will probably free you from the first charge of carrying a gun without a permit."

And with that Tod had had to be content. If he must find himself in jail in order to meet his two unknown antagonists face to face, there was some consolation there, at least.

Footsteps in the passage outside roused him from his reflections. He glanced up to see wavering candlelight appear behind the grille in his cell door. A key turned in the ancient lock. The door opened and the jailer entered with a tin plate of food in one hand and a lighted candle in the other. His dark bare feet were thrust into leather sandals; his muscular frame was only partly covered by white baggy trousers; and his friendly black eyes revealed a readiness to give his American prisoner every comfort and courtesy.

"Enchiladas, señor."

Tod stood up and gave the man a coin. "How about some light in here?"

When the fellow finally understood, he turned the candle upside down until there was a pool of melted tallow on the bench, then he set the candle in it. By the time the door banged shut Tod was already sampling the warm food. It consisted of tortillas—the flat corn bread of the Mexicans made like thin pancakes—and enchiladas, which were tortillas rolled around meat and cheese and then covered with chili sauce. It was so good and so hot to the taste that by the time the jailer returned with a tin cup of water he grabbed it out of the man's hand and drank with a swift sense of relief. Not until he put down the empty cup did he remember the warnings about drinking only bottled water along the highway. Well, for the present he felt better, anyway.

A few minutes later he had a visitor. The jailer ushered in the clerk of the Casa Grande.

"Señor Moran, I came to see if there was anything I could do. And I brought you a letter which just arrived."

"From San Francisco?"

"From Mexico City, señor."

"One minute. Maybe after I've read it I'll know better what can be done."

In surprise Tod recognized the large firm handwriting of Captain Jarvis. He tore open the envelope, sat down on the bench and held the paper toward the candlelight.

> Hotel Geneve
> Mexico City, D. F.
> Friday, May 12

DEAR JOE MACARONI:

Jim Blakemore's idea of my being a passenger on a liner all the way from New York was too much for me to stand, so I took a plane to New Orleans where I made connections with a cargo and passenger ship that landed me in Vera Cruz yesterday. Arrived here this morning to find an air-mail letter from J. B. telling about your wire from Laredo, so I'm sending this to Valles on the chance you'll get it.

Speed up your trip if you can. I need those letters of introduction. Can't very well start without them, though gossip among Americans here leads me to believe Martin Welch is correct. Things are getting hot for foreign interests in Mexico. Still, we can't decide about the mine until we really investigate.

Hope your car is holding up. Have been making inquiries about motor hotels here and suggest you go directly to the Shirley Courts at 151 Calzada Manuel Villalongin. It was formerly Emperor Maximilian's country estate and seems to please Americans who come here for a short stay. Give me a ring when you arrive. I'll stick close to my hotel until I hear from you.

I have been somewhat uneasy because J. B. writes that you thought you were being followed. However, I've about decided you were imagining things. (Forgive my frankness.) A pleasant trip—and please hurry. We want to finish up this affair as soon as possible so we can shove off with the *Araby* three weeks from now. If we take a week to drive back to San Francisco, that only leaves two weeks here. And that means full speed ahead.

Best regards,

TOM JARVIS

"Is it bad news, señor?"

Tod looked up. "No, not exactly. It means, though, that I must hurry."

The clerk threw out his hand in an expressive gesture. "If there is anything I can do——"

"Yes, there is." Tod's brows were drawn into a thoughtful frown. "Did you tell my friends in the dining room where I was?"

"Not yet, señor. I told them you would be a trifle late for dinner and for them not to wait. I thought it better to let them finish their meal without being disturbed."

"They are still in the dining room?"

"Yes, señor."

"Then please tell them where I am. Say I'd like them to come here as soon as they finish."

"Yes, señor. I shall tell them. It is only a short step from here to the hotel."

"One other thing." Tod held up his hand as the man turned to the door where the jailer stood waiting. "Please send my luggage here with Mr. and Mrs. Whipple. Have one of your boys get it from my room and tell him to be careful to bring all of it. I've a suit case, a traveling bag, and a brief case. Three pieces. If you let the Whipples know, they can bring it with them in their car."

"Yes, señor. Anything else?"

"No, thanks. My friends will take care of anything that comes up. I can expect them here in ten minutes with my bags?"

Behind Bars

"In five minutes, señor. Depend upon me. Our government, señor, has sent English-speaking people to work at the hotels and service stations along this highway and we are all ordered to look out for the comfort and well-being of our guests."

"Yes, I've heard that before." A twisted smile touched Tod's lips. "Right now I'd most appreciate a little speed."

"Ah, even though it is warm, señor, I shall hurry."

When the clerk had gone and the key turned in the lock again, Tod got up and peered out the high barred window. Clouds were blotting out the stars. A light breeze touched his cheek and brought to his nostrils the pleasant tang of wood smoke. He took off his tie and opened his shirt at the throat. It was hot.

His thoughts turned to Jarvis in the Mexican capital. If Captain Tom was to get that brief case so he could begin his work, it would perhaps be a good idea to entrust it to the care of the Whipples. Two more days of travel should bring them to Mexico City. That would be on the evening of the fifteenth. Yes, they could telephone to Jarvis at the Hotel Geneve, tell him to come to the Shirley Courts to pick up the brief case, and then they could let him know what had happened in Valles. The American consul could be notified before Jarvis started on Mr. Blakemore's job. In any case, Captain Tom must not delay his investigation by coming to Valles to get his third mate out of jail.

Jail? Tod grinned wryly. This was certainly a nice

mess. The important thing, however, was not Third Mate Moran but the brief case which would allow the investigation to get under way. And in the morning, when Lopez and the American owner of the Buick appeared, there might really be information important enough to wire to the Geneve. For if Jarvis received a telegram saying *I am in jail. Help me out*, what would he think of his young third mate? No, such a wire would never do. He had come to Mexico to help Captain Jarvis, not to hinder him.

Voices sounded in the corridor. Footsteps came his way. He turned, expectant. Ben Whipple entered first, his head bare, his black alpaca coat open, his hands in his pockets, his thin face grim. Just behind came Ma Whipple. She was wearing a small straw hat with its crown flaunting two blue flowers that matched the tiny dots in her white dress. The hat bobbed vigorously as she stopped short inside the door and glanced round the dark cell. A look of outrage appeared on her plump face. "It's awful!" she breathed. "Just awful. We won't stand for it. I told the chief what I thought of him when we came in."

Tod could not repress a grin. "I'm afraid the chief didn't understand a word you said. He doesn't know English."

"He doesn't?" Ma Whipple's eyes flashed fire. "And why not? Does he expect us to talk Mexican? This is all nonsense. I told him so. I'll tell him again."

Behind Bars

"Now, Ma!" Ben Whipple raised a thin hand in protest. "You jest calm down. Hadn't we better find out what this is all about, first?" He looked at Tod. "You tell us what happened. Now, Ma, you let Frisco do the talking."

"Have a seat, Mrs. Whipple." Tod smiled. "Don't sit too near my candle. My quarters are compact, just like your trailer, but not quite so homey, perhaps."

"Perhaps!" Ma Whipple snorted in disgust as she sat down. "I already know what I intend to do. I'm wiring my congressman in Washington tomorrow morning. He'll get in touch with the Department of State. We'll get things moving fast."

"Now, Ma, don't get excited. You don't even know your congressman's name."

"Paw, you mind your own business. Remember that rich Mrs. Parker we met in Florida? Remember her story of getting arrested in Morocco and wiring her congressman? Well, if she could get action that way, I can, too." Ma Whipple suddenly ceased speaking and wrinkled her nose. "Land sakes, what a smelly place! I don't like it."

"Neither do I," Tod admitted, "but I'm here because of my own fault." He went on to tell what had occurred, then added, "There is something you can do for me, though—something more important than trying to get me out of jail right now. You can carry my brief case to Mexico City. Go directly to the Shirley Courts and telephone my friend, Captain Jarvis, at the Hotel Geneve.

Here's a letter from him that'll tell you just what to do. After you've given him the brief case, then you can tell him where I am. But I don't want him chasing down here to Valles when he has more important business of his own. How long will it take you to get over the mountains?"

"I figure two days," Ben Whipple said quickly.

"Here comes your baggage," Ma Whipple put in as footsteps sounded in the passage. "We brought the boy along with us in the car."

Tod brightened. "I don't know how I'd get along without your help. You'll do what I ask?"

"Shucks, Frisco, we'll be glad to."

The door swung open, the jailer stepped to one side and a white-clad bell boy from the Casa Grande entered. "Your luggage, señor."

Tod drew a coin from his pocket. Abruptly he gave a start. Only a suit case and traveling bag were on the floor. "Where's my brief case?" he asked.

The bell boy looked at him in surprise. "But, señor, these two pieces were all you had in your room."

Tod's glance crossed to Ben Whipple and his wife. Their hands were empty. For a moment he stared in dismay. A tremor of fear ran through him from head to foot. "But I left my brief case in my room with these two bags! Didn't you find it?"

Ma Whipple broke in. "Your brief case was gone, Tod. Maybe it hasn't got here yet. The clerk showed me your note."

Behind Bars

"My note?" Tod's voice was low, tense. "What do you mean?"

"Land sakes, don't tell me you didn't write that note. Why, the clerk showed it to me. It was signed with your name and asked the clerk to give your brief case to the bearer."

"What clerk? The clerk that was just here?"

"No, I don't think so. The regular clerk came up to us in the dining room and told us where you were. He asked us to take your bags along when we came to see you. And when only your suit case and bag were brought out, I asked about the brief case. No one seemed to know anything at all until another clerk was called. He was the one who showed us your note."

Tod sank down on the bench. The candle flame wavered smokily. "Ma Whipple, I didn't write any note."

"You mean someone else did?" She turned a white strained face his way. "You mean someone stole your brief case?"

In silence Tod nodded.

Ben Whipple brought a gnarled hand down with a smack into the palm of his other hand. "It was those men in the Buick! So they got what they wanted!"

"Yes, they got it." A weary sigh escaped Tod's lips. His gray eyes seemed dazed. "And what can I do—in here!"

"Do?" repeated Ma Whipple. "We can set the police on those men. Didn't they steal your brief case?"

Tod stood up. "Of course. Where's that bell boy?"

The jailer in the doorway met his glance without understanding.

"The bell boy's gone," said Ben Whipple. "He scooted out mighty quick. I guess he had an idea you thought he was guilty."

"But we'll need an interpreter," Tod cried. "We won't be able to make the chief understand what we want. Paw Whipple, you'll have to run over to the cantina on the highway and try to find the interpreter who was here this evening."

"And let that Buick git away?" Ben Whipple shook his head with decision and crossed to the door. "I know what I'm going to do. Right this minute, too."

"Land sakes, Paw, what?"

"I'm going to the Hotel Condesa. Maybe the Buick's still there."

"Paw!" Ma Whipple swayed to her feet. "What you up to?"

But her husband had already vanished into the corridor. She turned slowly to Tod and he saw fear, sudden and overwhelming, reflected in her eyes.

CHAPTER IX

The Chase Begins

THE black sedan is gone, Frisco, but I don't figure it'll git very far." Ben Whipple sank down on the bench and wiped a handkerchief across his damp forehead.

It was forty minutes later, and Mrs. Whipple and Tod were standing in the candlelighted cell looking down in perplexity at the pleased expression on the old man's face.

"Paw, just what are you talking about?"

"I'm talking about that Buick. She jest pulled out."

"But, Paw, nobody would start over those mountains at this time of night."

"Oh, yes, they would," Tod put in. "Those two men would take to the road as soon as they got hold of my brief case."

"Now, wait a minute." Ben Whipple flashed a keen glance from his wife to Tod. "Ma's right, Frisco. That

Buick ain't starting over the mountains tonight. Why, it's more'n sixty miles from here to the village where the climb begins, and that car won't git that far."

Mrs. Whipple regarded her husband with suspicion. "Why not?"

The old man's face was keen and knowing. His brown eyes twinkled. "You see, nails ain't so good for tires."

"Nails! Paw, what'd you do?"

"Oh, I jest hammered some nails into the rear tires of that Buick. I remembered what Frisco told us about his own car, so I says to myself, 'If nails is bad for Ford tires they're jest as bad for a Buick's.' So I drove the Chevvy over to our trailer, picked up a hammer and some nails and then sped round to the Hotel Condesa."

Hope, sudden and joyful, surged up within Tod. "And the black sedan was still there?"

"She sure was. It was kinda dark in front of that hotel, so I fixed those tires right away. I did a mighty good job. Two nails in each rear tire. If the Buick only carries one spare, what'll the driver do about the second tire when it goes flat, too?"

"Paw Whipple, I didn't think you had it in you!"

"Go on," Tod urged. "Did you go inside the hotel? Did you see the two men who drove away?"

Ben Whipple shook his gray head. "No, I didn't git a chance. While I was asking the manager about 'em, I hears a motor start up all of a sudden. It was in a big hurry, too. So I runs outside jest in time to see the Buick drive away. I watched her. She turned south on the highway toward Mexico City." He chuckled deep in his throat. "But she won't git far."

Tod's hopes were on the wane. "But we can't be sure. That car would carry a repair kit. The chauffeur would be able to do the job by the side of the road."

"I thought of that," Ben Whipple admitted, "when I was hammering in those nails. So jest to make sure, I put a handful of dirt in the gas tank."

"Paw Whipple!" Fear and pride were mingled in Mrs. Whipple's tone. "You didn't!"

"Yes, Ma, I did. Didn't I help to drain Frisco's gas tank? It was tit for tat, and I don't feel sorry, either."

Over Tod swept a sudden uncontrollable desire to laugh. A sense of relief gripped him, too, but at the same time he realized that his chances of getting back his brief case were becoming more remote every minute. His glance strayed up to the window where the bars, in the candlelight, stood out plainly against the night sky beyond. It came over him suddenly that even if the Buick were delayed on the road, he himself was still in jail.

"Mr. Whipple," he said, "it isn't right for me to allow you to get mixed up in this affair. I appreciate what you've done, but I certainly don't want to see you locked up, too. Please don't take any more chances. Anyway, here I am—maybe for several days. And the Buick will reach Mexico City long before I can get out."

"Now, don't be too sure about that." Ben Whipple

cocked an amused eye his way. "You see, I had a little talk with the manager of that hotel."

"You did?" Tod's voice was vibrant with eagerness. "Did you learn what those men looked like?"

"The manager was kind of vague about that. He said the chauffeur was Mexican and the owner was a well-dressed American with plenty of money. Richard Smith was the name he used. He spoke some Spanish, too, and seemed to know this country pretty well. But I did learn something that's important to us jest now. The manager told Mr. Smith he'd better not try to start over the mountains tonight, and Smith said he didn't intend to. He only wanted to drive as far as Thomas and Charlie so he'd be ready for the climb in the morning."

"Thomas and Charlie?" asked Ma Whipple. "Land sakes, what's that?"

"Now, Ma, please don't interrupt. It's the name of a place about sixty miles south of here on the highway. That's where the climb begins."

Tod's mind flashed back to the road maps he had studied. "Of course. I know the town you mean. It's Tamazunchale."

"Well, it sounded like Thomas and Charlie to me," Ben Whipple declared. "Anyway, I figure it'll take time for the Buick to fix those tires and drain the tank. Now, if Frisco could git out of here early in the morning, maybe we could overtake them."

Ma Whipple said quickly, "Go ahead and tell me how

The Chase Begins

Tod is going to get out in the morning."

Ben Whipple's voice was low and restrained. "Shucks, Ma, didn't he tell us what the chief of police said about those two charges against him?"

"Of course." Tod broke in eagerly. "The first charge for carrying a gun without a permit could be taken care of by paying a fine. But the second one about firing on the Buick was mighty serious. The owner of the Buick was supposed to come round here in the morning and sign a complaint."

"That's it, Frisco. And the Buick's gone. Those fellers checked out half an hour ago. That'll only leave the one charge against you. Can't you pay your fine and go free?"

"I'm not too sure." Tod's tone was doubtful. "The chief said I'd have to appear before the judge."

"Now, listen, Frisco." Ben Whipple leaned forward. "Ain't these hotel people all along this Pan-American Highway always saying they got to look out for American tourists? Don't they tell us their government says they gotta treat us nice? You know why? So we'll come traveling down here and spend good money. Mexico needs that money. Now, I figure in the morning we can get the manager from the Condesa and that clerk from the Casa Grande and set 'em both to work on the chief of police. The chief told you he wished you could settle this affair with that other American, didn't he?"

"Yes." Tod stared unseeingly down at the floor. "Yes,

it's a chance. It might work." He raised his head, and new resolution flashed in his eyes. "But why wait till morning? If I could only start out tonight, I'd be sure to overtake that car."

Mrs. Whipple nodded until the blue flowers on her hat bobbed up and down in the candlelight. "No time like the present, Tod Moran. The chief's outside in his office waiting for us to go. He'll do it. He's been right polite to us—even when I told him what I thought of him." She paused, and an engaging smile touched her lips. "I'm glad now that he didn't understand English."

"We can try," said Ben Whipple, getting to his feet.

Tod said eagerly, "Jump into your Chevvy, Paw, and bring back the manager from the Condesa. Have him tell the chief that the Buick and its passengers have already left for Mexico City. Then bring the clerk from the Casa Grande. He promised me he'd do anything."

Ma Whipple crossed to the closed door and shook it. "Where's that jailer? I can walk over to the Casa Grande while Paw goes to the other hotel. It'll be quicker. I'll bring back that clerk if I have to drag him here. What time is it?"

Tod drew out his watch. "Nearly midnight. Won't everybody be in bed?"

"If they are," said Ben Whipple, "we'll rout 'em out. You jest leave this to me and Ma. We'll bring 'em."

"Paw Whipple," said Tod as the jailer let the old couple out the door, "you're smart as a whip."

The Chase Begins

Ma Whipple's departing words came through the iron grille. "Paw didn't build our trailer and get away from home for nothing. He's plenty smart—only the children haven't found it out yet."

At the end of ten minutes Tod heard the sound of raised voices from the office at the end of the little corridor. Pressing his face close to the door, he listened. He recognized Ma Whipple's feminine tones now wheedling and now demanding; he caught the sound of Ben Whipple's conciliating words; he heard other voices raised in excited Spanish. He sighed. The Whipples had evidently brought the men, all right. The argument went on and on without a pause.

At last a door opened and footsteps came hurrying down the passage. Ben Whipple's voice came out of the gloom. "It's fixed, Frisco. The chief is glad to forget that second charge, now that the Buick has gone. But he thought he ought to hold you for the judge to decide how big a fine you'd have to pay."

Tod strained his eyes through the grille. "Is he going to hold me?"

"No. Not if you pay fifty dollars American. Will you?"

"Will I?" Tod's eyes glowed with hope. "I'll give him a traveler's check right now."

"Ma tried to beat him down on the amount, but I told her to shut up. I said it wasn't money you wanted to save; it was time." He paused. "Here comes the jailer."

Highroad To Adventure

When the hotel men were gone, the fine paid and the three of them were finally outside on the narrow street where the Chevrolet was parked, Tod drew in a deep breath of the fresh night air. "Now for the Casa Grande! Paw, I want you to do something for me. Buy two boxes of good cigars in the morning and present them to these hotel men who helped us." He pressed some Mexican currency into the old man's hand. "Come on. Let's get going."

As the car bumped over the dirt road, Ma Whipple said, "You better get something to eat before you leave, Tod."

"Already had enchiladas. Not hungry now. I only want to get my hands on the wheel of my Ford."

"I hate to see you go," Paw Whipple remarked. "We'll follow you first thing in the morning."

A single light shone in the entrance of the Casa Grande. Tod jumped out. "Wait till I bring my car here so I can pick up my bags. I'll be right back."

His footsteps sounded loud in the stillness of the night as he crossed the patio and went through the passage that led to the open garage in the rear. His glance swept the dark sheds where the cars were parked. His pulse quickened. Suppose something had happened to the Ford? Suppose the young Mexican he had hired had not stayed by the car? With rapid footsteps he approached the red coupé.

"Rico? Are you still here?"

The Chase Begins

Something stirred within the darkness of the little car. A voice replied, "I have been asleep, señor. But nobody came near."

"Good. I'm going on tonight."

"To Mexico City, señor?"

"No, just to the next town. To Tamazunchale."

"But it is not wise to drive alone on these roads at night, señor. All *turistas* are advised against it."

Tod stepped in behind the wheel, and the young man moved over on the seat. "Want to come along with me, Rico? I'd prefer not to be alone, too. I'll pay you well if you do."

"I will be glad to go, señor."

"You know the road? You know the next town?"

"Yes. Very well."

"Good." Tod thrust his key into the ignition lock. A moment later he was backing out. "I want to pay my bill, pick up my bags outside, and then we'll be off. How far to Tamazunchale?"

"About a hundred kilometers, señor. The highway is good. No bad grades."

Tod's eyes were on his gasoline gauge. "Plenty of gas to get me there." He drove across the patio and brought the Ford to a halt in the entrance passage. "One minute while I pay the clerk."

When he came out, Ben Whipple was waiting at the rear of the Ford. "I got your two bags here, Frisco, and one of my five-gallon cans of gas. You might need it.

No, not now. Pay me back later. Open your trunk and we'll put 'em in." He leaned closer and whispered, "Who's that with you?"

"Oh, just a young fellow who's been watching my car." Tod threw open the trunk compartment and lifted the can of gasoline inside. "I thought I'd rather not drive alone."

"You're wise." Ben Whipple held out his hand. "Good luck, Frisco. If we don't see you on the road, we'll look you up at the Shirley Courts."

"I'll be there. Where's Ma?"

"She's talking to your friend."

Tod locked the trunk and went round the car. "Good-by, Mrs. Whipple. We'll have a good dinner together yet."

"I'm glad you'll have company. Be careful, won't you?"

Tod jumped in, slammed the door to, and waved his hand. "I can't ever begin to thank both of you enough."

"Forget it," Ben Whipple growled. "I'm sorry you ain't got a gun on you, though. You might need it."

"Nothing doing." Tod pulled the gear into low. "It's safer without firearms. Good-by!"

Ma Whipple's troubled tones rang out over the throb of the motor. "Go careful, Tod."

Go careful? He turned onto the pavement, slipped the gear shift into high and headed south into the night. He must wait and see what happened when he overtook that

The Chase Begins

black sedan. He glanced sideways at his companion. In the faint glow from the dashboard lights he saw a clear-cut profile under the wide brim of a sombrero, eyes dark, cheek bones high, mouth full but well formed. A light gray poncho covered the young man's body to the knees. Two dark hands rested on the poncho.

"Sleepy?" he asked.

"A little, señor. But I can sleep while you drive."

"You might as well. Do you mind a fight?"

"A fight, señor?"

"Yes, I'm trying to catch up with a certain black Buick. Two men in it stole a piece of luggage from me."

"Did you inform the police, señor?"

"No, I was too busy getting out of jail. Could they have telephoned ahead to have that car searched at Tamazunchale?"

"There is no telephone, señor."

"How about a telegraph?"

"No telegraph here, either."

"I see. It might be a good idea to stop at the police station in Tamazunchale. Could the Buick take another road there?"

"This is the only road, señor."

"Good. Then if we pass them on the road I can have police waiting for them when they reach the town?"

"But I thought the señor said something about a fight?"

Tod laughed. The speedometer was staying at fifty. Dark tropical growths flew past on each side. "I'm trying to take my friends' advice and be careful. I've made too many mistakes already. If the Buick is parked along the highway, we'll go right by and not stop. Without a gun I don't fancy meeting two men along the road."

"But I have something, señor." Rico's voice was low and resonant. "I have a knife. Here. Under my poncho."

"You mean a pocketknife?"

"No, señor. I always carry a dagger for safety. Look." The poncho moved and a dark hand held out a knife. The steel blade, slender and vicious looking, glittered in the dim light from the instrument panel.

Tod's glance came back to the highway. "Put it away, Rico. Don't use it. Don't use it even if we get into a fight."

"But why not? It is an excellent blade, señor."

"Please put it away." Tod raised his eyes.

Not a star was visible. Far ahead, lightning flashed across the sky. He listened for the sound of thunder, but only the low throb of the motor reached his ears. A storm was raging somewhere far back in the canyons of the Sierra Madres. He pressed his foot harder upon the gas. Wind whistled past the windows.

CHAPTER X

Night Drive

As the highway, under the headlight beams, rolled up beneath them, Tod put a question to his companion. "Rico, what do you do for a living?"

"I pick up odd jobs along the road, señor."

"With repair gangs?"

"No. I work for the tourists. I drive them over the mountains, help them with their luggage, guide them around Mexico City. That is where my knowledge of your language comes in handy."

"Where did you learn English so well?"

"In the States. My father, you see, sold his land in Mexico and took his family to Texas where he worked as a day laborer. I was born in San Antonio and went through school there. Then a few years ago, when the Mexican government asked for English-speaking Mexi-

[133]

cans to return home and take jobs along the new highway, I came back to my own country."

"But you are American, Rico."

"Yes, señor. But I am Mexican, too. Americans did not let me forget that. They did not let me forget for one little minute."

Tod glanced sideways at his companion. The young man's voice had been filled with a bitterness that plainly burned deep within him. There was no need to ask what it meant. The proud lift of his head, the stubborn line of his jaw, the flash of those eyes above the high cheek bones, all revealed how glad Rico had been to escape to a land where he was accepted as an equal—a Mexican among Mexicans. Tod, with warm understanding, brought the conversation back to a more pleasant subject.

"Just why should you drive tourists over the mountains? Most drivers today are familiar with all sorts of roads."

"Ah, but they have never seen mountains like these Sierra Madres. At Tamazunchale, where the climb begins, you drive a canyon road that swings round cliffs for a hundred kilometers before you come to another town. And then you climb still more through forests of oak and pine. There is no other highway like it on this whole continent. Many of the *turistas* are afraid to drive that mountain stretch."

Tod chuckled in derision. "I've driven over the Sierra Nevadas in California. This road won't scare me."

Night Drive

"No?" Rico's tone held a hint of laughter. "The Señor will see. If there isn't a storm, there is fog. And if the sun should come out and you look over the edge of the road, down thousands of feet to the Montezuma River, you'll stop your car because you'll be so dizzy."

"Rot! Heights don't make my head swim. Maybe it's the altitude that bothers some of the travelers."

"Maybe. From an altitude of five hundred feet the highway climbs up to nine thousand. You'll see. Many of the tourists have told me that in all the world there is no other road like this one. Some call it superb, spectacular. Others don't like it a bit. I've known some to go to Vera Cruz or Acapulco and ship their car home rather than return by this road."

"Then maybe it's just as well not to travel it at night?"

"Strangers do not attempt it at night, señor."

"But it can be done?"

"Yes, if there is no storm and no fog and if your car is in good condition."

Tod glanced ahead. Above the tropical growth alongside the highway the sky was black. Intermittent flashes of lightning far back in the mountains were a cheering sight to his eyes. "Then if your car needed repairs," he said, "you'd stop in Tamazunchale."

"You'd have to, señor."

"Good. Because, Rico, that Buick sedan ahead of us will need some repairs. And I could do with a little sleep myself."

Highroad To Adventure

During the next half-hour they sped through two sleeping villages without seeing a single light in any of the thatched huts. Once they passed a dirt road leading off to the left. Tod asked about it.

"The Tampico road, señor. It leads down to the gulf where you find the oil fields. Would the Buick be going there?"

"No, I think not. These men are not in the oil business. They're in mining."

Rico's next words came with an undertone of resentment. "Then they are foreigners, too?"

"One of them is. He's an American. Why do you ask?"

"Because most industries here are controlled by foreigners—Americans, British, French, or German. It has seldom been a Mexican who has found real money in the soil of Mexico."

"You sound bitter about it, Rico."

"All true Mexicans feel that way, señor. Would you feel any different if the great industries of the United States were owned by French or British or Germans? Suppose you American citizens were merely laborers who worked for rich foreigners, and worked from morning till night for thirty or forty cents a day?"

The picture Rico was painting was not at all pleasant. "I'm afraid," Tod admitted, "I wouldn't like it. In fact, I suspect I wouldn't like it at all."

"Ah, señor, you understand. You are not like most Americans who come down here. Most Americans say

Night Drive

a peso a day is enough for our people. But it isn't. We want to raise our low standard of living. We want to make Mexico a great nation. Give us time and we can do it. This is the age of the Reforma."

"Yes, I've heard of the Reforma."

Rico's tone turned friendly. "What is your name, señor? Moran? Listen, Mr. Moran. Let me tell you how my father happened to go to Texas to live. In the state of Guerrero he owned a small farm with some grazing land in the hills. His family had owned it for generations. One day an American came and offered to buy that land, but the price was too low and my father refused. Then soon after, a member of the government drove down from Mexico City and offered my father twice as much. My father had heard of this man, who was a *politico*, powerful in government circles. So my father, thinking he was getting a good price, sold out and moved to a near-by village. Then what do you think happened?"

Rico leaned forward. "American engineers came and surveyed that land, surveyed all the land around which had been bought by that rascally *politico*. The villagers were hired at a peso a day to go to work. Holes were dug. Wealth gushed forth. That land was worth a fortune, Mr. Moran—a fortune!"

"Oil?"

"Yes, oil. And that wealth was not flowing into Mexican hands, señor. The *politico* had bought it for a foreign concern and pocketed a nice wad of money for his trouble. That man was a traitor to his own country, to his own people. There were many like him in the old days. They would accept fees and bribes even though it meant cheating their countrymen. That was what hurt my father the most. He was working for twenty-eight cents a day on land once owned by him, on land that was making foreigners rich."

"Tough," Tod said. "I can't blame your father for feeling cheated."

"But all that is changed now, Mr. Moran. This is the day of the Reforma. We now have a president who thinks only of the good of his own people. *Politicos* who accept bribes are put in prison or shot. Generals who once had their own private armies and ruled great tracts of land without interference from the central government are now in exile and their armies disbanded. And the great plantations owned by a few rich families are being broken up and being given back to the Indians who once owned the land. It is the day of the Reforma, Mr. Moran, and I am helping to build it."

In surprise Tod looked at his companion. The dark, intense face was no longer clouded by a sense of grievance. Instead, it glowed with hope. The young man was staring through the windshield as though he saw a vision of future greatness for his country. Tod understood. He understood even while he realized that Rico ignored the drawbacks, the dangers, the injustices that such a plan would produce. It was Mexico for the Mexicans. Not for the foreigner and not for the few. Mexico for the people!

There was something vaguely familiar in this battle cry that struck a chord in Tod's memory. "Rico," he said, "I've often thought it must have been exciting for my own ancestors when they helped carve out a great nation from a wilderness, when they helped build up the United States. You'll find, though, that it won't be as easy for you as it was for the Americans. For you must tear down before you start to build. That makes it more difficult still."

"Yes, Mr. Moran, I know." Rico's voice was tremulous with emotion. "Just the same, I'm lucky. This is the beginning of a new Mexico. We are getting rid of corrupt officials, getting rid of the grasping foreigner."

"You evidently don't think much of foreigners."

"I don't, Mr. Moran."

"Even Americans?"

"I hate Americans more than all the others combined."

"Nothing like frankness," Tod said dryly. "But why should you hate Americans who come down here just to see your country? Don't they spend plenty of money?"

Rico's voice rang with furious intensity. "That's the very reason! They throw their money around like fools. They tip with a peso—a peso which is a whole day's wages to us. Don't you see that it drives home the fact that we are the under dog?"

Tod nodded. "I think I see what you mean. But what

about the individual American? What, for instance, about myself? Do you hate me, too?"

"I hate all Americans, Mr. Moran. I will work for them, I will take their money, I will be polite. But do not ask me to like them."

An amused glint came into Tod's eyes. It was evident that this young fellow riding beside him was somewhat hot headed. He laughed abruptly. "You certainly don't make me feel comfortable, Rico. Remember, I happen to know that you carry a long sharp knife under your poncho."

A swift smile broke over Rico's dark face. "Oh, I wouldn't think of using that, Mr. Moran. Not unless you were down here to bribe *politicos* and get land from our people."

Tod straightened up behind the wheel. A feeling of uneasiness crept over him. Until this moment he had listened with interest and with a certain amount of amusement to Rico's fiery words; but now it occurred to him that perhaps his companion, if he knew, would not look with tolerance upon this Blakemore mission into Mexico. Rico would not easily see another person's point of view. Certainly Rico could not be expected to show any sympathy for Mr. Blakemore's viewpoint or Captain Jarvis' or even Tod Moran's. For wasn't Tod Moran at this very moment carrying letters to men high in government circles, men whom Rico would doubtless call *politicos?* Well, if not exactly carrying letters now, he was doing all in his power to get them back. In any case, it was just as well that Rico knew nothing about the contents of the brief case.

When Tod spoke again, his voice was casual. "Isn't it about time we came to Tamazunchale?"

"Almost time, Mr. Moran." Rico, it was clear, had also decided he'd talked enough. He leaned back in the corner of the seat and closed his eyes.

It was after two o'clock when they crossed the bridge over the Montezuma River and entered the little town of Tamazunchale. No rain was falling, but high in the mountains that rose abruptly behind the town a storm was raging. Tod could hear the distant roll of thunder.

"The Hotel Azteca is just ahead," Rico offered. "You can get a good room there."

Tod slowed down. "I'd like to take a look around the town before I stop. Maybe we'll find a Buick sedan parked somewhere."

"Then turn to the right, señor. Drive down that street."

The town, Tod soon discovered, was really little more than a village. Low whitewashed buildings lined a single street that ended in a plaza opposite a church. They came to a tourist camp where Tod counted six cars parked in open garages. Not one was a Buick sedan.

"Any other hotels here, Rico?"

"Only the Azteca."

On their way back to the hotel Tod looked in vain for

a garage where a car could undergo repairs, but all he could find was an open service station, now deserted and dark. Even when they pulled up before the Azteca on the highway, he could see no hotel garage where a car might be hiding. In the darkness to one side of the building three cars were parked. Getting out to investigate, he found a huge limousine, a Ford sedan, and a small work truck. A lantern burning on the hotel porch revealed hanging baskets that held orchids glowing with purple and yellow tints. The thought of a room and a bed on the floor above was as attractive as those blooming orchids, but he gave a weary shrug, turned away, and climbed back behind the wheel.

"Rico," he said, "it looks as though that Buick had gone on up the mountain."

"I doubt it, Mr. Moran."

"Then where could it be hiding?"

"Maybe it stopped at one of those thatched villages along the road. Maybe your friends turned off their headlights when they saw another car coming."

Tod shook his head. "They'd more likely come out to the road and ask for aid." His hand pulled back the gear shift. "Suppose we keep going?"

Rico did not reply. Apparently it was a matter of indifference to him whether or not they started over the mountains. The little Ford rolled forward, gained speed, and almost at once began climbing. The low houses fell away behind and the Montezuma River appeared on the right. To their left, a cliff soared up into the darkness. A canyon opened before them.

The mutter of distant thunder echoed between the granite walls. But the highway was paved and the ascent so gradual that there was no need to shift from high. As the road curved to the left round the cliff, the headlights brought into view a uniformed soldier. Beside him in the center of the pavement stood a sign which read *alto*—stop.

Tod shifted to neutral and put his foot on the brake. The soldier stepped forward, rifle across his shoulder. In his hand an electric torch flashed on.

"*Turistas?*" he asked. "The road is closed to traffic, señor."

Tod blinked in the glare of the flashlight. "Closed? What for?"

"The rains have caused another slide far up the mountain. All traffic is held up here."

"How long has the road been closed? All evening?"

"Since five o'clock yesterday, señor. Only work trucks with their crews are allowed to pass this point. Tourists must stop tonight in Tamazunchale. You will be informed in the morning as soon as the road is open."

"I see." Tod's eyes became thoughtful. "Did you happen to stop a black Buick sedan during the last hour or so?"

The soldier hesitated. "How did the señor know about that car? I let it pass some time ago."

With an effort Tod restrained a start of dismay. His mind worked quickly. Courtesy, he had learned, brought a warm response from Mexicans. Well, he must be friendly and not too aggressive. To demand that he, too, must be allowed to pass would get him nowhere.

He turned off the motor and sank back in his seat. "That's hard luck," he murmured. "I had planned to meet them before they reached Mexico City. It was important."

"I am sorry, señor. I would not have allowed the other car to pass if the American in it had not been very sick. He was rushing to the American hospital in the capital."

"But they couldn't get by the slide, could they?"

"Not with his car. But the slide is just beyond the Montezuma Inn and he thought he might be able to stay there and so be the first one to pass when the highway is clear enough."

Tod leaned forward, his arm on the window ledge. "Would you let me do the same? It's vitally important. I must meet the two men in that car."

The soldier stepped back. His tone turned hard. "But, señor, there was only one man in that Buick—the American who was driving."

"That so?" Tod tried in vain to make his voice sound natural. He had made a bad impression and he knew it. "It's the American I must see, anyway. Did he mention having any trouble with his car?"

"Yes, señor, he did. He said a truck hauled his car to

Night Drive

Tamazunchale, but the repairs did not take long. He did not mention anyone else being with him."

"No matter." Tod forced a smile. "How about letting me pass so I can meet him at the Montezuma Inn?"

The soldier shook his head. "Señor, you are a *turista* who does not know this road ahead. And it is all *turistas* I am ordered to stop. This other American in the black sedan lives in Mexico City. He knows the highway. That is why he was allowed to pass."

"But my friend here knows the road." Tod motioned toward Rico, sitting silent and apparently uninterested in the corner of the seat. "My friend has traveled this mountain stretch many times. He can warn me about the curves."

The soldier stepped nearer and flashed a cone of light upon Rico. Quick Spanish words flew back and forth. Tod's hopes rose until the soldier said, "Your friend has only been over this road once or twice. He thinks it is safer not to go up the canyon tonight."

"What?" Tod turned in surprise and met Rico's dark glance.

There was a stubborn expression on the young man's face. "Mr. Moran," Rico explained, "it would be wiser if we waited here till daylight. In such a storm——"

Tod cut him short. "Rico, I've got to follow that car. You told me you drove tourists over this highway. Why change your story all of a sudden?"

"I do not change my story, Mr. Moran. We are both

[145]

sleepy. It is wiser to stop in Tamazunchale."

"But I can't afford to stop." Tod's voice was vibrant with earnestness. "Get me up to the Montezuma Inn tonight and you can name your price. How about twenty dollars, American?"

The stubborn expression vanished from Rico's face. He leaned forward and said something in Spanish. The soldier answered. Their conversation went on.

The soldier was standing with one hand on the window ledge, his torch pointed at Tod's companion. Rico was sitting erect, his woolen blanket drawn aside, his hands resting on his knees. And in surprise Tod now saw that Rico was wearing a linen-colored suit under the poncho.

But it was not the color of the suit that drew Tod's attention and held it. It was the coat with one button gone. His startled glance settled upon the lower button. It was light tan—a perfect match for the one he carried somewhere in his pocket.

Tod looked closer. At the spot where the second button had once been sewed, a distinct hole was now visible in the linen fabric—yes, as if the button had been torn away in a struggle.

In astonishment his thoughts flashed back to the incident that had occurred when he had put up at the Regina Courts in Monterrey. He remembered waking in the dark sometime after midnight and seeing an unknown person going through the dresser. So it was

Night Drive

Rico who had tried that night to steal his brief case! It was Rico who had driven south with Martin Welch in the black sedan. Cold rage surged up within him. Oh, what a fool he had been in Valles to accept this young Mexican at face value. Rico had been waiting so casually in the entrance of the Casa Grande—waiting too casually, Tod now knew. Well, he'd get rid of this impostor at once. He'd throw him out right here on the road while this armed guard could help.

The armed guard was speaking again in English. "Señor, your friend is willing to show you the way up to the Montezuma Inn. Were you a tourist driving alone I would not allow you to pass, but your friend agrees to warn you about the curves and the slide areas. Take your time. It is nearly seventy kilometers to the inn. The highway is blocked just beyond that point."

Tod stared at the soldier, his thoughts awhirl. Oh, if he only had a few minutes to think over what was best to do! To denounce Rico now would mean that he himself would be sent back to the Azteca for the night, while Martin Welch, alone in his Buick, reached the inn. And when daylight came, Welch would undoubtedly be the first one allowed to pass the slide, perhaps even before word was sent down the mountain that the road was again open for traffic. Tod's nervous fingers closed round the knob of the gear shift. No, he couldn't allow the Buick to escape him that easily. He must catch up with it at the Montezuma Inn. Yet here was Rico sitting beside him, with a knife hidden under his poncho. What had Martin Welch ordered this young Mexican to do?

The soldier's voice broke in upon his hurried thoughts. "The Señor would rather stay here?"

"No." With a quick intake of breath Tod spat out the word with decision. "I appreciate your kindness. I'll drive on. Rico will see that we don't plunge off the road." His foot came down upon the starter. He threw in the clutch.

"*Adios*, señor," called the soldier. "Good luck—and be careful."

"I'll be careful, all right," Tod said grimly. "Good-by."

CHAPTER XI

At the Montezuma Inn

BEFORE they had climbed many miles up the canyon road, the storm swept down out of the night to meet them.

Lightning streaked across the sky, followed almost instantly by thundering crashes that were deafening. Wind, howling along the canyon walls, whipped about the car until the wheel under Tod's hands pulled and quivered as if alive. Rain began beating in furious gusts against the windshield. But the fanlike motion of the wiper cleared the glass; and the headlights, piercing the downpour, threw a carpet of brilliance across the pavement. Tod held the Ford to twenty-five miles an hour.

At this rate, Rico confided in a loud voice, it would take two hours to reach the inn—if another slide did not block their progress in the meantime.

Highroad To Adventure

Any continued conversation was almost impossible. For the air in the little coupé vibrated with sound—with the protesting chug of the motor as the car labored up the grade, with the loud drumming of the rain on the roof, with the peals of thunder echoing from crag to crag far above. Tod was just as well pleased that he could not talk. He feared his tone of voice might give warning, might reveal that he was now aware of his companion's true identity—an employee of Martin Welch of the Tasco mine. And for the present he was determined not to let Rico suspect that he knew.

The highway had been cut out of the cliff on Tod's left, so that the Ford, as it climbed, kept to the outside edge of the pavement. Whenever the road curved to the right, the headlights swept across a rocky wall that soared straight up into the darkness. And whenever the road curved in the other direction, the headlights swept out over the edge of a dark abyss that yawned below. Sometimes a low guard rail, painted white, extended along the edge, but for most of the time there was only that dark abyss. How far, Tod wondered, would a car fall before it hit the river? Hundreds of feet, probably thousands. Drive steady, Tod Moran—drive steady!

Rico's voice pierced through the clamor about him. "I told you this road was no joke in the rain."

"We'll make it." Tod hunched his shoulders forward. "What sort of place is this Montezuma Inn?"

Rico leaned closer. "You won't like it, señor. It was

built for the engineers of the highway when the work first started. But now it's not much of a place. Very cheap. Tourists never stop there."

"Well, I'll stop there," Tod shouted back without turning his head. "I'd stop in a barn on a night like this."

"So you don't think much of this road, señor."

"The road's fine, Rico—what I can see of it."

Something hit the pavement ahead and bounced off into the darkness. "A rock, señor," cried Rico. "Watch out for them. One might hit the car."

As they continued to climb, Tod discerned gullies in the cliff where veritable waterfalls plunged downward into the narrow ditch on his left. Here and there piles of loose earth had also slid downward until the ditch was so filled that the water was crowded out upon the pavement. Perhaps an inch or two deep, it flowed with a swishing sound beneath the wheels of the car. With an uneasy gesture Tod pushed back his hat. Would they ever reach that inn?

So intent was he upon his driving that he had little time to make plans for his future actions. He only knew that he must keep Rico close to his side, keep him unaware of being under guard, and then attempt to discover the whereabouts of Martin Welch. For somewhere in Welch's luggage would be the brief case. The reason why Welch had ordered Rico to go in the Ford was a point Tod could not understand. It was one thing for Rico to watch Tod Moran's movements in Valles;

it was another thing entirely for the young Mexican to attach himself like this to the Ford's owner. On reflection, Tod decided that Welch and Rico had conferred after the brief case had been stolen. Probably it had been Rico himself who had taken it. But why then hadn't Welch ordered Rico to damage the car beyond repair? Even though the mine manager knew that Tod was in the Valles jail, he could not have been positive how long such a prisoner would be held there—especially since there would be no one to press charges in the morning. Well, no matter. The important thing was to overtake the Buick. And when he did meet Welch face to face, what then?

Another gust of wind swept with a whine down the highway. The windshield itself became a waterfall. Tod slowed up. The storm was increasing in violence. There was no chance to figure out anything now. He had enough to do if he kept the car safely on the road.

An hour later the rain lessened until it was merely a drizzle, and soon after that it stopped entirely. A star or two came out. Then the stars became tiny lights that moved in the distance far up the canyon above them.

"Is that a village up there?" Tod asked. His voice sounded loud to his ears.

"It's the highway, señor. Those lights must be trucks dumping earth from the slide. We'll get up there in about half an hour."

"Half an hour! That long?"

At The Montezuma Inn

"Yes, the road climbs nearly six thousand feet before we come to the inn. It is getting colder now, no?"

Tod noticed that the windshield was blurring with steam. He started to lower the window at his side when a truck appeared round a curve ahead. It came thundering toward them at a reckless speed. For a few moments its headlights blotted out all view of the road, then it roared past with a rush of wind. When the highway came into view again, the Ford's headlights were slanting over the edge of the canyon.

Pulling the wheel with all his might, Tod brought the car back toward the center of the pavement. Whew! Blinding headlights were surely a menace.

"That truck was empty," Rico announced. "Maybe it's going down to Tamazunchale to get more workers. The slide must be bigger than they thought."

During the next half-hour Tod drove without speaking. And always the highway continued its steady climb. The Ford's radiator began steaming, little puffs at first, then finally a sizzling escape of steam that flew back against the windshield.

"Maybe it's a hole in the radiator," Rico said quite cheerfully.

"Maybe." Tod pulled the car up against the low guard rail bordering the road. "There's water in the trunk. I'll get some." He reached over and pulled his key ring from the ignition lock.

"Can I help you, Mr. Moran?"

"Don't bother. You stay here."

Tod stepped to the rear of the car, unlocked the sloping trunk compartment and, reaching in, brought out one of the gallon bottles. As he was pouring the water into the radiator he called, "Well, Rico, we got this far without trouble. A pretty good car, eh?"

Rico did not answer.

"Care for a drink, Rico?"

"No, thanks, señor. We are almost there. I'll wait."

Rico's voice, Tod noticed, sounded muffled, strange. What was the matter with the fellow? Was he troubled by the thought of meeting his American employer at the inn? If so, it might be because Welch had ordered him not to allow the Ford or its driver to leave Valles. Thoughtfully Tod put the empty bottle back into the trunk and took his seat again behind the wheel. From now on he'd better be more alert than ever in watching his companion.

As the car took to the highway again, Rico settled himself back into his corner. His eyes were half closed; his hands rested lightly on his poncho. Ten minutes later he roused and peered out the window at his side. "We're coming to the inn, Mr. Moran. It's round this next curve, I think."

On the instant Tod's fatigue fell away, forgotten. A tremor of excitement ran through him. Martin Welch could not escape this time unless—unless the highway had already been cleared of the slide.

At The Montezuma Inn

A moment later, as the car rounded the curve, he saw there was no danger of that. Perhaps a mile ahead, road flares were clearly visible. Shadowy trucks, incredibly small in the distance, crawled down the road, turned and dumped their contents into the void. But between those trucks and his own Ford there was no sign of any habitation.

"Slow up," Rico urged. "We turn to the right just ahead."

"We go down?"

"Yes, you can make it. Put her in low."

The headlights revealed a graveled lane leading down off the edge of the highway; but where it led to or how far it went, Tod could not be sure, for it disappeared into darkness. In low gear he took the plunge, his foot hovering over the brake. For fifty feet the rough, narrow road hugged the cliff, then it turned outward and became a flat bit of ground extending the length of an unlighted building. Tod put his foot on the brake and peered out.

It was a forbidding sight that met his eyes. Perched on the edge of the abyss, the Montezuma Inn was a square, two-storied building without a porch of any kind. Its façade, pale and ghostly in the reflected lights of the car, was broken by two lines of shuttered windows, one above the other, and by a single door at one end on the ground floor. Adobe bricks showed through the whitewash. From the tiled roof water dripped. That was the only sound audible above the low purr of the motor—the soft drip-drip of water striking the mud-soaked ground.

Four cars parked there in the open drew his attention. The one nearest him was a tan Packard bearing a Texas license. Next to it was an old model-T Ford, and beyond that—yes!—a black sedan. His heart beats quickened. There was no need to investigate the numbers on that license plate. Martin Welch was somewhere inside the inn.

Tod eased the little Ford up beside the Packard, shut off the motor, and closed the window at his side. With his eyes on his companion he said in a tone he tried to keep steady, "Out we go, Rico."

"But I'll sleep here, Mr. Moran."

"In this car? Nothing doing. We'll get you a room, too—if there's one to spare. Anyway, I may need you to interpret for me. If this place doesn't cater to tourists, maybe there won't be anyone here who understands English."

"Of course, Mr. Moran. I'll see that you get a room, then I'll come back here and sleep."

"Rot!" Tod motioned Rico to the ground. "You need a good rest as much as I do. It must be getting on to morning, so you wouldn't be able to sleep very long out here."

With evident reluctance Rico stepped out. Tod followed. All at once he became aware of a swimming sensation in his head. It must be this altitude. He wasn't accustomed to being six thousand feet above sea level.

At The Montezuma Inn

As he locked the Ford he heard a voice speak out of the darkness behind him. He swung about. The door of the inn had opened, and in it stood a slouching figure. The man, no doubt the proprietor, was clad in dirty white shirt and trousers, his dark bare feet thrust into straw sandals. The candle he held aloft revealed his face lined and wrinkled, his eyes deep in their sockets, a mat of black hair over his forehead.

"*Turistas?*" he called.

Tod stepped forward. If this fellow spoke even a bit of English he must intervene before Rico replied in Spanish. "Can we get two rooms?" he hastened to ask.

"*Sí.*" Apparently the fellow understood, for a broad smile of welcome brought toothless gums into view.

"One minute, Rico." Tod turned to his trunk compartment and took out his bag containing his overnight things. Though he might not have a chance to sleep, he'd better act the part of a guest who intended to go to bed at once. As he locked the trunk, Rico picked up the bag and followed the proprietor inside.

Tod hurriedly joined them. He found himself in a vast shadowy room which was apparently a combination lobby, dining room, and bar. Near them stood a long bare table, and on this the proprietor set down his candle holder. The flame threw a wan light upon a bar at the opposite end where wine and beer bottles were stacked against a shabby mirror. Here also an open staircase led up to the second floor. Tod's nostrils twitched at the damp musty odor of the place.

Rico started to speak, but Tod cut him short. Looking directly at the proprietor, he asked, "You understand English?"

"*Si*, señor."

"How many people staying here tonight?"

The man regarded him blankly for a moment, then he held up both hands with some of the fingers raised.

Tod counted. "Six?"

"*Si*."

The toothless grin, Tod felt, lacked both mirth and intelligence. How could he be sure this fellow really understood? "How many automobiles out front, not counting mine?"

Again the man held up a hand, fingers pointing upward.

"Four?"

"*Si*."

"Is it possible to get around this slide?"

When this question only brought a look of perplexity to the man's face, Tod turned to Rico. "Ask him if I could leave my car here, walk around the slide on the highway, and then pick up another car that could take me to Mexico City?"

Rico shook his head. "No need to ask him that, Mr. Moran. No one could get around that slide, either above it or below."

"Just the same," Tod insisted, "I wish you'd ask him."

At The Montezuma Inn

Rico spoke swiftly in Spanish and the man, when he understood, threw up his hands in horror. He became so voluble and his voice so shrill that his words resounded under the raftered ceiling.

"Enough." Tod raised a hand. "I take it he says it can't be done?"

"Yes, Mr. Moran. He says anyone who tried that would fall to his death and the buzzards would get him. He says he could not allow any guest to make such an attempt. He says the government would send police to ask him why he allowed——"

"No matter." Tod nodded. "How about our rooms? Where do we register?"

When his companion did not at once reply, Tod threw him a sharp look. Rico was standing with the leather bag held against his poncho, his sombrero pushed back, his dark eyes intent upon something high at one end of the room. And on his dark handsome face was an expression of mingled surprise and fear.

Following that glance, Tod found his gaze resting upon the top of the staircase where an open door led to the second floor. The candlelight could not pierce the gloom of that long room, but enough light reached the spot to make visible the figure of a man standing in the deep obscurity. But even as he tried to discern the face, the figure, the man moved back into darkness and was gone.

"Shall we go to our rooms, Mr. Moran?"

Tod pulled his startled thoughts back to the matter on hand. "Yes. Suppose we turn in."

Rico spoke for a moment in low tones to the proprietor, then turned to Tod. "He says he will give us rooms seven and eight. We needn't bother to register until morning. A couple of his guests played cards so late he hasn't had much sleep, so he's in a hurry to get back to bed."

The proprietor picked up the candle holder and moved toward the staircase. With a muttered warning for them to be quiet, he led the way upstairs. Tod, following in Rico's shadow, held himself in readiness for any eventuality. But the doors that lined the narrow hallway above were all closed, the rooms silent. If the arrival of the Ford had roused one of the guests and brought him to the head of the stairs, he was now hidden behind one of those closed doors—and there was no way of telling which room was his. Yet it must have been Martin Welch, for who but Welch would be interested enough to get out of bed, walk to the end of the hallway, and peer below just to see who these late arrivals might be? Yes, that blurred figure at the top of the stairs had been the mine manager from Tasco.

Near the end of the hallway the proprietor threw open a door to his right, went inside and lighted an oil lamp in a bracket on the wall. Then he came out and entered the room directly opposite.

Rico said in a whisper, "Take your choice, Mr. Moran."

At The Montezuma Inn

"This one will do," Tod murmured, choosing the one that faced the front of the building. Rico's window, he suspected, would open upon that yawning abyss in the rear.

"Your bag, señor."

"Rico, ask the man for a key to my door."

The proprietor, lighting Tod's lamp with the candle flame, spoke over his shoulder. Tod caught the drift of the reply. No keys were necessary at the Montezuma Inn. Each door could be fastened on the inside with a hook.

Tod frowned as he glanced about the room. The whitewash was peeling from the walls and ceiling and lay in flakes on the bare floor. The bed was a huge affair, and beyond it near the window stood a single chair.

The proprietor went out with a muttered word. Rico paused in the doorway. "Good night, Mr. Moran." His voice was low, his eyes were sharp in the lamplight, his face grim. But there was determination, too, in the line of his jaw.

"Good night, Rico. I'll see you at breakfast."

Rico closed the door. Tod heard him take a step into the room across the hall. A door closed. The slap of the proprietor's sandals could be heard descending the stairs.

Tod sat down upon the edge of the bed. Before he went into action he'd better wait until the place was once more quiet. A few minutes would also give him time to perfect his plan. He looked at his watch. After four o'clock. Well, he'd turn his light out and wait until four-thirty, but not a minute longer.

All at once he tilted his head, listening. Rain was falling again. First lightly, then increasingly heavy, it pounded upon the roof and against the shutters at the window. An expression of satisfaction crossed Tod's face. This wasn't bad at all. The sound of the downpour would muffle his footsteps while he went downstairs to get his flash light from the car. His mind leaped on, pouncing upon one possibility, discarding another, preparing his defenses should Rico as well as Welch be awake.

Again he pulled out his watch. Nearly four-thirty. He let another minute pass, then stood up. The time for action had come.

CHAPTER XII

Before Dawn

Tod moved quietly to the door, opened it with the utmost care, and listened. Only the fall of rain could be heard. When he felt assured that the hallway was clear, he stole through the blackness to the stairs and, with one hand on the rail, went below.

It was not easy to find the door, but he dare not light a match. What he needed was the flash light. Once he had that, he would return to the floor above and find the room that hid Martin Welch. His hands came in contact with a door knob. After a moment he found the bolt, drew it and slipped outside.

Splashing through the rain, he reached his car. It took only a second to unlock the door and climb in. When his fingers touched the cold metal of the electric torch he felt a new confidence flow through him. He would leave the car unlocked so that he could jump in and start going at a moment's notice. Yet, suppose while he was upstairs facing Martin Welch, perhaps even fighting, Rico should steal below and damage the car? At the thought he leaned back in the seat, weighing certain alternatives. Did he dare move the car to a safer spot? No matter whether he moved it or left it here, there was danger. In any case, though, the car must be ready for instant flight. With the brief case safely his, he could drive back down the mountains to Tamazunchale where he could meet Ben and Ma Whipple in the morning. If any trouble arose with the police, the Whipples could vouch for the fact that the brief case had been stolen from him in Valles.

He peered out at the building, but it was so rainy and dark that he could only vaguely make out the nearest window. Which room above, he wondered, was occupied by Martin Welch? Rico at least was lodged in the rear. And it would most likely be Rico who would try to injure the car. It must be moved out of reach—at once. Now that his mind was made up, he thrust the key into the ignition lock and stepped on the starter. The low throb of the motor mingled with the sound of the rain. He switched on the lights, backed out, swung around, and headed for the graveled drive. Martin Welch, if he watched from an upper window, would surely believe that his pursuer was running away. Well, let him. Later on there would be a surprise.

In low gear the Ford climbed up to the highway. Tod

turned to the south as though he were going toward the slide and Mexico City; but, after driving for a short distance, he switched off the lights and stopped. By peering past the windshield wiper he could discern the white guard rail extending along the edge of the road. With intense care he backed the car against the cliff and swung about until he was facing downhill. Then, with the motor turned off and his head out the window so that he could keep his eyes on the low white fence, he let the car coast slowly back past the Montezuma Inn.

It was a nerve-racking job that made him press his foot on the brake more than once, but not until a turn in the highway had put the inn safely behind did he again switch on the motor and lights. Unless he had been followed, no one would see him now.

After traveling for ten minutes he drew the car up close to the cliff beside a pile of gravel where a turn in the highway made parking space available. He locked the car, opened the trunk, and took out the five-gallon can of gasoline given him by Ben Whipple in Valles. In case of flight he must be sure he had plenty of gas in the tank. Satisfied that he was prepared for any emergency, he soon started back for the inn.

With his Panama hat pulled low against the rain he hurried along close to the white rail, his only guide in the darkness. By the time he came to the road leading down the cliff, he was soaked to the skin. No matter. He would be on the move, anyway.

When he reached the inn he went directly to the Buick sedan. It was locked, of course. Sliding the flash light along the glass of the windows, he peered inside. There was a leather bag on the rear seat but no brief case. Although it might be locked in the trunk, it was more likely to be upstairs in the room with Martin Welch. He turned away.

The door of the inn responded to his touch. The proprietor, at least, had not been roused. Inside, he halted and pressed his thumb against the button of his torch. Slowly he let the cone of light circle the room. It revealed the table at the far end, the line of windows opening to the rear and, at the other end, the long mahogany bar and the staircase leading up to the second floor. The proprietor had said that the newcomers could register in the morning. That registry book must be found.

It was exactly where he had planned to look for it— on a shelf behind the bar. Stooping so that the flash light could not be seen from the head of the stairs, he opened the soiled canvas cover and flicked the pages to the last date used—May 13. Six names were listed there. As he studied them he realized that not one was familiar. Of the six people who had registered at the Montezuma Inn that day, four were Americans and two were Mexicans. There were a Mr. and Mrs. J. R. Sturtevant from Pittsburgh, Pennsylvania—they, obviously, were out. There were a Dr. Samuel Briggs and a Mr. James Foster, both of Houston, Texas. The two Mexican names did not interest him. Martin Welch, it was clear, had come in so late that he, too, had not yet registered. For if he had, he probably would have signed the same name he had used at the Regina Courts in Monterrey—Richard Smith.

Opposite each name were listed the room numbers. Tod let those numbers sink in. He would pass them when investigating. Welch would of necessity be in one of the apparently empty rooms.

With the flash light shining only intermittently on the floor, he stole across to the stairs and crept up. The hallway above was deserted. He flashed the light upon the closed door on his right. Number one. A Mexican, he remembered, occupied that room. Number two, directly opposite, belonged to Mr. and Mrs. Sturtevant. Number three held Dr. Briggs; number four, James Foster. Number five, if he remembered correctly, held a Mexican—was the name Torres? Number six was apparently empty. He and Rico had been given rooms seven and eight. Beyond lay nine and ten, both unmentioned in the register.

Deep in thought, Tod paused for a moment. One of those three rooms not listed in the register must be occupied by Martin Welch. He'd first try number six and see if the hook inside blocked his entrance.

When he stood before the door he loosed the button on his torch. Darkness closed down around him. From somewhere on his left he could hear, above the beat of the rain, the sound of someone snoring. But behind the door of number six all was quiet. Slowly he turned the knob. Under his touch the door swung inward. This easy entrance, he realized, meant that the room was probably unoccupied. In disappointment he heard no restless movement from the bed, no heavy breathing, either. Still in absolute darkness he pushed steadily on the door until it struck the wall a light blow. At once he pressed his thumb against the button on his torch, and the cone of light leaped forward. The bed lay untouched, unused. The light flashed from corner to corner. No, the room was unoccupied. Not a single piece of hand luggage was to be found, and there was no closet in which anything could be hidden.

Thoughtfully he closed the door and turned back. There were still those rooms beyond his and Rico's. But rooms nine and ten, he soon discovered, were also empty. Strange! What room could have been given to Martin Welch? As he thought it over, it occurred to him that possibly Welch had not yet gone to bed when the little Ford had driven up before the inn. If that was the case, the man might have gone to Rico's room for a report, dressed and ready to leave with bag and brief case. At least the fellow hadn't gone yet, since the black sedan was still below. Only one thing remained to do—Rico's door must be opened.

Well aware of his danger, Tod hesitated outside number seven. His pulse quickened as he leaned against the wood, listening. No sound came from within. Again in absolute darkness, he pushed on the door. Slowly it swung open. Had Rico turned in without securing the hook? A more reasonable assumption would be that Rico had left his room. But, no. He could hear the sound of a long-drawn breath.

Rico was asleep. Or was he? Maybe the fellow was simply feigning sleep, waiting to leap out and overpower him with the help of Martin Welch. Stepping backward, Tod pressed the torch. The light shot forward to the bed. To his surprise he saw that it was unoccupied, although the covers had been thrown back. Quickly he moved his wrist and the light swept to the left. He caught his breath and stared, transfixed, while his heart rose up and pounded in his throat. On the floor lay the outstretched body of a man.

For a moment Tod did not move. Rico, in shirt and trousers, lay on his back, inert, his arms outflung. Labored breathing issued from his lips. The torchlight swayed and quivered. Tod's gaze had fastened upon Rico's shoulder. The white shirt was crimson with blood.

Through Tod ran a shiver of apprehension. His first thought had been to do something for Rico. Now, as he took in that crimson spot and all that it meant, the thought swept into his mind that perhaps Rico's assailant was still here in the room. He flashed the light around. Nothing there but an overturned chair with clothes and shoes near it. Pulling himself together, he stepped into the room, closed the door behind him and knelt beside the outstretched form.

Rico was unconscious. Tod, with trembling fingers, unbuttoned the shirt and revealed a wound made by the thrust of a knife. Rico's own dagger? Yes, there it was near the wall, glittering in the light. Tod dragged his eyes away from the stained blade. Looking down again, he saw that the wound was almost too close to the shoulder to have pierced any vital part. Yet Rico had been struck unconscious. Tod's glance moved up a trifle. On the olive skin of the throat were marks as though fingers had dug into the flesh.

Tod straightened up. He must call the proprietor, get help.

Outside in the hall he remembered that a Dr. Briggs had been listed as a guest. With an effort he tried to recall the number of the man's room, but he was so shaken by what he had discovered that he couldn't be sure. Numbers three or four—those were the rooms occupied by those two men from Houston. Dr. Briggs, of course, might not be a physician and surgeon; instead, he might be merely one of those college professors who insist upon carrying their university degrees around with them. Still, it was a chance.

At room number four he knocked. When no answer came he tried to open the door. It gave only a fraction of an inch. The hook inside was fastened.

Before Dawn

He kept his voice to a husky whisper. "Doctor Briggs! Wake up. You're needed."

After a moment a muffled voice replied, "What's that?"

"Open the door—please. I need your help."

Inside the room a bed creaked gently. A lamp chimney rattled. A hand unhooked the door. It swung inward to disclose a pajama-clad figure with pale blue eyes that blinked in the glare of the torch. The man was fair and curly headed and perhaps thirty years old. "What's all this rumpus?" he demanded. "Come in and close the door. You'll wake up everybody in the place."

"Doctor Briggs?" Tod spoke earnestly as he entered the room and shut the door behind him. "Are you a doctor? A friend of mine down the hall has been hurt—knifed, in fact. Can you come?"

"Knifed?" The resonant voice showed concern. The pale blue eyes widened. "I'm not surprised. No, not surprised at anything that happens in a rotten dump like this. Wait a minute. You've sort of unnerved me. I need a shot of whisky. How about yourself? You look sort of pale."

Tod shook his head. "I'm all right. Please hurry." His glance swept the room in search of a medical kit. "You're really a doctor?"

Before the man replied, he reached into a traveling bag on the floor, brought forth a flask and, lifting it to his lips, drank long and deeply. "Ah, now I feel better.

You gave me quite a shock. You see, I'm not a doctor. Not used to such things—even in Mexico."

"Then there's no doctor here?"

"Oh, yes, there is. Doctor Briggs is just across the hall. My name's Foster—Jim Foster." He thrust his bare feet into slippers and reached for a dressing gown. "I hope it's nothing serious. My friend and I are on a vacation. Doc's a great fisherman. But never mind. Let's go."

Jim Foster tied a cord round his slender waist as he stepped into the hall. Without knocking, he turned the knob of the door opposite. To Tod's surprise it swung open. "Hey, Doc! You're wanted. Swell vacation, eh?"

But Dr. Briggs was already awake. As Tod flashed the light into the room he saw that the man was seated on the edge of his bed and ready to dress. He was darker than his friend, Foster, and several years older.

"No need to dress," Jim Foster remonstrated. "Your patient's just down the hall. Put on your bath robe."

Dr. Briggs, pulling himself erect, responded with only a nod. His sharp-featured face, strong and dark and impassive, was that of a man always vigilant, always sure of himself. His black eyes turned to Tod. "Who the devil are you?" he asked in a pleasant voice.

Tod, stammering a reply, gave his name. The doctor motioned him out the door. "All right, Moran. Go ahead. I'll follow."

In Rico's room the doctor became brisk and efficient. "Foster, light the lamp. Hold your flash light closer,

Before Dawn

Moran. That's right. This chap has a wound that'll need some care. It appears to be superficial, though. Funny he passed out like this. His throat? So that's the reason. Who did this, Moran?"

Tod straightened up, aware that Foster had turned from the lamp and was eying him with a suspicious glance. "I'm not sure, Doctor Briggs. I found him like this a minute ago."

"I see." The doctor's nimble fingers felt Rico's neck, lifted the head, turned it gently. "I think he'll be all right. Just a little Mexican quarrel, I suppose. They pull a knife at the least provocation. Foster, get hold of the proprietor and have him bring some warm water. Moran, help me lift him to the bed. Yes, his legs. That's right."

Voices and footsteps sounded from the hall. Dr. Briggs said quickly, "Close the door, Moran." He scrutinized the still figure on the bed while he raised a limp hand to take the pulse. "He'll soon be coming round. I'll get my medical kit. The wound has stopped bleeding, so don't be nervous. Be right back."

"Can't I get it for you, Doctor?"

"No, it's in my car. You stay and keep that mob out of here. But there is no need to worry."

Tod drew a breath of relief. "Then Rico will be all right?"

"I believe so. Hold the fort while I'm gone."

The door closed behind him. Tod was alone with the unconscious Rico.

As he looked down at the olive face he saw the lips part and the eyes open. He leaned over the bed. "You're okay, Rico. There's a doctor here who'll fix you up. He says it's only a superficial wound. You're lucky it's so near your shoulder."

"It doesn't hurt—much." Rico's black eyes shone with recognition. His lips moved. "You heard us fighting, Mr. Moran?"

"No." Tod spoke quietly. "Rico, where is Welch? What room is he in?"

Rico lay perfectly still, but his eyes narrowed, and Tod could see that his mind was working swiftly. "That is my affair, Mr. Moran."

Tod spoke in haste, knowing that if he was to learn anything, it must be before Dr. Briggs or Foster returned. "But it's my affair, too, Rico. I know you took my brief case. I know you and Welch have followed me all the way from Laredo. Why did he do this to you, Rico? Why?"

The wounded man's glance moved to the lamp on the wall. His mouth was stubborn. "This is my affair," he repeated.

"Listen, Rico, we've only a minute before the doctor comes back." Tod leaned closer. "Why did Welch try to kill you? After all, those papers in that brief case aren't so very important. I can wire home for copies and get them here in a few days. What's this mean?"

"Mr. Moran?" Rico's voice was low, tense.

Before Dawn

"Yes?"

"Keep out of this. Those letters are more important than you can ever know. They mean life and death to a certain man."

"To Welch?" Tod's voice conveyed his surprise. "But that's silly. Those letters might mean money to Welch—might mean the loss of his job, but surely nothing more than that. I don't understand."

Rico's glance met Tod's in a look of deep intensity. "Mr. Moran, those letters you brought from San Francisco mean death. Ah, you didn't know. Maybe your boss didn't know, either. But it's death just the same."

"Death—to you, Rico?"

"No. To someone in Mexico City. Later, you will know I spoke the truth. Now, please, no more questions. We'll tell these people it was just a little fight. Nothing important, eh? Then we shall not be held up by the police. You would not like that, Mr. Moran."

"No, I wouldn't."

"Then say nothing to these people here. The town of Jacala is only a few miles beyond the slide. If the proprietor should send word when the road is opened, we might both be held—for investigation. That must not happen."

"All right." Tod's voice was sharp. "But where is Welch? He did this, Rico. I know."

The young man's dark head moved a trifle. If he was in any pain he did not show it. "Mr. Moran, you want to do something? Then stop his car."

"But he can't get past this slide!"

"Just make sure he doesn't leave first. Will you?"

Tod nodded. "As soon as the doctor gets back, I'll fix that Buick. I'll let out the air in all the tires. Then he won't be able to sneak away without my seeing him. But I thought he was your friend."

"My friend?" Rico's lips curled in scorn. "I hate all Americans, Mr. Moran. They want to exploit my country. But even more I hate *politicos*. Because they are Mexicans who are false to their own country."

"Better stop talking," Tod broke in. He could see that this fiery youth on the bed was working himself up into a fury again—and this, certainly, was no time for that.

"Mr. Moran?" In Rico's voice was a beseeching note. "Don't leave me behind when you go. Take me over the mountains with you to Mexico City."

Tod stepped back. His eyes grew hard. "I don't know about that. You've brought me a heap of trouble."

Rico's glance wavered. "One other thing, Mr. Moran. Where is my knife? Is it still here?"

"Yes. It's on the floor."

"Get it for me—please. I might need it." His voice sank to a whisper. "You see, after I heard you go out, someone tried my door. I thought it was you. That is why I did not think of throwing the knife. Even when the door opened I did not throw it. That was a mistake I won't make again."

"Throw it?" Tod, in the act of picking up the knife,

turned a startled face toward the bed. "You would throw a dagger like this—at someone coming in your door?"

"Why not?" Rico raised a hand, his fist tightly clenched. "A knife like that can be almost as good as a pistol."

Tod kicked the knife into the far corner of the room. "Let it stay where it is. I don't intend to——" He ceased speaking. The door knob had turned.

Dr. Briggs came in, a basin of water in one hand, a medical bag in the other. "Close the door, Moran. I've stationed Foster out in the hall to see that no one comes barging in here."

Tod crossed to the open doorway. "I'll be back in a minute, Doctor. I'm sorry, but I've something I must do —right away."

"Then hurry, will you?"

Tod stepped into the hall. Not until he had every tire of the Buick flat on the ground would he feel easy.

"Oh, there you are!" It was Foster's cheery voice. "Everybody wants to know what happened, Moran. Maybe you can tell them."

Tod pushed his way past four or five guests who crowded the hallway. "I'll be right back," he said. "Nobody really knows what happened. Just a little Mexican fracas, I guess. Nothing serious."

He reached the stairs, brushed aside the proprietor who tried to stop him, and hurried down to the door. His footsteps did not slacken until he made sure that the

Buick still was parked in the drizzling darkness. Welch had not yet tried to run away, thank heavens. He stooped beside a rear wheel. When he was through with these four tires Welch would be safely bottled up.

He raised his head and let the rain fall gently on his face. Behind the clouds there was a hint of dawn in the air. This dawn, he thought, would bring a day of reckoning. At last he would be face to face with Martin Welch.

CHAPTER XIII

The Riddle

Tod sat at his bedroom window watching a misty rain sweep past. For more than an hour he had crouched there, silent, thoughtful, uneasy. The proprietor's competent little wife was sitting with Rico, who had dropped off to sleep. Dr. Briggs had gone to bed; Jim Foster had begged a cup of coffee and then turned in, also. Tod had heard the other guests talking behind closed doors. But so far, there was no sign of Martin Welch.

When Tod had cornered the proprietor and asked about the missing guest, the man's black eyes had regarded him with a puzzled frown. Either the question had not been understood, or the proprietor had been well paid to keep his knowledge to himself. In any case Tod was taking no chances. For the probabilities were that Welch was still in the hotel. Of course, he might

[179]

have escaped before Rico had been found; but how in thunder, Tod asked himself, had he gotten away without his car? The Buick with its four flat tires was still parked in the yard below. No, the mine manager must still be here. If he attempted to leave he could be seen from this window and be overtaken.

The bleak bit of landscape facing the inn was blurred by the mist. Tod could make out the graveled drive leading up the side of the bluff, the guard rail along the highway above, the brown rocky cliff that extended straight up to a distant fringe of pines. By leaning out the window he could see the cars parked below—the tan Packard, the model-T roadster, the black Buick sedan and, at the end of the row, a shining new Pontiac.

With an impatient movement, Tod pulled out his watch. Five to eight. For some time he had heard the rattle of dishes below, the murmur of voices, an occasional step on the stairs. It might be like Welch to go down brazenly to breakfast, to meet everyone there with a careless smile. Tod stood up and straightened his tie. If the fellow was willing to have this meeting occur before half a dozen guests, then let him have his way.

Outside in the gloomy corridor he paused in front of Rico's door and quietly opened it. The proprietor's wife, looking up with a smile from her sewing, inclined her head toward the bed. Rico was sleeping peacefully, his bandaged shoulder visible above the sheet.

Tod nodded, closed the door and went down the pas-

The Riddle

sage. Halting at the head of the stairs, he surveyed the room below.

Breakfast was in progress. Seated at the long table were five people—one woman and four men, all of them well-dressed travelers who had been held here by the slide. Martin Welch was not among them. Disappointed, Tod went down the steps. It was possible that someone at the table had seen this other guest who had arrived in the Buick after midnight.

As he started to cross the length of floor to the table at the far end of the room, he was hailed by a familiar voice close by. "Good morning, Moran. Have an eye opener?"

It was Jim Foster, leaning against the bar, dressed now in a brown business suit. Behind the bar, the proprietor was pouring out a drink.

"Had a rotten night, didn't we?" Foster continued. "Needed a bracer before I tackled that breakfast." His voice became low and confidential. "If you'd eaten dinner here last night you'd realize why breakfast doesn't appeal to me." He picked up his glass. "Join me?"

Tod refused with a word of thanks. At any other time he would have passed this fellow with a nod, but not now. A voluble person such as Jim Foster might give information of value. "What's the latest dope on the slide?" Tod asked.

"Oh, they expect to have the road cleared before noon. But you know these Mexicans. It probably means they'll need a week for the job. Sure you won't join me? Well, here's to you." He lifted the glass to his lips and downed the liquor at a gulp. Setting down the glass, he spoke in a lower tone. "We're not a very happy lot here, Moran. All of us had started up through the mountains before the slide occurred. Then when we found the highway blocked, we thought it would be simpler to put up here than go back to Tamazunchale. A mistake. Everybody knows it now." A smile moved on his lips. "Look at 'em! Nobody saying a word. Happy little group, eh?"

"Is everyone down this early?"

"Yes, I think so." Foster turned his gaze upon the table. His profile, Tod saw, was clear cut, though the flushed cheeks and baggy eyes more than hinted of too much liquor. "Yes, they're all there. That young couple eating without a word are from Pittsburgh. They don't like Mexico. They wish already they had stayed at home. The doctor, of course, you know. Probably he's thinking about the fishing he'll have if we ever get over the mountains past Jacala. The doc's a great fisherman—at least, he thinks he is. The fellow at the end of the table is an oil salesman named Cueva. The other chap in white is a White-cap."

"A White-cap?"

"Yes. One of those guides for the tourists. They'll drive your car, take you around, show you the sights. The tenderfoots hire them." Jim Foster paused, and his

The Riddle

teeth flashed in a smile. "Sorry. Your friend Rico is a White-cap, too, isn't he?"

Tod hesitated. "Maybe. I'm not quite sure."

"Not sure? But it's easy to tell. They all wear the official white cap with their license just above the visor. Didn't your friend have one?"

"I really don't know," Tod said desperately. "I picked him up at Valles."

Foster eyed him in surprise. "A mistake. You want to be mighty sure who you give a lift to here in Mexico. But never mind. That fight is no concern of yours. Anyway, the doc says he'll be okay in no time. Let him rest here for a couple of days—that's all he needs. Well, shall we attempt the breakfast? I'm warning you. You won't like it."

Tod held the man back for a moment by asking, "Did you play cards late last night, Mr. Foster?"

"Yes—with the doc. Why?"

"Oh, I was just wondering if you happened to see who drove up in that Buick outside."

"Let me see." Foster's face became thoughtful. "That White-cap was the last guest to arrive. He came in just before the doc and I went upstairs—sometime after midnight. But I'm sure I don't know what sort of car he drove up in. A Buick, you say? I don't seem to remember any Buick here yesterday afternoon."

"Oh, señor." The proprietor shoved the register across the bar toward Tod and turned the pages to the last entry.

[183]

Tod took the pen the man held out. "Go ahead, Foster, I'll join you at the table in a second. I have to register."

As Foster moved away, Tod studied the page before him. Directly under the date of the day before, three lines were filled with the names of the American guests—Mr. and Mrs. Sturtevant of Pittsburgh, and Dr. Samuel Briggs and James Foster of Houston. A space of several lines followed, then the names of the two Mexican citizens were written. The proprietor, it was obvious, kept the names of his foreign visitors separated from those of his countrymen. Now for the first time Tod looked closely at the two Mexican names.

The first one was Miguel Cueva of Tampico; the second, Pedro Torres of Mexico City, D. F. Cueva must be the oil salesman and Torres the White-cap. Señor Torres, if he had been the last guest to arrive, would bear watching.

Quickly Tod wrote his own name under the list of Americans. As his pen moved down to the Mexican citizens he hesitated. He must register for Rico—but what was Rico's real name? Well, Enriques Lopez or Ricardo Lopez—what was the difference? He scratched down the latter and gave back the pen to the waiting man.

Leaning across the bar, he said in a low tone, "Señor Martin Welch? Is he here?"

The proprietor's dark eyes widened. This time it was obvious the man understood the question. He closed the book with a slap. "No, señor. No."

The Riddle

So that was that. With a shrug Tod turned away and went over to the breakfast table.

Dr. Briggs was just arising. "Good morning," he said with a nod. "I'll go take a look at the patient." He paused, his dark face expressionless. "You've met these other guests, Moran? Mrs. Sturtevant, may I introduce a fellow countryman—Mr. Moran. From San Francisco."

"Really?" Mrs. Sturtevant was a sleek little creature who plainly thought her make-up would conceal her age. "How do you do?" she murmured. Her husband, when introduced, nodded briefly.

Dr. Briggs flung out a hand. "Mr. Torres. Mr. Cueva. I hope, Moran, you enjoy your breakfast more than I did." With a mirthless smile he left. Mr. Torres, the White-cap, rose, too, and excused himself.

Tod sat down on a bench next to Jim Foster. An elderly Indian woman at once came on bare feet from a door near the bar and poured dark steaming liquid into his cup.

"They call it coffee," sighed Mrs. Sturtevant. "See what you make of it, Mr. Moran."

The coffee, Tod decided, was unlike any he'd ever before tasted—strangely bitter and unappetizing, though Jim Foster seemed not to mind. Still it was hot, at least. Tod buttered a warm tortilla and rolled it. Eggs followed. Somehow the food did not interest him. He drank a second cup of coffee, while the silence around him continued.

[185]

"I told him," Mrs. Sturtevant piped up suddenly, "that it was a mistake to come to Mexico. No accommodations. No food fit to eat. And then look what happened last night! Why, any one of us might have been stabbed, too. Who did that stabbing, anyway?" Her questioning glance traveled down the table.

No one answered. At length Foster spoke up. "Oh, it was possibly one of the gang that hangs round the kitchen. There are three or four peóns out there."

Mrs. Sturtevant nodded with decision. "There you are! It could have happened to any of us."

"Nonsense." Her husband's voice expressed annoyance. "If you insist upon traveling, you've got to put up with a few inconveniences."

"Inconveniences! Why put it so mildly? It's utterly outrageous to expect civilized people to eat a meal like this. And just look at what that automobile association told us—fine accommodations all along the road. Do you call this fine accommodations? Do you——"

"My dear," her husband broke in, "I don't imagine these people are at all interested in your reactions. Let's call this trip a mistake. Let's turn round and go back home."

"Turn round?" Mrs. Sturtevant's shrill voice rose. "I'll not turn back till we've seen Mexico City. What would my friends say? Why, the bridge club would laugh behind my back! I'll simply——"

Tod heard a low chuckle at his side. Glancing at Jim

The Riddle

Foster, he saw a broad grin on the man's face. "I told you this was a happy little group, Moran."

Tod tried to smile. But his head felt hot, his eyes burning. He wasn't hungry, he told himself. Furthermore, though he didn't like to admit it, there was a queer feeling in the pit of his stomach. If he could only lie down for a while and rest! With an effort he stood up and excused himself.

Across the table Mr. Cueva, the oil salesman, said in sympathy, "It's the altitude, señor. It bothers lots of people."

The stairs seemed endless, and when he reached the dark hallway above, his head was swimming. A door on his right was open. As he started to pass it Dr. Briggs called out, "The boy in number seven is almost fit again. He wants to go on with you to the capital. I told him he might as well."

Tod paused in the doorway. "When do you think— we'll be leaving?"

"Oh, by noon, I expect." Dr. Briggs stepped forward, his dark face alert. "What's wrong with you?"

"I—I'm afraid I don't feel so well. Maybe I need—a little sleep."

Dr. Briggs's gaze was intent. "You haven't been eating Mexican food—or drinking water along the road, have you?"

"Yes. In Valles."

"At a hotel?"

"No. Not at a hotel." Tod's voice sounded strange to his ears.

"Look here." The physician's tone was professional. "You climb into bed and stay there. If you don't feel better I'll fix up something for you to take. You may have picked up a dysentery bug. Many travelers do. No joke, either."

Tod shook his head. "I can't afford to be sick. I've got to drive to the city as soon as the highway is open."

"Young man, you go straight to bed." Dr. Briggs spoke with emphasis. "I have a feeling it'll be some days before you ever reach Mexico City. Now, don't try to squirm out of it. I'm advising you as a doctor. I've been down here before and I know. Go to bed."

"All right." Tod gave in. "Until the road is open, I will. But no longer."

An understanding smile crossed the dark face. "I'll make a professional call on you in half an hour. Now, turn in."

"Thank you. I will." Tod continued down the hall, realizing with a pang of despair that he was truly sick. Yes, he had to admit it—he felt awful. As a wave of nausea swept over him, he put out a hand for support.

Down the hall a door opened. Pedro Torres, the White-cap, came out and passed him without a word. Through a blurred vision Tod looked at the door that had just closed. It was number seven—Rico's room.

The thought went vaguely through his mind that it

was queer the White-cap should be calling upon Rico; but a moment later he lost interest in Rico, in the brief case, in everything except the overwhelming feeling of sickness that gripped him. He reached his door, tottered inside, slammed it shut and fell, fully clothed, onto the bed.

How good it felt—just to rest there. Not to think. Not to think of Martin Welch or the Buick or his own Ford convertible parked up there on the highway. This sickness wouldn't last. Why, he was never ill—never. He was simply worn out. Let him rest a while and he'd be better.

In silence he lay there listening to the sounds in the building. He heard steps on the stairs and in the corridor. He heard the rattle of dishes from the kitchen below. He heard a car draw up before the inn. A door slammed.

After a brief interval, the tempo of life increased. Footsteps hurried along the corridor. Voices called. Someone shouted, "The road's open! Make it snappy." Mrs. Sturtevant's reply came, sharp and clear: "We're leaving? Thank heavens!"

Leaving? Tod raised himself to an elbow, swung his legs to the floor and sat up. If he was going to be sick, he would be sick in Mexico City, not here. He must get in touch with Captain Jarvis at the Hotel Geneve before he allowed himself to give in to this pain, this nausea, this baneful sense of inertia. Pull yourself together, Tod Moran! Get going.

Highroad To Adventure

A knock sounded on the door. It swung open, and Dr. Briggs entered. He stopped short when he saw Tod seated on the edge of the bed, and his lean face expressed disapproval. "I thought I had ordered you to turn in. Get off those clothes and tumble into bed. Here's a little dose of something I've fixed for you. It'll set you right —that is, if you haven't picked up some of those poisonous dysentery bugs."

"I feel better, Doctor Briggs. I'm really all right."

"Nonsense. Don't fight against it. Just take it easy." The doctor handed him a glass half filled with a whitish liquid. "Swallow this. If this doesn't make you feel better by tomorrow, perhaps you ought to get someone to drive you the rest of the way to the capital. You could go to the American hospital there."

"But I'm not that sick!"

"I hope not." Dr. Briggs regarded him with a speculative glance. "Listen here, Moran. Do you realize that nearly half the tourists who come down here pick up intestinal germs? Now if it happens to be only the usual food poisoning, you'll be all right in a few days—if you take care of yourself and stay in bed. But there's just a chance it might be amoebic dysentery. You can't fool with that. Of course, you drank water that wasn't bottled?"

"Yes."

"Foolish of you. Very. I don't suppose it had been boiled, either."

The Riddle

"No, I don't suppose it had."

"All right, take this. Go ahead. I'm waiting."

Tod gulped down the thick fluid. It made him feel worse than ever. He put up a hand and found his forehead damp with sweat. His cheeks were hot. "Thanks, Doctor," he murmured. "I'll soon be okay."

"I trust so. Well, good-by and good luck. I'm leaving."

"You're off—for Mexico City?"

"Not today. Foster and I want to do some fishing beyond Jacala."

When he was alone again, Tod struggled to his feet and crossed to the open window. Sitting there in the chair, he watched the Sturtevants back out their Pontiac and swing up to the highway. The oil salesman left next in the model-T roadster. Tod leaned over the sill and looked down. The White-cap was prowling around the Buick, and Dr. Briggs and Jim Foster were stepping into the tan Packard. Foster took the wheel, and a moment later the purr of their motor was audible as their car climbed up to the highway and turned toward the slide. Still no Martin Welch.

A knock sounded on the door. "Come in," Tod called out.

Rico entered, fully dressed, his arm in a sling. "Aren't you going, Mr. Moran?"

"Yes." Tod pulled himself erect. It occurred to him that this young Mexican was his only contact with the lost brief case. Somehow he must manage not to lose

Rico, too. "I don't suppose you could drive my car, Rico?"

"With one arm? I'm afraid not."

"I guess I'll have to, then."

Rico stepped closer, his face showing concern. "What's wrong? You're sick?"

"I was—a little. Feel lots better now, though."

"It's the altitude. It oftens bothers the tourists. You'll get over it in a few days."

"Oh, sure—just the altitude." Tod's tone was sarcastic. "That's what all you Mexicans say. That's because you're used to bugs."

Rico spread out his hands in a gesture of resignation. "Of course there is no sanitation here, Mr. Moran—not like the States. And the laws concerning water and milk and such things are not what you'd approve of. But we're trying to make things better. We're trying."

"Of course." Tod nodded. "Skip it. Did that White-cap offer to take you with him?"

"Why, yes. How did you know?"

"Oh, I happened to see him coming from your room."

Rico's glance was expectant. "I told him I was hired by you, Mr. Moran. Though, of course, with only one arm, I'm not much use."

"Oh, yes, you are. I'll get my bag packed, then we'll have to take a little walk to my car. Let's hope it's still there!"

"It isn't below?"

The Riddle

"No. It's parked up the highway. I thought maybe Martin Welch might try some more of his foolishness."

Rico's eyes wavered. "Martin Welch? But he isn't here, señor."

"No? Well, he was here. Maybe he's gone by this time. Maybe he walked around that slide and picked up another car on the other side."

"But no one could walk around that slide, Mr. Moran."

"Yes, you told me that before." Tod flung his shaving things into his bag, locked it, and picked up his Panama. "Let's get going."

By the time he reached the lower floor he was feeling more like his old self. His interest in the riddle of Martin Welch's invisibility, lost while he lay upstairs on his bed, now quickened to life again. "Rico," he said as he paid the proprietor at the bar, "what would happen if this fellow failed to register every guest who stayed here?"

"He'd lose his license, señor."

"Ask him if I can see the register, will you?"

But the canvas-covered book, when opened, revealed no new name added. Martin Welch, no matter what name he had used, had not signed that register. Yet he must have been here. For hadn't the soldier who had stopped them at Tamazunchale the night before said an American had been driving the Buick—and wasn't the Buick outside right now? How could Welch have disappeared into thin air between that little town and the Montezuma Inn?

"I'll take your bag, Mr. Moran. Don't worry about me. I bet I feel better than you do."

Tod tossed his companion a quizzical look. "I'd be surprised, Rico, if you didn't."

Outside, a single car was left—the Buick sedan. Before the open trunk stood Pedro Torres, a white military cap pulled jauntily over one eye. "Have you a car around here, sir?" he asked. "I'd like to borrow an air pump."

"Sorry, I haven't one."

"Then I'll have to hail someone on the highway. It'll be some time before the traffic gets up here."

"Too bad." Tod's memory of his own troubles on the road still rankled. He started on, then paused. "Is the slide all cleared away?"

"No. Just a one-way road for the present. The highway won't be entirely clear until tonight." The White-cap was gazing straight at Rico, and Tod thought he saw a look of understanding pass between them. No matter. Rico might yet lead him to the brief case.

"We're certainly a fine pair, aren't we?" Tod smiled wryly at his companion as they splashed through mud puddles, side by side. "Both of us sort of under the weather. Not even good friends. Yet we're traveling together."

"But we are friends, Mr. Moran. That's why I prefer to go with you."

"Are you sure?" Tod gazed up at the leaden sky. The mountain peaks were hidden by the mist. "Aren't you riding with me because that Buick happens to be stalled?"

"No, Mr. Moran. If you believe that, why do you take me along?"

"I'm sure I don't know." Tod sighed. "Maybe it's because I want company. Maybe it's because I feel so blamed rotten nothing else matters. Maybe I think there's a chance to get my brief case back while you're around."

"Brief case, señor? But I have no brief case."

"Let's not waste any more breath in talking." The graveled incline now before them appeared steeper and longer than it had from his window. "My mind is too muddled to think, anyway. But I'm sure of one thing— I've had enough of this Montezuma Inn."

CHAPTER XIV

Jacala

THE sight of the Ford convertible, parked close to the pile of gravel, made Tod quicken his pace. One glance informed him that his car had apparently been undisturbed. Nevertheless, his fingers trembled as he unlocked the door; and not until the motor had taken up its low, steady beat did he feel relieved.

"She's okay—I think," he called out to his companion.

Rico, standing on the running board, was using a corner of his poncho to wipe the moisture from the windshield. "She's a good car, Mr. Moran."

"Good? Why, she's perfect!" Tod lowered the window at his side. "Hurry up. We'll have to switch on the wiper, anyway."

Rico placed his sombrero upon the floor and, folding his poncho as best he could with one hand, flung it to the ledge behind the seat. As he climbed in, Tod was acutely aware of the linen-colored coat draped around the bandaged shoulder, aware also of the tear in the cloth where one button was missing.

"We'll soon climb out of this mist, señor. Then you'll see some real country."

Tod threw in the gear, swung the car round and headed up the highway. The tires whined on the damp pavement. Visibility, in spots, was not more than a hundred feet.

When they passed the inn, he saw Pedro Torres, the White-cap, coming up the drive, doubtless with the intention of flagging someone who passed. Yet cars that had already been delayed for hours would scarcely stop long enough for a stranger to inflate four tires.

No, it would likely be quite a while before the black sedan succeeded in getting under way.

Beyond the inn they met the first of a line of northbound cars which had been allowed to pass the slide. "These people," Rico observed, "must have stopped at Jacala. It's only a few miles farther on."

Twelve cars went slowly by, nine of them with licenses from the States. Of the nine, Tod counted four California plates. "Californians are great travelers," he remarked. "They're always on the move."

At the slide, a huge steam shovel and several trucks were still busy. Armed soldiers allowed one-way traffic to pass. Tod's Ford was alone, but beyond the slanting pile of earth were three cars waiting to proceed down the mountain. Tod glanced at his watch. It was nearly eleven o'clock. These Mexicans with their modern equipment hadn't done so badly, after all. Rico was no doubt right when he asserted that his country would one day be great, if given half a chance.

Several miles beyond the slide the cliff gradually gave way to a forest of pine, dark and dripping in the misty light. There was such an eerie atmosphere about the place that Tod was glad when it, too, fell away behind and fog-drenched clearings came into view. Then the clearings slipped downhill; the highway climbed round the edge of a bluff, and the sun was out.

Tod caught his breath. Against a clear blue sky rose mountain peaks as far as the eye could see. It was a stupendous sight that left him speechless. He felt small and unimportant. Failure or success—what difference did it make! Casually he glanced down off the edge of the road to a floor of gray mist. That mist, he knew, was a ceiling for a valley hundreds of feet, perhaps thousands of feet below. Yes, Rico had been right. These wooded mountain sides, these crags and peaks were more breath taking than any he had seen before.

Still the road climbed. It curved through another forest, swung to the right, and began a descent into a little valley filled with sunshine.

"Jacala," Rico announced, pointing to the red-tiled roofs of a town. "It is beautiful, yes?"

Jacala

Tod agreed with a nod. "How far beyond is Mexico City?"

"About a hundred and fifty miles, señor. The road keeps going up beyond Jacala, but there are not many slide areas. You should make it in four hours. Do you feel able to drive that far?"

"Oh, sure. This sunshine and air make me feel fit as a fiddle. I'll be all right so long as I don't try to eat. Maybe a cup of coffee would taste good, though. Any chance of getting some in Jacala?"

"Yes. An American named Simpson has a good lunch room there. We'll come to it before we enter the town."

At Simpson's service station Tod stopped for gas and oil and then drove on past the line of modern tourist cabins. A tan Packard was just leaving the lunch room. Jim Foster, at the wheel, waved a cheery greeting, but Dr. Briggs, seated beside him, turned toward Tod a face stern with disapproval.

On a thatch-covered porch overlooking the valley, coffee was served by a young Mexican clad in white. Under the influence of the hot drink Tod almost forgot that his legs felt weak, his head slightly dizzy, and his cheeks too warm. The beauty of the valley surrounded by its pine-clad mountains brought him a sense of peace —until he recalled that his brief case was still missing. Yet there was nothing else to do but report to Captain Jarvis in the capital. It would be, of course, an admission of failure. Here he was, arriving in Mexico City, a messenger without any message, a courier with his documents lost.

With a sigh Tod put down his cup. "Did you notice," he asked his companion, "the dirty look Doctor Briggs gave me when we drove up?"

When Rico did not reply Tod flashed him a glance. The young man's gaze was turned in the other direction, an expression of uneasiness on his face. Following that gaze, Tod beheld a soldier coming toward the porch, coming in fact straight toward their table. Tod glanced round. Yes, all the other tables were empty. Yet why should a soldier wish to speak to them, and why, too, should Rico be so concerned?

The soldier stopped before them, shifted the rifle strap on his shoulder, and spoke quickly in Spanish. Tod, listening intently, caught his own name mentioned.

"What's the matter, Rico?"

"This highway guard is asking about us, Mr. Moran. He says the proprietor of the Montezuma Inn reported us to one of his men up at the slide, and word was sent down here to the station. He wants to see our identification cards." Rico reached into the inside pocket of his coat and brought forth a small leather case. Opening it, he handed it to the man.

Curious, Tod asked, "What sort of identification do you have?"

"Just a license for working with the tourists."

Jacala

"Then you're a White-cap?"

Rico nodded. "You might call me that."

Tod did not need to ask his companion what had become of the official cap. It was no doubt locked in the trunk of the black sedan—left there when Martin Welch had provided him with the poncho and sombrero to use as a disguise. With an impatient gesture Tod brought out his tourist card. When the soldier had looked it over he spoke again in Spanish.

"He says," Rico explained after a moment, "that the proprietor was informed you are not just a tourist, Mr. Moran."

"Then what am I?" Tod retorted.

"He says he was told you came to Mexico on business."

"Well, what if I did?"

Rico leaned across the table. "But, Mr. Moran, no foreigner is allowed to enter this country on business without a special government permit."

"I've never heard of that before!"

"But, señor, it is true. No longer can foreign mining engineers come here, because our government demands now that all important work be done by our own citizens. That is why so many of our students go to American universities. When they complete their studies, they return home and take the places of the foreign engineers who have been here for years. Every day you find fewer and fewer foreigners working at the big-paying jobs."

"But that doesn't concern me, Rico. I'm no mining engineer."

"I know, señor, but this may be serious. No American can come to our country on business without first applying for admission and stating what that business is. You failed to do that?"

Tod's tone revealed his irritation. "Rico, I'm no business man. I'm third mate on an American cargo steamer. I came down here merely as a sort of messenger—to bring a brief case to a friend of mine in the capital. You know that as well as I do."

"Then you are not really a tourist, Mr. Moran." Rico sat back in his chair and, to Tod's surprise, there was a troubled expression on the dark handsome face.

Puzzled, Tod glanced up at the soldier. The man smiled, handed back the tourist card and, turning on his heel, departed.

Rico lowered his voice. "The guard said you will not be allowed to enter the city. You will be detained when we reach there."

"Detained? What do you mean?"

"Listen, Mr. Moran. On the outskirts of Mexico City is a station where the police stop all cars for identification. You are certain to be held for entering the country under false pretenses."

"You mean arrested?"

"Maybe. Or they might order you to turn round and

drive back the way you have come, reporting at every station along the road."

"Rot!" Tod's tone was sharp. "This is Welch's work, of course. He couldn't stop me on the road, so he's trying to have me sent out of the country before my work is done."

"Then you do have work down here!"

"Yes. What of it? Anyway, my friend in the city has contacts with men high in government circles. He'll manage to straighten out this misunderstanding. We'd better get going." Tod stood up. "Suppose we get past that station before they know?"

"Ah, I thought of that, but it is too late now." Rico threw out his hand in a gesture of resignation. "A patrolman has already left on his motorcycle for the capital. The report will be at the station long before we can get there."

With nervous steps Tod crossed to the rail of the porch. Welch's work again! The whole thing was a mere technicality. Yet from the viewpoint of Mexican officials it might appear as though he were trying to enter the country under false credentials. Could he explain to their satisfaction?

He swung about. "Why is your government so blamed particular? Would they stamp my card and let me pass the station if I explained?"

Rico shrugged, then winced as the movement jarred

his shoulder. "Señor, in years past it was the big foreign interests that ran my country. That is why your business men must now get a special permit to enter this country. Why should we trust you? Why?"

To Rico's fiery question Tod found no reply. A few Americans, it was clear, had earned so much dislike and suspicion that years must elapse before their fellow countrymen could allay that feeling of distrust.

"Rico," he said after a moment, "could we enter the city on another road?"

"We might be able to. I'll do all I can."

Tod's eyes narrowed. "Just why are you so eager to have me reach Mexico City?"

"Me?" Rico smiled disarmingly. "Why I merely want to see you get there. I want to earn the twenty dollars you promised."

"Are you sure that's the only reason?"

"What other reason could I have, señor?"

"Never mind." Tod turned back to the table and sat down.

Rico slid into the chair opposite. "You are in no hurry, Mr. Moran?"

"No. I've decided to stay here for an hour or two. I think certain friends of mine will soon be coming along the road. At least they ought to be here by midafternoon, maybe sooner. You know them. They drive a Chevvy that pulls a trailer. I'll sit here where I can watch the road. Want to wait here with me, Rico, or do you want me to pay you off so you can catch a ride into Mexico City?"

"I'll wait here, Mr. Moran."

"You're a funny fellow, Rico. I can't make you out. How about some lunch?"

CHAPTER XV

The Brief Case

FRISCO, we're sure glad to see you. We've got news."
Ben Whipple leaned out of his car, his eyes alight.

Beyond him Ma Whipple nodded with vigor. "Real
news, Tod. I'm glad we can let you know before the
black sedan overtakes us."

Tod came up to the car and put one foot on the running board. It was late afternoon and the Chevrolet and
trailer were pulled up beside the highway near the lunch
room. Rico was dozing in the Ford safely out of hearing.

"I've been waiting for you," Tod explained. "Now,
what's the news? Is it bad?"

"Bad, nothing!" Ma Whipple spoke with scorn. Her
stout little figure was tense and her blue eyes shone.
"Paw, you go ahead and tell him. Begin with the pump."

Ben Whipple cleared his throat. "It's this way, Frisco.

The Brief Case

We came on from Valles early this morning and found that no cars was allowed past Thomas and Charlie; but when word came down the mountain that the road was clear, we started right up. There was a regular parade of cars. You must of seen 'em go by here. Well, when we got to a sort of hotel alongside the road, there was a feller flagging us."

"The White-cap, I'll bet," Tod exclaimed. "At the Montezuma Inn?"

"Maybe. Anyway, this feller wanted to borrow our pump so he could put some air in his tires. I was jest going to say we didn't have time when Ma gives me a poke in the ribs and points down to the front of that place. You could of hit me in the eye when I sees what's there. The black sedan! So I turned off the motor and got out the pump. That feller seemed real nice, even though he was a Mexican, but I wasn't taking no chances so I goes with him down to his car. Then I saw it." Ben Whipple flashed Tod a look, brown eyed, keen, knowing. "Yes, sir. I saw it."

Tod's voice was excited. "Saw what?"

"The brief case. There it was—right in the Buick's trunk."

"You're sure?"

"Sure as I'm alive. The trunk was open so I jest fooled around it while the driver was pumping away on a tire. And there it was—mixed up with some baggage. Oh, I didn't make no mistake. Didn't I see that brief case when

[207]

you toted it around that night in Monterrey?"

A thrill of hope surged up in Tod. "And the black sedan is on the road behind you?"

"You bet. She ain't passed us yet." Ben Whipple lowered his tone. "I had an idea I ought to try to sneak the brief case outa that trunk, but I knowed it was no use. That feller would of seen me and give chase. So I walks up to the highway where Ma's sitting in the car and tells her."

"Exactly." With a click of her teeth Ma Whipple took up the story. "I says to Paw right away we ought to drive fast and see if we could catch up with you. You see, I didn't figure your car would get very far, seeing as how it's always stalling along the road."

Tod overlooked this slighting remark. "Go ahead," he urged. "What then?"

"Well, Paw went down to the sedan and told the driver we'd go on and he could give us back the pump when he caught up with us. We drove as fast as we could. We beat him here."

Tod glanced back up the highway. Under the afternoon sun the pavement lay empty and glistening. He turned his head and looked the other way. Beyond the lunch room began the first of the tile-roofed houses of Jacala. In broad daylight, in such a place as this, how could he hope to get the brief case? Could he appeal to the authorities here in Jacala? Hardly. He was already a suspicious character to the military police on the highway, and it was obvious that the soldiers worked in collaboration with the police in the towns along the route. No, he must work out his problem without their help.

"We got to think fast, Frisco."

"That's what I'm trying to do." Tod's voice sank to a whisper. "When the Buick overtakes you, Paw, that driver will stop to give you back your pump, won't he?"

"I figure he will."

"Well, he'd better. Suppose he comes up behind you when you're driving along a lonely stretch of road? That would give me a chance to get at his trunk."

"How?" Ma Whipple spoke in a skeptical tone.

"I don't know yet," Tod admitted. "We'll have to plan everything in detail. But I've got to be riding with you when the Buick comes along. Can you drive a car, Mrs. Whipple?"

"Me?" Indignation flared on Ma Whipple's round face. "Of course I can!"

Her husband smothered a cough. "Ma never drives when the Chevvy is pulling the trailer, though."

"I was thinking about my Ford," Tod explained. "If Ma could drive it, I could ride inside your trailer. Then that White-cap wouldn't see me."

A frown settled upon Ben Whipple's face. "I don't fancy Ma trying to drive any car on these mountain roads. How about your friend driving, Frisco?"

"Rico? He's only got one arm."

"One arm?" Ma Whipple's voice rose in horror. "Land

sakes, he had two when I saw him in Valles. What you been up to, Tod Moran?"

"You ask him when you're driving the Ford. He'll tell you—maybe."

"I don't like this idea," grumbled Ben Whipple. "It's bad enough having Ma driving a strange car all alone, but with that Mexican riding with her——"

"Now, Paw, stop wasting time. Land sakes, before we know it, that black sedan will be sneaking up behind us. I'll get out right now and take over the wheel." She leaned forward, her eyes intent. "Tod Moran, you don't look so well yourself. What's the matter? Been fighting?"

Tod forced a smile. "Oh, I'm all right. Just tired and sleepy." He wasn't going to admit, even to himself, how sick he felt. "Come on. I'll take you over to my car."

As Ma Whipple climbed out, her husband warned, "Now, you keep just ahead of us, Ma, so I can see you."

"Fiddlesticks!" Ma Whipple waved a plump hand. With a sigh, she trudged along at Tod's side toward the red convertible. "Paw's always got to worry about something. If it isn't one of the children, it's me."

Tod opened the car door. "This is Rico, Mrs. Whipple. He can tell you all about his country."

Ma Whipple got in behind the wheel. "You don't mind a woman driving, do you?"

Rico's dark eyes showed surprise. "You stopping here, Mr. Moran?"

The Brief Case

Tod did not answer. The less Rico knew of his plans, the better.

Ma Whipple stepped on the starter, threw in the clutch. With a series of jerks the Ford rolled ahead. A plump arm waved a quick good-by.

As Tod slipped into the seat beside Ben Whipple, the old man growled, "Ma oughtn't to drive with one hand. That's jest like her, though. Look at her go! She'll get arrested, speeding through a town like that."

Ben Whipple shoved the gear into low, and the Chevrolet with its trailer slowly forged ahead. They passed through the edge of the little town at fifteen miles an hour; then, as open country spread before them, the car gained speed and took an easy incline in high.

"Always climbing," muttered the driver. "That's all you do on this road. We're up five thousand feet now. Four more thousand to go. I can't make it very fast, Frisco."

"Don't worry." As the highway curved up the side of a mountain Tod glanced back. In relief he saw that the road was deserted. "We've got to make plans, then I'd better hide in the trailer. Any ideas?"

"If I'm going to think," Ben Whipple replied, "I gotta be smoking. Fill my pipe for me, will you? Ma always does it on the road."

Once more the highway swung up through forests of pine. Jacala in its little valley fell away behind. The sunlight slanted through the trees. Occasionally the little Ford came into view on a curve far ahead.

"Now, if you only had a good gun," Ben Whipple suggested, "you could jest hold up that feller and take away the brief case."

"No guns, thank you," Tod retorted. "I've already had enough trouble because of one."

"Suppose, Frisco, you jest hit him over the head with a nice heavy wrench? I got one in my tool box."

"Nothing doing." Tod started to laugh, but the mirth died on his lips as a wave of sickness swept over him. He must fight off this feeling until he had regained the brief case. After that, he didn't care what happened. With an effort he controlled his voice. "I can't afford to get mixed up any more with the police. They're on my trail right now."

"You mean they're following you?" Ben Whipple's tone was grave.

"No. They're waiting for me ahead—at Mexico City." Tod went on to explain about his tourist card.

"Shucks," said Ben Whipple. "You leave that to me. I'll sneak you into the city. The trailer's jest filled with nice places to hide. The shower bath would do." He puffed for some moments on his pipe, his gaze upon the little round mirror outside his window. "I can see the road a long way behind, Frisco, so you'll have plenty of time to hop out if the black sedan comes along. I'll pull up beside the road and you keep out of sight behind the trailer."

"No, I'd better be inside it. But we've got to know exactly what we intend to do." Tod took off his Panama and ran a hand through his hair. He mustn't let Paw Whipple know how he felt—that his head ached and his ears rang, that his mind refused to work and his muscles were too weak to attempt a hand-to-hand encounter. Wearily he looked out at the passing forest.

The sun sank behind a mountain top. Still no car came up from the rear. The Ford, with Ma Whipple and Rico, had long since disappeared ahead. Once an Indian went by on bare feet, his back bent under the weight of a huge load of fagots, his baggy trousers flapping. Otherwise, they met no one at all.

At dusk they sighted an adobe house alongside the road.

"Suppose we stop here a minute?" Ben Whipple suggested. "You kinda worry me, Frisco. You don't seem like yourself. You don't say a word. Ain't you even interested in your brief case?"

"Of course." Tod roused himself from the lethargy into which he had fallen. "This altitude sort of bothers me."

Ben Whipple looked at him shrewdly. "It ain't the altitude. You're sick. I'm a-going to make up the bed in the trailer and tuck you in."

"Not yet." Tod sat erect. "Wait till the Buick comes along. Then I'll turn in."

Ben Whipple brought his little caravan to a stop before the adobe building. A sign over the door announced *cantina*, and another on the roof read *gasolina*—liquid refreshment for man and automobile. A slouching figure in the doorway wore a bartender's apron.

Tod's mind seemed to leap awake. "Paw, there's a bar inside."

"Well, I don't drink very often," Ben Whipple said doubtfully.

"It was the White-cap I was thinking of, Paw, not you." A plan, full fledged, swept into Tod's mind. "Suppose we wait here?"

Ben Whipple scratched his head. "I'm beginning to think that Buick ain't coming. Maybe she's stopped in Jacala."

"But not for the night, I'll bet. Listen, Mr. Whipple. This is my plan. I'll get inside the trailer and wait. You stay here. When the Buick comes along . . ."

Night closed down. Above the pines the sky became a luminous blue. Then slowly the blue deepened and the stars came out.

From the rear window of the trailer Tod watched the road. When he saw the headlights of an approaching car in the distance he ran to the door and shouted, "Someone's coming! It might be the Buick."

In another moment he was at a side window, waiting. The headlights grew larger. The glare made him draw back to one side. The sound of a motor was audible. Drawing aside the curtain, he looked out. A large black sedan slowly passed and stopped beside the Chevrolet.

The Brief Case

Ben Whipple was standing there with upraised hand.

"Got my pump, mister? I need it. Had a little trouble myself."

"Señor Whipple?" The White-cap's voice revealed no suspicion. "I thought it was you. Very much, señor, do I appreciate your help." He turned off his motor, jumped down, and opened the tonneau door. His white-clad figure was clearly visible.

Ben Whipple took the pump. "Going on to Mexico City tonight?"

"Yes, señor. My boss said to be in Mexico City in the morning, but I wish to hurry. You staying here?"

"No, I'll move on pretty soon. How about something to drink in the cantina? It'll only take a minute."

"Ah, señor, it is I who shall buy you a drink. One minute, señor. I must turn off my lights."

Tod grew rigid. This was exactly what they had feared. For if the White-cap turned to his instrument panel to click off the lights, he might at the same time pull his keys from the ignition lock. And without those keys the trunk would never be opened without a fight.

But Ben Whipple met the occasion with a quick reply. "Aw, don't bother about them. Come along. We'll make it snappy."

The man did not hesitate. With a laugh he strode off at Ben Whipple's side toward the cantina.

Tod waited only until they had disappeared inside, then he cautiously opened the trailer door, stepped to the ground, and darted round to the other side of the trailer. Without pausing, he made his way through the darkness toward the Buick. When the long black sedan was safely between him and the lighted windows of the cantina he breathed easier. His hand touched the chromium handle of the door. For a moment he stood still and listened.

A soft breeze was whispering through the pine tops. The distant murmur of voices came from the cantina. Well, Ben Whipple could be depended upon to keep the White-cap busy for a few minutes. He swung open the car door. The faint glow from the instrument panel revealed a key ring hanging from the ignition lock. Bending his head so he would not be seen, he jerked out the key and drew back.

In another moment he was standing at the rear of the car, fitting the key into the trunk lock. His gaze crossed to the cantina doorway. Two vague figures could be seen leaning against the bar, a lighted lamp above their heads. If that White-cap turned now and looked this way, everything would be lost. Everything? No. He'd have that brief case out of the trunk before the man could rush outside.

His fingers turned the key. He threw up the cover. Reaching in, he felt a leather traveling bag. His hand moved across it and came in contact with a woolen top-coat. Flinging this aside, he searched on. Then his fingers closed round a familiar leather handle. With a mur-

The Brief Case

mur of triumph he drew out the Blakemore brief case.

It was heavy, too. Thank heavens, the letters and papers were still there. He lowered the cover of the trunk, locked it and pulled out the key ring. Then he ran forward and slipped the key again into the ignition lock. When he had softly closed the door once more he took a deep breath. Ben Whipple and the White-cap were laughing together at the bar. His eyes narrowed. Maybe he'd better make sure now before it was too late.

Seating himself on the running board, he unfastened the straps of the brief case. His fingers felt inside. Yes, there were the half-dozen letters, all in the legal-size envelopes, and there, too, were the copies of the business negotiations wrapped in paper and held together with rubber bands. All at once he lifted his head in sudden alarm. Voices sounded through the still night air. The two men were coming out.

With fear giving speed to his weary legs, he ran back for the protection of the trailer. When it stood between him and danger he halted, holding his breath in suspense. Had he been seen? But surely a person stepping from the lighted cantina would not be able to adjust his vision at once.

Ben Whipple's anxious tones came to him. "Why the hurry? Have one on me."

"Thank you, señor. But when you drive this mountain road you do not drink more than one."

Tod crouched close against the trailer wall. As footsteps approached he slid round to the rear. Would Pedro Torres be suspicious? Had the man been ordered to guard that luggage with his life? The moments dragged as he waited, the brief case hugged under one arm.

He heard Ben Whipple's nervous laughter, the sound of a car door slamming, a cheery good-by. A motor roared. Wheels ground on the gravel, then took up a whine as they reached the pavement. The headlights moved away between dark walls of pine.

"Got it, Frisco?" Ben Whipple's whisper reached him from near the trailer door. "He's gone. But shucks, he was in a terrible hurry."

Tod moved round the corner to meet him. "I got it." His words, though low, rang with a feeling of triumph. "Think he suspected anything?"

"Shucks, no. Why should he? Climb in, now. We'll pick up Ma and keep going. You'll be in Mexico City tonight."

CHAPTER XVI

Captain Tom Jarvis

UNDER THE TROPICAL STARS the caravan wound up through the mountains on the last lap of the journey to Mexico City. Ben Whipple, riding alone, kept his gaze on the Ford ahead; and whenever the tail lights became too distant he sent a frantic note from his horn through the night. That warning for Ma Whipple to slow up always brought a response that pleased her husband—a toot on the Ford's horn and a few moments' wait by the road. Then Ma Whipple would speed up once more and Paw had to do it all over again.

Still the highway kept climbing. At an altitude just under nine thousand feet the summit was reached. Then the road began a gradual descent into the Valley of Mexico, cradled in the high Sierra Madres.

Sound asleep, Tod lay in bed in the trailer while his

cabin on wheels creaked and groaned around him. The hum of the tires came to his ears in an undertone not unlike the wash of water along a steamer's hull. In his feverish dream he was once again at sea. He stood on the bridge of the freighter, *Araby*, gazing across a wide blue expanse of water as a tropical island drew near. He raised his binoculars to his eyes. Now he could see it! There was Mexico City towering above the buildings along the water front.

"We're arriving on schedule," came the voice of Captain Jarvis, deep and resonant and strong. "We're almost there."

He opened his eyes. The cabin of his ship was dark and strangely quiet. Why, the engines had stopped. The *Araby* must be lying outside the harbor waiting for dawn before entering the channel. He turned his head. A vague figure stood in the doorway.

"We're almost there, Frisco. Are you awake?"

It was Ben Whipple speaking, not Captain Jarvis; and he was in the Whipples' trailer, not on the *Araby* at sea. Raising himself to an elbow, he managed to say, "Sure I am."

"We had to take Rico into our confidence, Frisco. We needed his help. We're jest outside the city. The police station's a little bit ahead."

Tod rubbed his eyes. "How am I going to get past the station?"

"You stay right in bed and cover up. When they look

at my tourist card they might ask where Ma is. I'm a-going to say she's asleep in this trailer. It's eleven o'clock, so it ain't likely they'll ask a poor woman to git up and dress at this hour of the night."

"I hope not," Tod muttered.

"But if they do, you jest squeal like Ma would. Rico says, though, there ain't much danger."

"But what about the Ford? How are Rico and Ma getting through?"

"Oh, Rico's going to show her a dirt road that leads into town another way. They'll meet us at the Shirley Courts. That's quite a drive across town, Rico says." The old man paused and then anxiously inquired, "How you feeling? Any better?"

"Oh, sure. All I needed was a little sleep."

Ben Whipple sighed. "Ma says if you ain't better she'll give you some medicine. If she does it'll sure lay you out unless you're as strong as an ox. Where's your brief case?"

"Under my pillow."

"Keep it there." Ben Whipple appeared to be enjoying himself. His voice was brisk and cheerful. "We won't stop again till we get to the station. Let's hope those police will be polite."

When he was gone, Tod pulled up the covers and turned his face to the wall. Once again his little room began moving. The bed shook. Tires hummed. A door rattled. A built-in cabinet near him kept up a persistent

murmur of protest. Now and then a light flashed by outside and he heard a car whizz past. They were meeting
traffic, all right. A thrill of expectancy went through him.
Mexico City—at last!

Abruptly he became aware of a brake taking hold.
Voices sounded. The trailer came to a stop.

Tod pulled his sheet still higher. If the door opened,
he must lie absolutely quiet. And if anyone questioned
him—oh, how in thunder could he hope to reply like Ma
Whipple! But the door did not open. He soon heard
Paw's cheery good night, and at once they got under
way again. A sense of relief swept over him. They had
passed through the line.

Getting to his knees, he peered out between the draped
white curtains of the window above his bed. They were
bumping across a dozen railroad tracks; then the Chevrolet came into view for a moment as its driver turned to
the right down a wide street. How, he wondered, would
Ben Whipple ever find his way to the Shirley Courts if it
was some distance across town? But when they presently
turned a corner and entered a street between low whitewashed houses, he saw on the corner building a yellow
arrow with a notation, reading *Shirley Courts*. At the
next corner a street lamp revealed another arrow. Not a
bad idea. He'd better get dressed at once.

But it was half an hour more before the Chevrolet and
its trailer reached its destination, going through narrow
back streets such as he had seen in seaports in southern

Spain. Another series of railroad tracks were crossed; another turn; and they drew up before an arched gateway in a long white wall.

The trailer door opened and there stood Ma Whipple. "I been waiting for you slow pokes," she said. "How you feeling?"

"Lots better." Tod's weary voice did not support his words, but as he stepped out he managed a grin. "Have any trouble getting into the city?"

"Not a bit. Rico knew his roads. He jumped out at the corner and ran for a street car."

"Why the rush? I haven't paid him yet."

"Oh, he said he'd be back in the morning. He went in such a hurry he forgot his poncho and sombrero."

Tod looked around. Immense trees lined the sidewalk. Through the arched gateway he could see a courtyard with wide lawns and low white buildings. An electric light revealed several cars parked there in the open, his Ford among them.

Tod accompanied his two friends through the gate, where a night watchman pointed out the office. After registering, he was given a cabin with a sitting room, bedroom and bath.

"Now you go right to bed and sleep till noon," Ma Whipple ordered. "Don't you be in a hurry to ring up that Hotel Geneve, either. Your eyes look tired and your face sort of pale. You take good care of yourself or I'll send for a doctor."

[223]

A twisted smile moved on Tod's lips. "Don't you worry. I'm okay. Nothing but bottled water for me after this. I've learned my lesson."

"Here's the key to your car." Ma Whipple dropped it into his hand. "I locked it up good and tight and gave the guard at the gate a peso to keep his eyes on it."

Ben Whipple touched his wife's arm. "Come on, Ma. You're keeping Frisco awake by your chattering. See you in the morning! We're going down the block to the trailer camp."

"Wait a minute." Tod crossed to the door and turned, his eyes bright. "You can't leave here till I've thanked you."

Ben Whipple waved him aside. "Shucks, Frisco, forget it. We'll be round in the morning."

When his friends had gone, Tod took a warm shower, then put on his pajamas and bath robe and slippers. Except for the fact that his mind seemed somewhat hazy, he felt almost fit. Tired, perhaps, but nothing else. He even hummed a tune as he picked up the brief case and unfastened the straps. The sight of its contents made his spirits rise still more. A glance at his watch on the table told him it was already after midnight. Why, this was the morning of May fifteenth! He had kept his pledge to Captain Jarvis. He had arrived in Mexico City on time.

All at once he raised his head as the wheels of a car sounded on the gravel outside. He went to the window and pulled aside the blind. A taxi stood before his door.

Captain Tom Jarvis

"This is the number," came the driver's voice. "Two pesos, señor."

A man stepped out with bent head, then as he straightened himself and stood erect, Tod beheld a breadth of shoulder, a towering height. There was only one such figure as that—Captain Tom Jarvis'.

With a quick intake of breath, he rushed to the door and unlocked it. He flung open the screen. "Captain Tom!"

A huge paw closed about his hand. "Joe Macaroni! So you're really here!"

"Come in—come in! How in thunder did you know?"

"The clerk in the office phoned me. I'd left word to give me a ring, no matter at what hour you arrived." Two strong hands gripped Tod's shoulders. "Sufferin' catfish, it's good to see you! You look sort of tired. The third mate of the *Araby* isn't used to traveling on dry land, eh?"

As Jarvis loosed his grip, Tod stepped back. "It was a change, all right. Yes, quite a change."

A deep chuckle came from Jarvis' lips. "About ready to ship out again—is that it?"

Tod nodded. He was feasting his eyes upon the familiar figure of his friend. Standing well over six feet in height, the master of the *Araby* was a magnificent specimen of manhood. The dark serge suit he wore only accentuated the surprising length of limb, the broad shoulders, the muscular arms. But it was the poise of the head, the expression of strength in the light blue eyes that best revealed the personality underneath. The room now seemed dwarfed by that commanding presence; the walls resounded with the voice.

Tod threw out an excited hand. "Take a chair—sit down. But get rid of that hat. You don't look right in a hat, Captain Tom."

A delighted grin spread over the captain's rough-hewn face. He flung himself into a chair, stretched out his long legs and, tossing his hat to the floor, leaned back with a sigh of contentment. "I was really worried about you, Joe Macaroni, after I got that word from Jim Blakemore. J. B. thought you might be having trouble on the road. Did you?"

"Plenty." Tod dropped into a chair opposite and leaned forward, his hands on his knees. "It was my own foolishness, though. I saw Welch in San Francisco and I didn't figure from his looks he was quite so smart as he is. I lost the brief case once, but got it back. There it is—on the table."

"Good." Jarvis nodded his closely cropped head. "Something funny happened to me, too, today. I had a visit from a Señor Juan Tomaso."

"Who's he?"

"Oh, one of the men I was to get in touch with. You have a letter to him in your brief case. That was what the fellow was worried about. He'd received a note from J. B. saying I would come to his office with a letter of introduction and to expect me. Señor Tomaso was quite upset. Yes, quite upset."

Tod's voice was sharp. "But why?"

"Because he said if such a letter got into the wrong hands he'd lose his position in the government. He even admitted it might endanger his life."

"But I don't understand!"

Jarvis' light blue eyes grew thoughtful. "He didn't explain fully, but I got the impression that when Blakemore and his American associates bought that silver mine, this Señor Tomaso acted as go-between for its sale. That was long before the present government here took over control. I suspect there was something crooked in the way he bought that mining property. Otherwise, why should he be so disturbed? But I told him not to worry; there was nothing to fear. I pointed out that you were bringing the letters, and I'd vouch for no one seeing them but the two of us." Jarvis reached out a hand and slid the brief case off the table. Setting it upon his knees, he took out several long thick envelopes. "Yes, here's one addressed to him. Señor Juan Tomaso. Not exactly a pleasant gentleman, if you ask my opinion. Too smooth."

A frown creased Tod's brow. "You mean to say Mr. Blakemore bought mining property by crooked methods?"

"I'm not sure, Joe Macaroni. But you must realize that in years gone by, some of the American business men who came down here were not always particular how they acquired Mexican property—so long as they acquired it."

"No wonder," Tod said bitterly, "we're not popular down here."

Jarvis nodded. "Oh, we're learning. In troubled times like these we can't afford to have our neighbors south of the border anything but friendly. We've got to treat them as equals—not as inferiors. We need Mexico as a friend, not an enemy. Blakemore realizes that, too—now."

"Do you think he knows the part this Señor Tomaso played in getting hold of the mine?"

"Probably he isn't sure—or he wouldn't at this time have written him. Oh, J. B. is absolutely scrupulous, but when he was younger he probably didn't know the ways of Americans in Mexico." Jarvis paused for a moment. "Just the same, I wish I didn't have this letter. I don't fancy Juan Tomaso. He's one of those *politicos* any good government could do without."

"*Politicos?*"

"Why, yes." Jarvis threw him a quick glance. "What are you excited about?"

"Oh, nothing important. I just remembered something."

Jarvis looked down at the letters lying on the brief case in his lap. "Were all of these envelopes sealed when you got them from the Blakemore offices? J. B. doesn't usually seal letters of introduction."

"Sealed? I'm not sure." Tod plunged into reflection. "I remember looking at them when I was given the brief case in San Francisco." All at once he gave a start of dismay. His voice was low, tense. "They weren't sealed then, Captain Tom! I'm sure."

"That's funny." Jarvis lifted his head. "Every one of them is sealed now."

"But they can't be!" Tod stood up. "Open one, Captain Tom. Quick!"

With hurried movements Jarvis thrust a hand into a trouser pocket and brought out a knife. He pulled open the blade and slit one envelope across the top. "This is Señor Tomaso's letter. We'll just see what it says that might worry him so much." He drew out the contents.

Tod stood perfectly still, while the color drained slowly from his face. For Jarvis was holding a folded bit of newspaper in his hand.

"Captain Tom, it's been stolen!"

"One minute, Joe Macaroni. Let's make sure. J. B. would hardly send a newspaper clipping to this Juan Tomaso, but there's no knowing." He unfolded half of a newspaper page, which had evidently been hurriedly torn across. "This is in Spanish." He looked up at his third mate. "A Mexico City paper, three days old."

"Look at the others." A strident note crept into Tod's voice. "See if—see if they're all gone."

Swiftly but with calm fingers Captain Jarvis slit the other five envelopes. The contents were all the same—

torn bits from a newspaper evidently bought somewhere along the Pan-American Highway. The big man looked up and met Tod's frightened glance. "Yes, not one single letter is left."

"The packages, Captain Tom." The words came, stifled, from Tod's lips. "Take a look at them, too."

Jarvis reached into the brief case and lifted out two thin packages wrapped in brown paper. He pulled off the rubber bands. In each was a folded newspaper.

Tod, with a step backward, slumped into his chair. He had arrived in Mexico City with the brief case—but the letters and documents had gone. In despair, he closed his eyes.

"There's more behind this than we understand, Joe Macaroni." Jarvis' deep voice brought him up with a start. The big man tossed the brief case and its worthless contents to the floor, pulled himself out of the chair and stood erect. "We can get copies by wiring and having them sent by air mail. But that's not it—that's not it!"

"What do you mean?" Tod's hands were gripping the arms of his chair. "Let me tell you what happened on the road, Captain Tom. Maybe that'll explain."

"No." Tom Jarvis took a step across the room, turned and faced him. "Get dressed. Quickly. You can tell me later. I've got to get back to the Geneve and find an address."

Tod flung off his bath robe. When Captain Tom Jarvis gave an order, Tod Moran obeyed. "Whose address?"

"Señor Juan Tomaso's. He's staying at some hotel, but I never thought to look. He wrote it down on his card. I left it in my room."

Tod was already struggling into his clothes. "You're afraid—afraid something might—might happen to him?"

"Yes. Tomaso was scared out of his wits. He said if we lost that letter, his life would be in danger." Jarvis strode to the door. "I'll telephone for a taxi. Let's hope we won't be—too late."

CHAPTER XVII

Rico's Strange Actions

B Y THE TIME Jarvis' footsteps again sounded on the walk outside, Tod was slipping into his coat. "Be right with you," he sang out. He picked up his hat and threw open the door. "Why order a taxi, Captain Tom? We could take my car."

"Not tonight." Jarvis shook his head. "Neither of us knows this city and we can't be stopping to ask our way. Come on. The cab will be at the gate in a minute. Time presses."

With a feeling of apprehension Tod fell into step at his friend's side. "You really think there's danger?"

"Tomaso seemed to think so. If we warn him, though, we've done our part. It won't take ten minutes to reach my hotel. I should have put his address in my pocket."

Rico's Strange Actions

Jarvis was gazing across the dark lawns. "Surely that can't be the taxi driver already?"

Following his glance, Tod saw two figures in animated discussion at the gate. One he recognized as the night watchman, an elderly Mexican with a friendly smile and a shrill voice. The other appeared to be a White-cap. At least the man wore a light linen suit and a cap somewhat like a naval officer's. Then, coming closer, Tod saw that the White-cap had an arm in a sling.

"Why, it's Rico!" he exclaimed.

Rico stepped forward to meet them. "I forgot my poncho, Mr. Moran." In the dim light his face twitched with emotion. "I thought maybe if you weren't asleep, you'd let me—you'd let me get it—from your Ford."

"Of course." Tod paused. "Captain Jarvis, this is Rico, who came over the mountains with me. One minute. I'll get the things from the car."

Tod hurried across the gravel to the Ford, unlocked the door and took out the sombrero and poncho. As he again locked the car, the thought struck him that perhaps Rico would also like to be paid. His glance turned toward the lighted window of the office. Maybe the night clerk would cash a traveler's check.

But Rico, when questioned, shook his head. "In the morning will do, Mr. Moran. I'll stop in on my way to the White-cap Association."

Jarvis' eyes lighted up with interest. "You guides don't work for a company, then?"

"No, sir. We're our own bosses." Rico's voice was low, abrupt. He flung the poncho over one shoulder and took the sombrero in his hand. "We White-caps have formed an association, Captain Jarvis. The taxi men have done the same." He looked up, and his tone grew stronger, almost belligerent. "This is a new Mexico, señor. This country now belongs to the people, not to the few who are rich."

"I see." There was a curious expression upon Jarvis' face. "Come on, Tod. Here's our cab."

The watchman at the gate ran to the curb and flung open the taxi door. "That White-cap wanted to wake you," he growled, "but I wouldn't let him." Anger flared in his eyes as his gaze followed Rico's departing figure down the sidewalk.

"Good night, Rico," Tod called.

Rico did not answer. Neither did he turn. Nonplused, Tod stepped into the taxi.

As the car picked up speed Jarvis spoke to the driver. "To the Hotel Geneve! Get there as quickly as you can."

"*Si*, señor."

"Listen, Joe Macaroni." Jarvis' voice turned earnest. "What in thunder was the matter with Rico?"

"Did you think he was upset?" Tod asked.

"Upset? I'd say he was scared to death. Didn't you notice his voice—and his eyes? Is he a friend of yours?"

Tod sighed. "I wouldn't call him a friend. Yet, somehow, I rather like him. He's so filled with ideals about

Rico's Strange Actions

his country—this Mexico he and his friends are making over. He's pretty hot headed, though. I wouldn't be surprised if his temper got him into trouble."

"He appears to be a true Mexican," Jarvis observed. "Probably he has both Spanish and Indian blood in him. Oh, his ancestors aren't the same as the California Indians that you know. Rico, most likely, has blood of the Aztecs in him—a race as proud and as cultured as the old Egyptians. These modern Mexicans are doing things. Look at this." He pointed out the window.

The taxi had left the dimly lighted street behind and was swinging round a huge statue into a tree-lined boulevard. "This is the Paseo de la Reforma. Doesn't it remind you of the Champs Élysées? This city takes me right back to Paris."

Tod leaned forward with interest. Although after midnight, the great boulevard was still alive with traffic. Horns honked. Tires hummed. Taxis and busses and motor cars of every description shot out from lanes of traffic with no regard for rules.

Jarvis chuckled. "Mexican drivers are what I'd call wild."

"Wild?" Tod sat back. "They're crazy."

But the immense avenue along which they traveled was a thing of increasing beauty. On each side were lawns studded with tall dark trees; and behind the line of trees, windows shone from hotels and apartment houses built in the modern manner. This capital of Mexico, it seemed to Tod, was more beautiful than San Francisco, more exciting than New York, more interesting even than New Orleans. For, while its buildings of steel and glass pointed to the future rather than to the past, it yet retained the trees and gardens of an older civilization. As the charm of the place caught him in its grip, Tod asked himself why his own people could not do as well as these Mexicans. Why did Americans always cut down trees when they built a city? And why did Americans prefer concrete pavement even when there was space for a strip of lawn?

Suddenly he swayed as the taxi turned to the left and entered the Avenue Insurgentes. A few minutes later they drew up before the Geneve, one of the city's great hotels.

Jarvis sprang out with a word to the driver. "Wait!"

Tod looked at his watch. It was a quarter to one. Impatiently he leaned back in his seat until his friend returned.

"The Hotel Luxor," Jarvis told the driver. "Step on it!"

The motor roared again as they got under way. Jarvis raised his voice. "As soon as I found the card, I telephoned to Tomaso's hotel. He wasn't in. That may be good news. If we can't find him, maybe no one else will, either."

Tod drew a long breath. "I was beginning to feel as guilty as a murderer," he admitted.

"Oh, forget it." Jarvis sounded annoyed. "You and I

can hardly be held responsible for Tomaso's crooked dealings. It's his affair, not ours."

"But if anything happens, Captain Tom, it'll be because I lost those letters."

"Just how did you lose them? Start at the beginning and tell me what happened."

A reflective look came over Tod's face. "Nothing happened at all until I reached Laredo. Then, at the office where I was given my tourist card——" He stopped and turned to his companion. "I almost forgot. Did you enter Mexico on a tourist card?"

"No. I was given a special form. Did you have any trouble with yours?"

When Tod had told him in a few words, Jarvis smiled. "We'll fix that up. Once I have some introductions from J. B., I can get in touch with the proper authorities. Go ahead. What happened at Laredo?"

Tod continued, "Somebody had been to that little office asking if I'd crossed the border yet—and then when I went to the telegraph office to send you a wire, someone tried to see what I was writing." Again he stopped.

"Go on," Jarvis urged. "What about it?"

"I was trying to remember if that fellow in Laredo looked like Rico. But I'm sure he was taller. No, I must have been imagining things."

Jarvis leaned back and laughed. "Joe Macaroni, you're worn out from your trip. Before you tell me anything more, you're going to have a good night's rest. Anyway, here's the Hotel Luxor. You come in with me. If Tomaso is back, he may want to ask you a question or two."

Although the lobby of the Luxor blazed with light, only the night clerk was present. Jarvis spoke in a businesslike voice. "Is Mr. Juan Tomaso in yet?"

The man behind the desk hesitated, while his glance wavered. "No, señor. He is out."

"He hasn't left town, has he?"

"Oh, no, señor. He is in the city."

Jarvis turned to Tod. "We'll wait a while. If he doesn't come back soon, we'll leave a note."

The clerk leaned across the desk. "I am afraid Señor Tomaso will not be in tonight. You see——" He paused and cleared his throat, then added in a lower tone, "You see—there has been an accident."

Tod drew his body taut. "An accident?"

The man nodded slowly, his dark eyes wide.

"Just what do you mean?" Jarvis demanded.

After glancing round, the clerk brought his gaze back to Jarvis. "You are friends of Señor Tomaso?"

"Yes. I've come to Mexico City in order to see him."

"Ah, señor, I fear you may never see him again—alive. Tonight he was stabbed. He has been taken to a hospital."

Tod's hands closed round the edge of the desk. As from a far distance he heard his companion ask, "Is he seriously wounded?"

Rico's Strange Actions

"Yes, señor. They are not sure he will live till morning."

"Where did this happen? Here?"

"Oh, no, señor." The man threw out his hands in a quick gesture. "The hospital attendants informed the police, of course, and the police came here to make inquiries. They have only just left."

"And what did they say? Was Tomaso able to talk to them?"

"A little. They said the señor was walking here after visiting friends near the Plaza de la Republica. He was crossing the Reforma when his assailant struck. Out of the darkness, señor. Without warning."

"The police caught this man?"

"Not yet. But they have a description of him."

"Good." Jarvis' tone was calm. "What did he look like?"

"He was a White-cap, señor—a White-cap!"

"You mean he was one of those guides who show the tourists around?"

"Yes, señor. The police will have him in jail by morning."

Tod turned away, his hands clenched. His gaze swept round the modernistic lobby, but he did not see the chromium chairs or the palms or the open staircase that rose as if unsupported to the mezzanine above. He was repeating a name over and over to himself—the name of someone he would have liked to call a friend.

"Let me leave my telephone number," Jarvis was saying. "If you get any news of Señor Tomaso's condition, please let me know—will you?"

"Most assuredly, señor."

Tod waited, while his heart rose up and pounded in his throat. A hand touched his arm. "Let's go."

As they moved off across the tiled floor, Jarvis asked, "Any idea who that White-cap might be?"

Tod nodded. "Yes, I think I know," he answered wearily. "Rico."

CHAPTER XVIII

What Jarvis Discovered

Mr. MORAN—Mr. Moran!"

The urgent summons cut through Tod's dreams. Opening his eyes, he looked around. Sunlight filtered through the curtain at his window. The door shook as a loud knock sounded.

"Mr. Moran! Wake up!"

Sleepily Tod raised himself out of bed, crossed to the door and opened it. Outside the screen stood a boy from the office of the Shirley Courts.

"A telephone message, señor. Captain Jarvis says to tell you he will be over in twenty minutes with a guest. He says it is most important."

"Thank you. I'll be ready."

As he flung off his pajamas he wondered whom Jarvis could be bringing. Was it Rico, or perhaps even Martin Welch?

Fifteen minutes later, after a hasty breakfast in the coffee shop, he was waiting at the door of his apartment when Jarvis stepped from the taxi. A man Tod had never seen before accompanied him. Tod took in the stranger at a glance. A Mexican of perhaps fifty years of age, he might have been a prosperous broker, somewhat portly, more than a little pompous in manner.

"Señor Madero, this is the third mate off my ship—Tod Moran."

"A pleasure." Señor Madero inclined his head in acknowledgment. There was no hint of pleasure, however, in his voice. His plump dark face was tense, his eyes abstracted. He lighted a cigarette with a hand that shook.

"Had breakfast?" Jarvis inquired.

"You bet. At the coffee shop. Come in." Puzzled as to the meaning of this visit, Tod pulled out the sitting-room chairs and motioned his two guests toward them. "Any news, Captain Tom?"

Jarvis, easing his long body into a chair, met Tod's gaze with a somber glance. "I phoned the hospital at eight this morning. Juan Tomaso had died one hour before."

Tod's hands gripped the arms of his chair until the knuckles grew white. He tried to speak, but the words refused to come.

Señor Madero took quick short steps across the room. "I'll be the next one!" Turning, he threw out his hands in an eloquent gesture. "I'll be the next one, and you do nothing—nothing!"

What Jarvis Discovered

Jarvis frowned. "Cool down, Madero. You're safe with us. We'll get to the bottom of this affair right away."

The man's face moved with emotion. "I have a family, Captain Jarvis. I am not like Tomaso. He had no one but himself. But think of my poor wife, my poor little daughter, my poor son, my——"

Jarvis interrupted. "Just a moment, Madero. I've come here to thresh out this matter with Moran. Give us a chance, will you? If you won't, I'll have to ask you to leave."

"But not alone!" Fear, sudden and overwhelming, flashed across the man's features. "It wouldn't be safe, Captain Jarvis. My life, too, is in danger!"

Tod pulled himself erect in his chair. "But I don't understand, Captain Tom. What has Señor Madero to do with this?"

Obviously annoyed, Jarvis nodded his head toward their guest. "He'll explain. He's already explained three times to me."

"Yes, Señor Moran." Madero looked down, his black eyes filled with anxiety. "I received a note from Mr. Blakemore saying Captain Jarvis would soon bring me a letter of introduction—that since I and Juan Tomaso had assisted him years ago in acquiring certain properties, perhaps we could assist again."

Tod was beginning to understand. "You are afraid you will be treated like Tomaso?"

[243]

"Exactly. When I got Mr. Blakemore's note, I was uneasy. I was so uneasy I telephoned to my friend, Juan. He laughed at my fears—and see what has happened to him!"

Tod leaned forward. "But why did you fear for your life?"

"Ah, that is the point. It is difficult to explain, señor."

Jarvis interposed dryly, "You had no difficulty in explaining to me."

"True." Señor Madero sat down in his chair. "I will tell you everything, Mr. Moran, just as I tell the captain. This is no time for untruths, yes? Years ago Juan and I arranged to buy certain mining properties for an American company headed by James Blakemore. Juan handled the Tasco end. Oh, I admit we made much money. Those were the good days in Mexico." He sighed. "Those days, alas, have passed away."

"Too bad." There was a hint of sarcasm in Jarvis' tone. "Don't forget to say also, Madero, that you bought that land cheaply as farm land and sold it to Blakemore as mining property at a great boost in price."

"Even so, he got it for a mere song, Captain Jarvis!"

"Probably. Just the same, you also took a nice commission on the sales price, too. Working both ends, you see."

Tod looked across at the man sitting opposite him. "You have never been in any danger before?"

"Not until these last few years. About the time the

What Jarvis Discovered

Pan-American Highway was opened, Juan and I began hearing rumors. Somebody was investigating that old affair. Oh, we have been on guard, because Tomaso held a fine position with this present government—and he did not care to lose it."

"Naturally not."

Señor Madero's voice became more friendly. "We did not feel really frightened until these notes arrived from Mr. Blakemore. Should he sell the mine? he asked us. Was the government really intending to take over mining property held by foreigners? What would we advise? At once I got in touch with Juan, as I told you. We realized that the danger was increasing. For suppose Mr. Blakemore put down in black and white what he had paid us—and suppose those papers got into the hands of those who watched us?"

"But what difference would that make?"

"Ah, señor, those peóns from whom we acquired the property never had any proof that we knew the land contained silver. But what if they obtained proof? And what if they learned that Juan and I had sold at a figure far above what we paid them?"

"Speak plainly," Jarvis cut in. "You raised the price twenty thousand dollars on the land, then also took a fat commission from Blakemore besides."

Madero nodded eagerly. "You see, these men long ago had vowed revenge on us. We feared if they learned this, too, their anger might increase. Juan thought it was just a matter of his losing his government position, because if this was reported to high authorities, he would be—what you say?—out on his feet. But I pointed out that peóns think nothing of throwing knives. I said our very lives might be in danger. Juan laughed. He didn't believe me." A sigh escaped Madero's lips. His fingers twitched on the arm of his chair. "Yes, I shall be next. Ah, my poor wife! My poor little daughter! My son! My grandchild!"

"Enough." Jarvis raised a peremptory hand. "I'll promise that no attack will be made on your life."

An eager look came into the man's dark eyes. "You will? But how, Captain Jarvis?"

"Give me a chance to talk to Moran. I'm sure we can figure this out. Perhaps, Tod, Mr. Madero might wait in your bedroom?"

"Of course." Tod got up and ushered the man into the next room. "It's not made up yet, I'm afraid, but if you don't mind——"

"No matter. I wait—gladly."

As soon as they were alone, Jarvis leaned back in his chair and stretched out his long legs. "He wears me out. Though maybe it's the altitude. Seventy-five hundred feet up does make a difference. You know it's not sea level." He threw Tod a quick look. "You do the talking now. I'll listen."

"You bet." Tod sat up straight. "You want to hear all about my trip?"

"Exactly. Begin at Laredo and tell everything that

happened. Don't forget a single detail, no matter how trivial it may seem to you. I want to know everything about that black sedan, everything about Rico. How he looked. What he said. Fill in all the parts you left out last night. Understand?"

Without hesitation Tod plunged into his narrative. At first his voice was excited, but by the time his story had progressed to the events in Monterrey, his tone had grown calmer, more reflective. In clear detail he told of his trip south along the Pan-American Highway. He lingered over the events in Valles, then hurried on through his pursuit of the sedan to Tamazunchale and the trip up the mountains.

"Wait a minute." Jarvis sat up. "You say your radiator began steaming and you got out to put in some water. Did Rico make any effort to leave you at any time?"

"No."

"He always stuck close to you and the Ford?"

"Yes."

"Did he ever have an opportunity to steal your car?"

"No, I kept the key in my pocket whenever I got out and left Rico sitting in it. And when we were both out, I always locked it."

"Good. Now, try to remember. When you got out on the road to fill the radiator, you used water from a bottle in the trunk?"

"Yes."

"Did Rico seem at all uneasy about anything then?"

"No, I don't think so. Still, I do remember I asked him if he'd like a drink and when he answered, his voice sounded sort of funny."

"Funny?" Jarvis caught up the word with an eager look. "Just what do you mean?"

"Well, I'm not too sure, myself. I remember thinking his voice sounded queer. But is that important?"

"Anything might be important. Go on. Now, when you reached this Montezuma Inn . . ."

The happenings at the Montezuma Inn brought forth many more questions. "You say Martin Welch was there, yet you never once saw him?"

Tod nodded. "I can't understand—unless the proprietor was paid to hide him away."

"Never mind. Tell me about the other guests there. All you can remember about this Doctor Briggs. About his friend, Jim Foster. About Mr. and Mrs. Sturtevant."

"But surely," Tod protested, "the Sturtevants and the other guests couldn't be mixed up in this!"

Jarvis answered in a reflective tone. "We can't be sure of anything yet. Leave out nothing, Joe Macaroni. Nothing at all."

Once more Tod took up the thread of his story. When he had finished, he leaned back in his chair. "That's about all, Captain Tom. Make of it what you can. I can't fathom how Welch disappeared."

Without a word Jarvis got to his feet and took a turn

about the room. "Welch never did disappear, Joe Macaroni."

Tod looked up with a start. "But he must have!"

"No. He didn't disappear because he never was there."

"What do you mean?" Tod sprang out of his chair. "You've seen Martin Welch? You know something?"

"No. I've never met the man. I've only heard of him through Blakemore. But I'm sure of one thing. Welch did not follow you down the Pan-American Highway."

"Then who did?"

"That's the question." Jarvis' eyes shone bright and hard as steel. "I'd like to meet this Doctor Briggs."

"But why Doctor Briggs?"

"Oh, I have a hunch he could tell me something—if he would. Now, think back a moment. Did Rico ever try to hide his coat from you? How about that button you found on the floor of the Regina Court in Monterrey? Was it ever mentioned between you?"

"No. Why mention it? It was obvious that Rico had been the one who tried to steal the brief case."

Jarvis spoke in a sharp tone. "But did the boy ever make any effort to hide the coat? Did he try to keep you from seeing the spot where that button had been torn loose?"

"Why, no. I don't think so. When I first met him in Valles his coat was covered by the poncho, but later he folded the poncho and put it behind the seat. No, he didn't seem to care whether or not I noticed that one button was gone."

Jarvis crossed to the window and looked out, but Tod knew he was not seeing the wide green lawns, the immense trees, the line of cabins opposite. When next the big man spoke, his voice was low, thoughtful. "Suppose Rico did not enter your room in Monterrey?"

"But he must have." Tod took a step toward his friend. "It's clear as crystal, isn't it?"

Jarvis swung round. "Don't be too sure. Somehow, it doesn't fit into my pattern."

Tod waited. He knew what the captain meant when he mentioned his pattern. Jarvis always said that any problem could be worked out, once you were given all the facts. Once get started correctly and the pattern would take shape before your eyes, just as rugs were woven by those men in Eastern bazaars. Jarvis, Tod realized, was already shaping that pattern. It might be the right one; it might not if there were missing strands he hadn't yet got hold of. Tod's mind leaped back along the trip he had made. Had he left out anything—anything at all?

Jarvis left the window and took a stride across the room. "I'd like to use the telephone in the office, Tod. I'd like to ring some of the hotels here and see if a certain person is registered at one of them."

"You mean Martin Welch?"

"No. I mean one of the men who stayed at the Montezuma Inn that night—Doctor Briggs." He stopped short. "Maybe Señor Madero would do it for me. He'd know the hotels where a prosperous doctor would most likely put up."

"But you won't find Doctor Briggs in Mexico City. He and Jim Foster were going fishing somewhere around Jacala."

"Yes, you told me that before, but I have the feeling that Doctor Briggs may not have gone fishing, after all." Jarvis crossed to the bedroom door and flung it open. "Señor Madero, would you do something for me?"

"Certainly." Madero came out, his dark face eager. "Anything, Captain Jarvis."

"Come on. I'll walk with you over to the office, so you won't be alone. Then I'd like you to do some telephoning. It may take you quite a while."

Señor Madero bowed. "If I can show my gratitude, Captain——"

Tod watched them go out the door and disappear along the path toward the office. His mind was in a whirl. Why need Jarvis treat the fellow as though he needed protection? It was utter nonsense. Or was it?

The question came back with full force when he heard steps and looked up to see Rico standing outside the screen door.

"Good morning, Mr. Moran."

"Hello, Rico." Tod could scarcely keep his voice from trembling. "Come in. I didn't expect you here."

"Why not?" Rico entered the room, his white cap in his hand. "I've come for my pay. I'm leaving the city this morning."

"So you won't be put in jail?"

Rico gave a sudden start. "Why do you say that?"

"Why?" In Tod's voice was a tone of menace. "Because of what happened to Juan Tomaso last night."

"But I did not stab him, Mr. Moran."

"Oh, so you do know he was stabbed! Have you heard yet that he died this morning?"

"Died?" Rico flinched. His cap dropped with a soft thud to the floor.

"It's murder." Tod pressed on without pity. "Now do you understand what it means for you?"

Rico's head jerked erect. His eyes blazed with fury— or was it triumph? "But I'm not sorry, Mr. Moran! Not sorry one little bit. He deserved what he got—the cheat, the blackguard, the traitor!"

"But I'm sorry," Tod said slowly. "And most of all— for you."

There was a scornful twist to Rico's lips. "You needn't feel sorry about me." He paused, and his gaze took on a deep, searching quality. "You don't believe I did it, Mr. Moran—do you?"

"Yes." Tod nodded. "I haven't forgotten your telling me about your father being cheated out of his oil land. But it wasn't oil land, Rico. It was mining property."

Rico's voice dropped low. "I didn't want to tell you

at first. But now I might as well. My father's land was rich with silver—near Tasco. But just the same, I did not kill Juan Tomaso." He put out his hand. "If you'll please pay me now, Mr. Moran, I'll go."

"Oh, no, you won't!" In a stride Tod reached the door and stood before it, facing Rico. "You're staying right here until we settle this whole affair."

"But I can't stay here." Rico's dark eyes shone with entreaty. "I've just time to catch a bus, Mr. Moran. By this evening I must be a long way from here."

"Understand this, Rico. You're not leaving this room."

Rico drew his body taut as he surveyed his antagonist from head to foot. "You can't stop me, Mr. Moran."

Tod's gaze fastened upon Rico's bandaged shoulder. "If your arm wasn't in a sling, we'd fight this out. Don't try to draw a knife on me."

"But I never carry a knife in the city."

Cold anger surged up inside Tod. "I suppose you didn't have it with you last night, either!"

"Now, Joe Macaroni!" The familiar voice reached Tod's ears as the door behind him was shoved open. "What's all the rumpus? Oh, it's your friend, Rico."

With an effort Tod controlled himself. "He's been lying to me so blamed much, I suppose I got mad. But look at his coat—still with one button gone!"

Jarvis' face was impassive. "Are you sure that your button matches the other?"

"Of course." Tod strode across to the bedroom. "I'll get it. One minute."

[253]

When he came back he had the coat button in his hand. Rico did not move when Tod held it against the coat. "A perfect match! And yet he says he's leaving town!"

"Don't worry." Jarvis' tone was at once light and contemptuous. "I don't believe your friend will leave the city just now. Will you, Rico?"

A baffled expression came over the young man's face. "If Mr. Moran will pay me, I'll leave. I need the money for bus fare."

"Very well. Pay him, Joe Macaroni. We'll see whether or not he'll go."

Tod reached into the rear pocket of his trousers and brought out his wallet. "I haven't enough Mexican currency, Captain Tom. I'll have to cash a traveler's check at the office."

"Never mind. I'll pay him." Jarvis thrust a hand into his own rear pocket. "How much do you owe him?"

"Twenty dollars, American."

Rico took the two ten-dollar bills Jarvis handed him. "Thank you, Captain Jarvis. If you'll excuse me now, I'll go."

In dismay Tod looked at Jarvis. But the big man made no move. His gaze was fastened upon Rico as though waiting for something. Rico stuffed the bills into his coat pocket, stooped for his white cap on the floor, and crossed to the door. Without a word he flung open the screen and hurried out.

What Jarvis Discovered

Tod protested harshly, "Why did you let him go?"

Tom Jarvis reached the door in a stride and stood looking out. "I still think he'll stop. Unless—unless I'm wrong."

"But of course you're wrong." Tod's gaze was following Rico's rapid strides toward the gate. "Rico is the only connection we have with those lost letters. If he gets away, we'll never get them back."

"He's gone, all right." A perplexed frown settled upon Jarvis' brow. "Got your keys to the car?"

"Yes. In my pocket."

"Come on, then. Quick. Don't bother with a hat."

Pausing only long enough to snap the catch on the lock, Tod slammed the door shut after them and hastened along at his friend's side. The Ford was parked on the gravel between two other cars.

"Where are we going, Captain Tom? To follow Rico?"

"No. We're not going any place. Unlock your car. They must be hidden somewhere in the Ford."

Tod thrust the key into the lock of his car. "How could anything be hidden in the car? I've had my bags in and out of the trunk half a dozen times."

Jarvis leaned inside and pulled open the door of the little compartment in the instrument panel. "No, not big enough. Have you had your battery checked in the last day or so?"

"Not since I left Laredo."

[255]

"Then they've got to be here." Two strong hands tugged at the seat.

Tod tried to peer over his friend's shoulder. "What's got to be here?"

"The documents. And here they are! Under the seat all the time." Jarvis swung about with a sheaf of papers in his hand.

Tod's eager gaze fastened upon them. Of legal size, they were bound together at the top with brass pins. And protruding from their midst were half a dozen folded sheets of paper.

"The missing letters, Joe Macaroni." Jarvis drew them out and glanced quickly through them. "Only five left. Juan Tomaso's must be gone. But here is one for Madero. We'll give it to him right now, then maybe he'll breathe a little easier—not that he deserves to, though."

Tod cut in abruptly. "So this was what Rico was after?"

"Of course. I really didn't think he'd leave without them. Evidently something mighty important is taking him away. But we'll follow him. Get your hat while I'm giving this letter to Madero. Then we'll go."

"But Rico will be out of sight by now."

A shrewd look came into the light blue eyes. "There's only one place he could be heading for. Can't you guess?"

Tod hesitated. "Tasco?"

"Yes—Tasco. We've got to get there before Rico does. It's full speed ahead from now on."

CHAPTER XIX

Journey's End

THE RED CONVERTIBLE slid through the maze of traffic toward the suburbs, Tod at the wheel, Jarvis directing him. As soon as they gained open country the paved highway began climbing to the south. The Valley of Mexico fell away behind.

Tod settled back into his seat with a sense of relief. A mountain road, no matter how new to him, was preferable to the mad traffic of the city. "Now maybe we'll have a chance to talk, Captain Tom. Why are you so sure Rico didn't stab Juan Tomaso?"

"Two things, Joe Macaroni. First, the time element and second, Rico's own story. He wasn't acting a part. He was telling the truth."

"But I wouldn't believe a word he says!"

Jarvis took a tobacco pouch from his pocket and filled

[257]

his pipe. "Let's check up on the time. If we find it physically impossible for Rico to have been on the boulevard at the moment Tomaso was stabbed, you'll believe he told the truth, won't you?"

"I guess I'll have to."

"Very well. When the clerk at the Shirley Courts phoned me, he said you had checked in five minutes before. I remember looking at my watch, because I wondered if it was still early enough to run over and see you. It was exactly ten minutes before midnight."

Tod interrupted. "But Rico wasn't there when I registered. Mrs. Whipple said he had jumped out at the corner after pointing to the Shirley Courts."

"I know. That's why I stopped at the trailer camp on my way to your place this morning with Madero."

"Then you saw the Whipples?"

"I did. You had said so much about them last night that I felt as though I knew them. We were friends at once. In fact, I had a bad time tearing myself away from all their talk. But I learned what I was after. Mrs. Whipple arrived at the Shirley Courts ten or fifteen minutes ahead of you. Rico had jumped out of the car at the corner near by. That places him there at about eleven-thirty."

"But wouldn't that have given him time to find Juan Tomaso?"

"Hardly. According to hospital records, Tomaso was brought in by the ambulance at eleven-twenty—at a moment when Rico was still seated beside Mrs. Whipple in your Ford. No, Rico is definitely out."

"Still, he was scared, Captain Tom—scared stiff about something."

"But not for himself. For someone else. Who that person is, we don't yet know. Perhaps we'll learn when we reach Tasco."

"And how long will it take us to get there?"

"That depends on your car. It's a hundred-mile trip. If we stop for lunch in Cuernavaca we ought to arrive in Tasco around three."

Tod leaned forward. The paved highway was climbing through a pine forest and curving out of sight through the trees. Around the curve a huge bus careened into view. With its exhaust popping, it shot past at breakneck speed. Tod leaned back again. "One other thing, Captain Tom. You said Welch wasn't following me on the road. Then who was?"

Jarvis' tone was thoughtful. "I know the man, but I don't know who he is."

"You know the man? What in thunder do you mean?"

"He was a guest with you at that Montezuma Inn."

Tod ran over in his mind the people who had been staying there. "Doctor Briggs? But it couldn't have been! Then there were only Jim Foster and the Sturtevants and two Mexicans."

"Joe Macaroni, you must have been so tired out by driving that your head didn't work."

"I was sick," Tod admitted. "My mind felt all muddled. But Doctor Briggs fixed me up. Still, I can't figure how it could have been any of the people I met."

"Work it out by a process of elimination," Jarvis continued. "We don't know who the man is, so for the present let's simply call him Mr. X. Now, this Mr. X must have driven the black sedan up through the mountains from that town with the unpronounceable name."

"Tamazunchale."

"Okay. Call it anything you want. But if Mr. X drove the Buick to the Montezuma Inn, he must have been there—granting that there was no way he could get around that slide."

Tod cut in firmly, "No one could walk around the slide. Several people told me so."

"All right, then. Mr. X was stopping at the inn—and you must have seen him. You must have talked to him, too. Let's eliminate all those we can and see who's left." Jarvis took a puff at his pipe, then resumed. "We know he was an American, so the two Mexicans can be overlooked for the moment. Then who is left? Briggs, Foster, and Sturtevant. But Sturtevant has a wife who is very much in evidence, so he, too, can be crossed off our list of suspects. Who's left?"

Tod nodded. "Just Briggs and Foster. Go on. Tell me it was Doctor Briggs. I know you tried to get Madero to ring him up."

"I did. And do you know why? Because if Doctor

Journey's End

Briggs was really the medical man he appeared to be, he is also excluded from our list of suspects. A doctor, I figure, simply won't do."

"Then there is only one person left," Tod cried. "Jim Foster!"

"Exactly. Jim Foster, whoever he was, is the one man left on our list."

"But he came from Houston with Doctor Briggs," Tod protested.

"Yes? And who told you that?"

"Why—why, Foster did." Tod shot a quick glance at his companion. "Still, Doctor Briggs spoke of going fishing with him. They were old friends."

"Don't be too sure about that, Joe Macaroni. Remember the names of the guests in the registry book at the inn? Which name was last in the list of Americans? Jim Foster's. You told me so yourself."

"I know I did." Tod's brow was creased in a frown. "But still, they were both listed from Houston, Texas—Doctor Briggs and Jim Foster."

"And would that be so difficult? Listen. Foster comes in late and registers. He sees Doctor Briggs' name. Perhaps he even knows the man. He may have met him on the road—at Valles, at Monterrey, even at Laredo. He may have struck up an acquaintance just as you did with the Whipples. So what does Foster do? Why, he signs his own name under Doctor Briggs' and puts ditto marks under the place of residence, which happened to be Houston. If you came along, that would throw you off the trail. Simple, isn't it?"

"Too simple, Captain Tom. Because both Doctor Briggs and Foster are on a fishing trip—near Jacala."

"I'm afraid you're wrong. You see, when I went into the office at the Shirley Courts to give Madero his letter from Blakemore, he'd already found some trace of the man I wanted. Doctor Briggs and Foster both put up at the Ritz Hotel last night."

Tod's hands tightened on the wheel. "Did you have a chance to talk with either of them?"

"No. The telephone operator told Madero they had checked out early this morning—for Tasco."

"For Tasco! Then maybe—maybe you're on the right trail, after all."

"I'm sure I am." Jarvis struck a match and again lighted his pipe. "My pattern is taking shape. Only, I don't think I have all the strands to work with. Something is missing. Joe Macaroni, have you forgotten to tell me some little detail?"

"I don't think so. I've told you everything."

"Perhaps you're right." Jarvis shifted his legs in the cramped quarters of the car.

After a brief interval of silence Tod spoke up. "I just can't believe it's Jim Foster we want. I still think Martin Welch was in that Buick and somehow he managed to disappear—just where or how, I don't know. But we'll find out before this affair is over."

"Have it your own way." Jarvis' tone again turned thoughtful. "There's some missing fact about the events at the Montezuma Inn I haven't yet got hold of. Where, for instance, does that White-cap come in? I mean the fellow who drove the Buick away from the inn."

"You mean Pedro Torres? Oh, he was just picked up by Welch and paid to take the car into Mexico City. He was all right. He talked quite a bit to Paw Whipple in that cantina on the road." Tod stopped short. When next he spoke, it was with a sense of chagrin. "Captain Tom, you're right. I did forget to tell you something."

"What?"

"Just something I saw when I went upstairs from breakfast. I was feeling sort of sick at the time. I guess that's why it slipped out of my mind. When I reached the upper hallway Pedro Torres was coming from Rico's room."

"So they knew each other!"

"Don't be too sure," Tod warned. "All I know is that this Torres had been visiting Rico. Does that mean anything?"

Jarvis was in deep thought. "What I'm wondering is this," he said, after a moment. "Could that White-cap have gone up through the mountains with Mr. X in the Buick? Yes, he might have."

"But the soldier on guard at Tamazunchale would have seen him. He told me the American was driving alone."

[263]

"I know. But take this into account. Mr. X is no tourist. He knows the ways of this country. He knows that an American accompanied by a White-cap guide will be taken for a tourist—and no tourist will be allowed to pass that point. He knows, too, that perhaps you're on his trail. And he wants to lose you. So he tells the White-cap to crouch down on the floor by the back seat. Maybe he even covers the fellow over with a rug so his white clothes won't be seen. It might be done."

"I've got it, Captain Tom." Tod spoke swiftly, eagerly. "Now I know what happened. Suppose, after all, it was Welch who drove that car past the guard on the highway? Couldn't he stop half a mile past the spot, change places with the White-cap, and then get out himself and walk back to the town along the river? Why, it would have been simple. He could wait in Tamazunchale until next day and take a bus up to Mexico City."

"You may be right," Jarvis conceded, "but I don't think so. For one thing, the brief case was still in the Buick. Would he have left that behind? No. He would have taken it with him."

"But there was nothing of value in the brief case, don't forget. The letters were gone."

"Exactly. And that's why I'm sure our Mr. X reached the inn. Look, Joe Macaroni, this is what I feel must have happened. Mr. X is connected with Mr. Blakemore's mine. He learns—how, we don't yet know—that you are on your way down the Pan-American

[264]

Highway with letters and documents which may get him into trouble. For it is evident that someone at the Tasco mine is trying to put over a crooked deal on Blakemore. Mr. X believed he could outsmart you and me by getting hold of the brief case. Of course he was foolish, but remember that desperate men are often driven to foolish actions. So what does he do? He hires a White-cap with whom he has already struck up an acquaintance, a White-cap who has hung around Tasco and the mine for some time. But that White-cap is Rico, and Rico, unknown to Mr. X, is playing a little game of his own."

"Not a little game, Captain Tom. A big game. It led to murder."

"Yes, it led to murder. Rico, like most people when they begin their underhanded work, probably never intended it to go that far. Anyhow, Rico apparently became a tool for Mr. X, but only apparently, mind you. In Monterrey the two of them planned to get your brief case. They were unsuccessful. They tried to delay your progress. Again they had little success. Then, just before you reached Valles, Joe Macaroni, you played directly into their hands. You fired upon the Buick. You were locked up."

Tod sighed. "I hope I never see the inside of a Mexican jail again."

"It probably did you good," Jarvis retorted. "Up till then you hadn't realized the devilish cleverness of the unknown man whose wits were pitted against your own. Then you knew—when it was almost too late. For when you drove into Valles that night, the trap was ready to be sprung. Mr. X had already had Rico lodge a complaint with the police. So the police were waiting. But you arrived with Mrs. Whipple seated beside you in your car. That confused the police for the moment, and you were allowed to reach the Casa Grande. Probably the White-cap was watching and reported at once to his employer that you'd slipped through. Oh, you may be sure Mr. X was furious. The stupid police! I'll bet the air sizzled and crackled."

A grin spread over Tod's wide mouth. "At least for once I had him going."

"But not through any brilliance on your part," Jarvis slyly pointed out. "Never mind. Let's get back to X. What does he do? He decides to send Rico to the Casa Grande to watch. If the police don't intend to arrest you, maybe Rico can get a ride with you up the mountains. Again you play into their hands. You ask Rico to watch your car. But you may be sure it is not the car that Rico is watching; it is you. So as soon as the police finally decide you are the man they want and come to the Casa Grande and take you away, Rico reports to Mr. X at the Hotel Condesa. Now, you may be sure, both of them are delighted. Perhaps they can even get that brief case by the simple trick of sending a forged note to your hotel."

Journey's End

"Then it was Rico who stole my brief case?"

"Undoubtedly. We can hardly blame the clerk for not being suspicious. He knew you were in jail and he didn't want to advertise to his other guests that an American tourist had been arrested. His one mistake was in not looking up your signature on the register. He gave your brief case to the bearer of that note—and Rico now had what he wanted. He had those letters and documents which he wanted as badly as Mr. X—only for a different reason."

"So that's when the letters were hidden in my Ford!"

"Yes, it's logical, isn't it? Rico goes back to your car, takes the letters from their envelopes, and inserts pieces of a newspaper, instead. He does the same with the package of documents. He ties up the package again and seals the envelopes, thinking it will delay Mr. X's discovery of their loss. Then he goes back to the Condesa, gives the brief case to Mr. X, and both leave at once in the car. Mr. Whipple, you remember, saw them drive away."

"But Rico didn't leave Valles with this Mr. X. He stayed in my car."

"Of course. Mr. X dropped Rico on the highway near the Casa Grande and drove on alone."

"But what about this other White-cap, Pedro Torres?" Tod argued. "Where does he appear?"

"I'm not sure," Jarvis admitted. "Remember that what I just told you is mere supposition. We can't yet be sure where Torres comes into the picture. Was it at Valles? Was it at Tamazunchale? Or didn't he appear until the Montezuma Inn? I'm inclined to believe now that he didn't enter the picture until the inn was reached."

"There's one point I don't understand," Tod objected. "Why would Mr. X allow Rico to stay behind with me, once they had the brief case?"

"They probably had some conversation on that very subject. Mr. X would take it as a matter of course that Rico would continue with him in the Buick. But Rico wouldn't want to do that for two reasons. First, the real contents of the brief case are hidden under the seat of your Ford and Rico must get them. Second, if Mr. X should ask Rico to drive while he opened the brief case to examine the letters, then Rico was lost. We can be sure that Rico suggested it might be wise for him to go with you and so keep an eye on your movements. Mr. X probably would finally agree and make an appointment for them to meet in Mexico City. So Rico goes back to your car."

Tod threw a quick look at his friend. "But you wouldn't think he'd care to ride over the mountains with me, would you?"

"Probably he didn't intend to. Probably he was merely sleeping in your car with the idea of picking up a ride in the morning. But you got out of jail unexpectedly. You came back to the car. What is there for him to do but go with you? Especially until he can get those letters from under the seat. Was there time for him to do this while you went into the Casa Grande to pay your bill?"

"I don't think so. When I came out Mrs. Whipple was talking to him."

Jarvis shrugged. "It's of little importance, anyway. Rico is more than willing to be taken to the city that night, for he figures he can get hold of the papers once you reach your destination. One letter, though, he must have put in his pocket. I mean the letter to Juan Tomaso. That letter has disappeared. Of course to Rico that was the most important of the lot because it pointed to the guilt of the *politico* who had cheated his father years ago."

"It's plain now," Tod said, "what happened at the Montezuma Inn. Mr. X opens the brief case and discovers he's been tricked. But how does he know it is Rico who tricked him?"

"Probably he doesn't. He may think you are the one, though he can't be sure. He goes to Rico's room, and the boy's answers make him suspicious. They fight. You know what happened after that."

"Yes, but what about those letters, Captain Tom? Who sealed them? Rico?"

"That's a point we can't yet be sure of. Though I believe, as I told you, it was Rico—in Valles. Probably Mr. X, when he gets to his room at the inn, opens the brief case, takes out the package of documents, and finds nothing but a newspaper inside. Perhaps he did not try to slit open the envelopes, for the documents, after all, are what he wants. With the documents he figures he can delay the investigation until he's made a quick get-away—if it becomes necessary. Perhaps he believes he can still engineer his plan to have Blakemore sell the mine at a loss—and he'd still be able to pocket a nice share for his work. This is mere supposition, of course. But it explains Mr. X's actions. It explains the attack on Rico at the inn. It explains why the brief case was thrown into the Buick's trunk and left there as worthless."

Tod slowly shook his head. "I can't quite see your pattern yet, Captain Tom. It's not yet clear."

"Of course it isn't." Jarvis chuckled. "There are too many facts still missing. I need every strand to weave that pattern into shape. But with luck we should get those facts today—when we arrive in Tasco."

They stopped for lunch in Cuernavaca, then sped on down a road that descended for miles until they came to Tasco in midafternoon. The little town was perched on the side of a mountain, its cobbled streets winding and steep.

"You'd never think we were in the Americas," Jarvis remarked as they parked before the Hotel Tasqueño. "This is like a village in Spain. Market place, red-tiled roofs, burros, chickens—it has all the atmosphere of an Old-World town."

Journey's End

Martin Welch, they learned from the hotel owner, was a well-known resident of Tasco. They wished to go to his home? Then they must walk. No automobiles could make the sharp turns necessary in getting there.

"Is Welch home from the States yet?" Jarvis asked.

Yes, he had returned three days before. But he would probably now be out at the mine, several miles away. No, they could not phone. There were no telephones in Tasco.

"We'll walk up to his house and see," Jarvis said to Tod. "Come on."

The narrow winding street ascended sharply past a market place where Indians displayed their wares in stalls—woven baskets, soft woolen ponchos and serapes, pottery painted with primitive designs, fruits and vegetables carried in from the surrounding valleys. Captain Jarvis and Tod climbed a stone stairway to a street high above, and here the cobbles underfoot were laid in designs. Through open doorways they could see silversmiths bending over their intricate work, and from the kitchens of the homes in the rear came the slap-slap of tortilla makers and the enticing odor of chili boiling over a fire. They plodded on past a fountain where a woman was dipping up water in a jug, and still climbing, finally came to the house pointed out to them as Martin Welch's.

At a wooden door in a whitewashed wall, Tod pulled a bell cord. After a long interval the door was opened by a native woman. Señor Welch? Yes, he was in. She ushered them through a tropical garden and into a dim cool room filled with old Spanish furniture. Almost at once a door opened and Martin Welch came in.

He appeared the same as Tod had remembered—short and heavily built, his face florid, his hair thin almost to baldness. He wore a white linen suit and a dark blue tie. "You didn't send in your name," he began, then his eyes lighted up. "Captain Jarvis?"

"Yes. This is my friend, Tod Moran."

Martin Welch was all eagerness. He pulled out chairs; he clapped his hands and ordered iced drinks; he insisted their luggage must be brought from the hotel at once. Tod kept silent. He didn't intend to allow Welch's apparent friendliness to throw them off the track.

"I have been expecting you, Captain. When Mr. Blakemore said he was sending you down here I immediately wired the mine to give you every assistance, to have you stay here as my guest. But finally I thought I'd better come back myself, so I cut short my visit and took a plane down. Arrived three days ago."

"You still feel that Blakemore should sell?"

"Oh, absolutely. No doubt about it." Welch crossed his hands over his paunch and leaned back in his chair. "It is impossible for foreign capital to stay here longer. Why, the government is demanding that we build a hospital for our workers, that we even build a school for their children. It's outrageous."

Journey's End

"You advised Jim Blakemore against doing that?"

"Certainly."

"Yet you could do that much for your workers and still make a profit, couldn't you?"

"Not the profits we've been making, Captain Jarvis. The present government of Mexico is, unfortunately, not like the old ones."

"Do you mean," Jarvis asked, "it is unfortunate for Mexico?"

"No, indeed." Welch sat up. "Unfortunate for the foreign interests."

Jarvis smiled. "A government should represent its own people, don't you think, Welch?"

Welch almost squirmed. "Nevertheless, Captain Jarvis, the present administration asks altogether too much."

"Probably you're right," Jarvis agreed. "But isn't it a matter of chickens come home to roost? Foreign interests for years have bled this country white, taking immense profits, paying wages hardly better than those given to slaves. And now when a responsible government comes into power, it isn't surprising if it calls a halt too soon, if it oversteps, if it makes demands that seem to you outrageous. We Americans, Welch, have only ourselves to blame."

"Yes, I suppose you're right." Welch looked suddenly over his shoulder as a door opened. "Come in, Doctor Briggs. I want you to meet some friends."

Tod's eyes widened. Behind Doctor Briggs's tall form another figure was visible.

Highroad To Adventure

Welch's voice reached his ears from a far distance. "Captain Jarvis—Mr. Moran. I want to present Doctor Briggs, a guest of my assistant manager. Come in, Jim. My assistant manager, gentlemen—Mr. Rickman."

Tod sprang from his chair. The assistant manager, hesitating there in the open doorway, his face suddenly drained of color, was Jim Foster of the Montezuma Inn.

CHAPTER XX

Explanations

"Do you know this man, Tod?" Jarvis' tone was sharp. "Is he our Mr X?"

"Yes. You were right. Up at the inn he called himself Jim Foster."

Martin Welch interrupted. "What are you talking about? Jim is my assistant manager."

"I fear he won't be your assistant much longer," Jarvis snapped. "He has many things to explain."

"Rot!" The assistant manager had regained his composure. His blond head went up. His eyes flashed. "The doctor and I are just leaving on a fishing trip."

Doctor Briggs fingered the hat in his hand. His voice was low as he spoke to Martin Welch. "I had a hunch this two-name business was phony. His insistence, too, that we fish near Tasco instead of Jacala as we'd first agreed." He took a step toward the door. "Perhaps I'd better go."

"One moment." Jarvis raised his hand. "Would you mind telling me where you met this man?"

Dr. Briggs swung about. "At the Hamilton Hotel in Laredo. We had a few drinks together. We met again at the Montezuma Inn."

"Then you know nothing much about him?"

Dr. Briggs shrugged. "Evidently not." He turned to the man in the doorway. "I'll travel on, Rickman. Sorry." With a quick nod to the others, he let himself out the door into the garden.

Jim Rickman started to follow. "Be right back," he said.

"No, you don't!" In a stride Jarvis reached the door and blocked the exit. "We have certain matters to discuss."

Martin Welch threw out a hand in a helpless gesture. "But I don't understand, Captain Jarvis."

"You will—in a moment."

It was Jarvis, Tod saw, who now took charge. In a manner so compelling that even Jim Rickman obeyed, the big man motioned them into chairs. "Welch, you have placed complete confidence in your assistant manager?"

"Of course. Always. He's been with me for nearly five years. Why, he's handled this affair of selling the mine."

"Oh, he has! And whom did he advise selling to?"

"To a Mexican company."

"Was their offer a good one?"

"I wouldn't call it exactly that. It would have meant quite a loss to the present owners."

Tod's gaze had turned with interest upon Jim Rickman. Could this be the man, he asked himself, who had played the part of Mr. X? It was hard to believe. For Jim Rickman, at least outwardly calm, sat back in his seat with an air of impatient boredom. Yet his pale eyes were slightly narrowed, and once or twice he raised a hand to stroke his light curly hair. Although he might be in a tight place, he nevertheless gave no sign of fear.

"Tell me, Welch," Jarvis was saying, "how your assistant knew that Moran was bringing me copies of those business negotiations to look over."

"Why, I wired Rickman, Captain Jarvis. I sent him a night letter saying Moran was driving down with the papers and would meet you in the city. I wanted him to assist you in every way."

"Blakemore told you we were coming? It was foolish of him."

A slow flush spread up Welch's cheeks. "Perhaps Mr. Blakemore trusts me, Captain Jarvis."

"I am glad that trust wasn't misplaced," Jarvis conceded. "Though it appears your judgment of men is not quite as good as Blakemore's. '

Rickman cut in. "There is nothing to explain, Martin.

[277]

I was only doing what I felt was best for Mr. Blake-more's interest. I thought he should sell this mine. I still think so."

"Don't interrupt, Jim." Welch frowned. "I am in charge of the mine and I intend to find out what you've been up to."

Rickman's tone was ingratiating. "There isn't anything to find out. These fellows have got me all wrong. Oh, I admit I was perhaps a little impetuous. But nothing more."

"Then please let me hear what Captain Jarvis and Mr. Moran have to say."

While Jarvis gave a brief outline of the events which had occurred along the Pan-American Highway, Tod kept his gaze on Rickman. Twice the assistant manager tried to interrupt. It was Jarvis who stopped him the first time. And the second time, it was Welch's grim face that made Rickman's words of protest die on his lips.

"But surely," Welch said toward the end, "my assistant had nothing to do with this murder of Juan Tomaso."

"I don't know," Jarvis admitted. "Have you, Mr. Welch, ever heard of Tomaso before?"

"Why, yes. He headed the company that wants to buy the mine."

"Up to his old tricks again, I see."

"What do you mean, Captain Jarvis?"

"Juan Tomaso engineered Blakemore's buying the property in the first place. It seems he wanted to make another clean-up."

Explanations

Somewhere in the rear of the house a bell sounded. "We must have a visitor at the gate," Rickman said, rising. "I'll see who it is."

"Sit down!" Jarvis commanded. "I prefer you to stay in this room."

Mr. Rickman subsided, and a moment later Tod heard a door open. "Mercedes is going," Welch explained.

Tod paid no attention to the words flying back and forth between Jarvis and the manager. His ears were strained to hear the murmur of voices outside. All at once a familiar intonation brought him to his feet. Eagerly he crossed to the door and threw it open.

"It's Rico, Captain Tom. Shall I ask him in?"

"By all means. He'll help us to get to the bottom of this affair."

Tod stepped out into the garden path. "Rico," he called. "Come here."

The boy stepped past Mercedes and came rapidly up the flagstone path. "Ah, Mr. Moran! I'm glad you're here." He threw a furtive glance over his bandaged shoulder as he adjusted his arm in the sling. "They're after me. They're following!"

"Who's following?"

"The police! They'll be here—any minute!"

"Come inside." Tod motioned toward the door. "Captain Jarvis is here. Tell him."

Rico's mouth twitched with emotion. He hurried inside, stopped short when he saw the three men seated

[279]

there, and then went up to the assistant manager. "You've got to help me, Mr. Rickman. The police—they're after me. They think Pedro or I murdered Juan Tomaso."

There was no hint of sympathy in Rickman's tone. "Well, maybe you did. You Mexicans are always throwing knives. It's a national accomplishment, isn't it?"

For a moment Rico looked around helplessly, an expression of defeat in his somber eyes; then, seeing Tod's empty chair, he slumped into it, and his hand came up to his face.

"I'm sorry, Rico." Captain Jarvis spoke in a tone that conveyed the depth of his feeling. "It's we Americans who are to blame for this. We brought all this trouble on you—by our actions years ago. You thought you were avenging your father, I suppose."

Rico raised his head. His eyes were misty. "We didn't murder anyone, Captain Jarvis. We only wanted to make sure Tomaso lost his position with the government."

"We? Who is this Pedro you mentioned?"

"My brother. Both of us are White-caps."

"So your brother is the White-cap who drove the Buick from the Montezuma Inn?"

"Yes, sir." Rico's breath came fast. "The police arrested him early this morning. Now they're after me."

"You came here by bus?"

"Yes, sir. I wanted to see Mr. Rickman."

Tod remained standing by the door. Everyone in the room, he saw, was listening to the boy's words with profound interest. Even Rickman. Yet there was almost a smile of satisfaction on the man's lips. Why, Tod wondered, should Rickman feel pleased by all this?

"What made the police pick up your brother?" Jarvis questioned.

"They found my official cap near the spot where Tomaso was struck down. It was lying on the grass. It had my license number on it. They checked up on the number and learned who owned it."

"Then why arrest your brother?"

Rico rubbed his hands nervously together. "I'd better tell you everything, Captain Jarvis. You see, when I left Mrs. Whipple last night I went straight home. Pedro was there; he'd just got in. He insisted that I go to the Shirley Courts and get—my sombrero and poncho."

"Don't lie, Rico." Jarvis' deep voice was stern. "This is no time for anything but the truth. You mean your brother insisted you try to get those letters from under the seat."

Rico gave a sudden start. "Yes, sir," he finally admitted. "That's it. I told him I would try, but I was sure the Ford would be locked. When I started out, Pedro threw me his cap because my head was bare. That was what got Pedro into trouble. When the police came for me and searched our room, Pedro's cap couldn't be found, so they decided he'd borrowed mine and lost it on the grass where Señor Tomaso had been—stabbed."

"Then they're not at all sure who did it. But, Rico,

how did you learn all this without getting arrested yourself?"

"My landlady told me. When the police took Pedro to jail, they left one man at the door to bring me in when I showed up. The landlady sneaked out the back way and went to a corner to wait for me. She warned me not to go home. Oh, she's a good friend to me and Pedro. She even took me to a neighbor's house to dress my shoulder. But it's lots better. It'll be all right in no time."

"Did she ask you how you'd got that knife wound?"

"Yes, but I wouldn't tell her. I guess I deserved it, all right. Mr. Rickman's got a hot temper."

"Evidently. So he's the one you had a fight with at the Montezuma Inn?"

"Yes. He came into my room and demanded everything that had been in the brief case. I told him I'd thrown them away—into the river where no one would find them. He came at me then, but I drew my knife. He got it away from me."

A grunt of disgust came from Rickman's lips. "The fool's making up a story for your benefit, Captain Jarvis. Don't believe a word he says."

Jarvis paid no attention to the interruption. "Go on, Rico. Where was your brother during this fight?"

"Asleep. It was raining and he didn't know Mr. Moran and I had come. He didn't know anything about it until it was all over. In the morning when he came into my room I gave him the letter."

Explanations

"What letter?"

"The one Mr. Blakemore wrote to Juan Tomaso. It was just what we wanted. It showed us that Tomaso had cheated not only our father but Mr. Blakemore, too."

"Some people wouldn't call it cheating," Jarvis observed. "It was a business proposition."

Rico threw out his hand. "Call it anything you like, but to me it was worse than cheating. That was why I had kept out the letter. I hadn't put it with the rest under the seat of the car. Then the police found it in Pedro's pocket. They said it connected him with the crime. It looks bad for Pedro."

"Your brother is certainly in a tough spot, all right." Jarvis regarded the boy thoughtfully. "Don't you think perhaps he is guilty? If it wasn't you who did it—and I know you were still riding in the Ford at the time the crime took place—then don't you think it might have been your brother?"

Rico met the older man's glance with an agonized expression. "I'm not sure, Captain Jarvis. Pedro says he didn't—but I don't know. I don't know what to think. He promised me in Valles he wouldn't do anything—anything like that."

"Then you were the one who got that brief case from the Casa Grande in Valles?"

"No, Captain Jarvis. It was Pedro. I was outside watching near the Ford." Rico paused and lifted his head. "I might as well tell you everything. I went with

[283]

Mr. Rickman north to Laredo. Oh, we've worked together for a long time. But he never knew why I was
so interested in the affairs of the mine. I wanted to be
his friend—and he thought I was."

"And your brother? Did he go along, too?"

"No. But I had told him what I suspected. Oh, I had
done little jobs for Mr. Rickman before, and this time
I had even seen the wire Mr. Welch sent from San
Francisco. Mr. Rickman had laughed. He said Mr. Welch
was a fool to be asking him to show every courtesy to
two men who were coming to investigate this deal."

Martin Welch sprang to his feet with a muttered oath,
but Jarvis cut him short. "Sit down, Welch. Please don't
interrupt. Go on, Rico. Where did you meet your
brother?"

"At the Hotel Condesa in Valles. That was where Mr.
Rickman decided I must try to get a ride with Mr. Moran
in his car. That was where Pedro joined Mr. Rickman
in the Buick."

"So you left your official cap there in Valles?"

"Yes, in the hotel room where I changed my clothes."

Jarvis' tone was sharp. "You say you changed your
clothes? Do you mean you took off the suit you were
wearing?"

"Yes, sir. A thin white suit. The kind all of us White-
caps wear."

"Then what became of this suit of yours?"

"I don't know. Mr. Rickman gave me one of his own

to put on. We didn't want Mr. Moran to think I was a tourist guide. We thought maybe he'd seen my white outfit when the Buick passed him and we didn't want him to get suspicious."

"Then this is Rickman's suit you are wearing."

"Yes. I haven't had a chance to get back my own."

"And there's one button missing from the coat, isn't there?"

"Why, yes." Rico touched the white cloth which was draped round one shoulder for a sling. "You can't see the place now, though. It's under the arm sling."

Jarvis turned to Rickman. "So you were the man who entered Moran's room in Monterrey!"

Rickman's lips curled in scorn. "Don't be foolish. I don't know what you're talking about."

"No matter." The big captain turned back to Rico. "Listen, my boy. Would your brother be apt to wear your cap and leave it at the scene of the crime—leave it so you'd be arrested?"

"Pedro?" Rico's dark eyes flashed. "Never, Captain Jarvis. Not Pedro! If he lost it there, he lost it in running away. You see, someone saw him."

"Yes, someone saw him." Jarvis got to his feet and took a step across the room. Suddenly he swung about. "What you mean, Rico, is that a passer-by saw a White-cap running across the grass. It was dark, you know. How could anyone tell for certain who that White-cap was? Now, I wonder." His gaze swept across to the assistant manager. "Stand up! Let me see how tall you are."

Rickman did not move. "What's that got to do with this affair?"

In Jarvis' deep voice was the unmistakable ring of authority. "Stand up, I tell you!"

With reluctance the man obeyed.

Rico leaned forward. "We're about the same size, Captain Jarvis. I'm wearing his suit, and it's a pretty good fit."

Jarvis nodded slowly. "Then your white suit would be a pretty good fit for Rickman."

"But surely," Martin Welch remonstrated, "you don't mean that my assistant killed Juan Tomaso!"

"I'm not sure. I don't yet see a motive, but neither can I believe that Rico's brother wore that cap and lost it. I have the feeling that the cap was deliberately left there at the scene of the crime—left there to throw suspicion upon an innocent person."

Tod's gaze left Jarvis and crossed to Rickman. The man sat down abruptly in his chair, but his chin was up and his eyes bright. "You're talking sheer nonsense, Captain Jarvis! You're using an active imagination without a shred of proof to back you up."

"Oh, yes, I've proof—and I'll soon have more. The pattern is taking shape. For the first time every fact is beginning to fit into its proper place. Yes, even Rico's white uniform. Probably in Valles you stuffed that suit and cap into one of your bags. Did you have those bags last night at the Ritz Hotel?"

When the man merely glowered in silence, Rico struck in, "He had them, all right. His luggage was in the Buick, but the first thing my brother did when he got to town was to go to the Ritz with those bags for Mr. Rickman. Pedro must have forgotten all about my suit and cap."

Jarvis caught up this information with an eager nod. "Then Rickman could have worn your uniform. Now, if only I could find a motive! Why should he want to get rid of Tomaso?"

"They had an awful argument last night," cried Rico.

"An argument? Did they quarrel? How do you know all this?"

"Pedro told me."

The boy's story, as brought forth by Jarvis, was straightforward. Rico's brother had found upon his arrival at the Ritz that Rickman was about to go out. The man had canceled the taxi he had ordered and told Pedro to drive him to the Hotel Luxor. At the Luxor he told Pedro to wait. Almost immediately, however, Rickman came out with Juan Tomaso; for it appeared that Tomaso had an appointment to keep, even though Rickman urged him to put it off. Both men stepped into the Buick, and Pedro was told to drive out the Reforma to an apartment house near Chapultepec Park. All the way out the boulevard Pedro heard them arguing in low tones. He heard enough to inform him that Tomaso wanted to withdraw his offer to buy the mine. When Rickman insisted upon going through with the agreement, Tomaso in a fury threatened to tell Martin Welch what his assistant manager was up to. They had ridden the last quarter of a mile in silence. At the apartment house Tomaso got out without a word of farewell. Rickman, in a voice of suppressed anger, ordered Pedro to take him back to the Ritz, and then put the Buick in a garage. That was all Rico knew.

"That's plenty," said Jarvis. He flashed a deep look toward Rickman. "So you felt you did have a reason to silence Tomaso!"

Rickman spoke with controlled emphasis. "I had no reason at all. You can't prove a single thing."

"Don't be too sure." Jarvis lifted his head, listening. A bell was sounding in the rear of the house.

Rico leaped up. "Maybe it's the police!" His face was distraught with terror. "They'll arrest me, Captain Jarvis! They'll charge me with murder."

Jarvis spoke rapidly. "Welch, don't let your servant open the gate. Perhaps you'd better go yourself. If it's the police, hold them off for a few minutes. I've still got some questions to be answered."

Even while Martin Welch was going out the door Jarvis pressed on with his inquiry. "Rico, you told me that when you changed your clothes in that hotel in Valles, you didn't remember what became of your white suit. Think back. Don't you remember?"

Explanations

"I'm sorry." Rico shook his head. "Is it important?"

"Very. For if Rickman stuffed your suit and cap into one of his bags, then your brother might have carried them both to Rickman's room at the Ritz. Don't you see where that gets us? Rickman returns to his room, beside himself with anger. Tomaso has refused to go through with the deal because he's suddenly afraid—afraid because he has received a note from Mr. Blake-more saying I'm on my way to investigate. Shall Rickman see his plans destroyed? Not only that, Tomaso has also threatened to tell Welch. And that would mean the end of Rickman. He'd be finished. Then in his room Rickman opens the bags—and sees your white suit and cap. At once a new plan leaps into his brain. He'll put on your outfit, leave his hotel by a rear door, and wait at the apartment for Tomaso to come out. He doesn't shoot as you might expect him to. No. He must make this crime appear to be the work of a Mexican. So he uses a knife, drops the white cap so it will be found, and gets safely back to his hotel again."

"Utter rot!" Rickman could not quite keep a tremor from his voice. "You're using your fancy again, Captain Jarvis. You haven't one single fact as proof."

"Don't be too sure of that." Jarvis' glance moved to the door. "Where's Welch?"

"He hasn't come back from the gate yet," Tod answered. "Shall I call him?"

"Please."

Highroad To Adventure

Tod swung the door open. Martin Welch was already coming up the garden path. "It was the police, all right," he whispered. "They'll give us exactly five minutes. Is Jarvis finished?"

Tod shook his head. "He wants to ask you something."

As soon as Welch entered the room Jarvis put his question. "Welch, is Rickman's luggage here?"

"Why, I'm not sure. A boy brought his bags up from the car. Jim was packing again for his fishing trip. Is it here still, Jim?"

Suspicion blazed in Rickman's eyes. "What do you want to know for, Captain Jarvis?"

"I'd like to look into those traveling bags," Jarvis answered. "I'd like to see whether you've had a chance to get rid of Rico's white suit. Is it in one of your bags, Rickman? Did you intend to bury it somewhere when you and Doctor Briggs were out on your fishing trip?"

Rickman's hands closed round the arms of his chair. His voice was low. "My bags were in Doctor Briggs' Packard. I don't know where they are now."

"Just the same, suppose we take a look. Rickman has a room here, Mr Welch?"

"Of course. He lives here. I'll go to his room."

"Oh, no, you don't!" Rickman was out of his chair in an instant. "You leave my things alone!"

"Oh, so you're worried, are you?" Jarvis challenged. "You only make me more eager to see what's in your luggage."

Explanations

Rickman took a step toward the door leading to the rear hallway. "Leave my things alone, Martin."

Martin Welch waved him aside. "We'll settle these charges right now. Please step aside."

Tod waited, one hand on the back of Rico's chair. Not a word was said as Welch went out. Jarvis kept his gaze fastened upon Jim Rickman, and Rickman himself flashed a quick look around the room as though seeking escape. Finally he threw up his head, and his lips curled in scorn. "Quite a nice little theory you've brought forth, Captain Jarvis. But the whole build-up is false. It's clear as crystal that Rico is the one who's guilty."

"I fear you can't make out a case against him," Jarvis retorted. "Rico happened to be riding in the Ford at the very moment the crime was committed. There's a witness to prove it!"

"Then it's his brother who is guilty!"

"We shall see." Jarvis' glance moved to the hallway as Welch appeared with two leather handbags. "Open them, Welch. I suppose they are both locked."

Martin Welch set them down on the floor and, stooping with difficulty, unfastened the straps of one. "This isn't locked." He reached in and brought out a dark woolen shirt, several pairs of socks, and some underwear. "No white suit here, Captain Jarvis."

"Try the other bag. A suit like the one we want wouldn't take up much space."

The second bag disclosed no white suit, either. "We could search his room," Welch suggested.

"No. He wouldn't hide that suit in his room. If it isn't in his luggage he's already got rid of it. But how? He must have been with Doctor Briggs. I feel sure he was planning to dispose of it on this fishing trip."

Rickman sat down in his chair. Tod, watching him closely, fancied he saw relief on the man's set face. There was a hint of a smile, too, at the corners of his mouth.

Jarvis looked at Welch. "Anything else besides these bags?"

"Just some fishing equipment on the floor."

"Do you mind bringing it here?"

Welch struggled to his feet and again disappeared down the hallway to the bedroom. When he came back he let fall to the floor a wicker fishing basket, a pair of high rubber boots, and a fishing rod in its canvas case. "That's all. Nothing there."

"Open the basket, will you, Welch?"

Tod suddenly sprang forward. The two boots had fallen to the floor, one over the other. He picked up one and thrust his hand inside. With a cry of triumph he brought out a tightly rolled pair of white trousers.

"Those are mine!" Rico cried.

Tod caught up the second boot. A tightly wadded coat came out, badly wrinkled. As he spread it out, a long knife rolled to the floor. Its blade was brown with stain, and on one sleeve of the white coat another brown stain was visible.

Explanations

A sudden rising clamor of voices filled the room. Rickman had sprung for the hallway and was fast disappearing toward the rear of the house.

"Wait, Captain Jarvis." Welch raised his hand. "He can't get away. The police have surrounded the house. I told them to let no one leave—no one!"

Rico stepped forward and caught up his coat. "But this will go against me, won't it? How can I prove I didn't do it—when my coat has blood stains on the sleeve?"

Outside a whistle shrilled. Voices rose. Someone shouted.

"They've got him, all right," Jarvis announced. "Don't you worry, Rico. You've got plenty of witnesses. I'll promise you that the Blakemore Company will see this thing through. And I'll recommend a little American coöperation on Blakemore's part. We'll see about keeping the mine and carrying out at the same time those demands of your government. We'll see, too, that you and your family are satisfied. From now on, all of us are going to be friends."

CHAPTER XXI

The Broad Highway

THEY were tramping up the highway in the gathering dusk, Jarvis with long easy strides, Tod doing his best to keep step with his friend. It was two evenings later and they were somewhere between Tasco and Cuernavaca.

"I think there's a truck coming," Jarvis said hopefully.

"What good will that do us?" Tod retorted. "We want someone to come up behind and take us into Cuernavaca. Then maybe we could hire a tow car to go back and bring in the Ford."

He glanced off to their right where a grove of pines sloped down a hillside to a stream. Far to the south the snowy crest of a volcano rose against the sky.

"It's a blue van, Joe Macaroni."

"A blue van?" Tod's weariness dropped away as his

[294]

gaze flashed up the pavement. "That's not a truck, Captain Tom. It's the Whipples with their trailer!" Stopping in his tracks, he waved his arms.

Down the highway toward them plunged the Chevrolet with its trailer in tow. With a grinding of brakes Ben Whipple brought his caravan to a halt.

"Maybe we oughtn't to stop, Ma," came Ben Whipple's voice. "They look like tough hombres—both of 'em."

Ma Whipple's little hat bobbed vigorously. "We never give hitch hikers a ride."

Tod hurried up to the car window. His voice was meek. "Not even a drink of ice water?"

"All right. Bring out that water you boiled this morning, Ma. It's still nice and warm."

"Maybe they're hungry, too, Paw."

"Hungry?" Jarvis came up behind Tod. "Did someone mention eats?"

Ma Whipple couldn't restrain herself any longer. She threw back her head and laughed till her plump body trembled. "Land sakes!" she finally gasped. "You both looked so funny!"

"Rico came round to the trailer camp this morning," Ben Whipple said. "He told us where you were. So we started right out for Tasco. Ma's just dying to know if all Rico said is really true." He craned out the window. "Where's that car of yourn, Frisco?"

"I'll tell you where it is." Jarvis raised a hand and

pointed up into the air. "See those three buzzards circling round up there? They're the only scavengers Mexico has, and so I suppose they are necessary. Just the same, I figure that by the time we get back to the spot where we left Tod's car, there won't be anything there but the bones."

"You didn't have an accident, did you?" demanded Ma Whipple.

Tod sighed. "No. The car just naturally sputtered and died right under us." His voice grew hopeful. "But we'll soon have her going again."

"Oh, sure," chimed in Jarvis. "She only needs a new battery and new spark plugs. Then her carburetor needs some adjustment, and I think her valves need grinding. Oh, sure! She'll soon be going again."

"How far you walked?" Ma Whipple asked, her voice warm with sympathy.

"Miles," said Tod.

"Leagues and knots and kilometers," added Jarvis.

Ma's voice rose sharply. "What you waiting for, Paw? Draw off there into that clearing. I'll have supper ready in no time. We've two big steaks in the ice box." She lowered her tone as her gaze turned to Tod. "Before we left Mexico City this morning I baked you a three-layer chocolate cake."

"Chocolate cake!" Jarvis' deep tones rang out in jubilation.

"It melts in your mouth," Tod cried. "And if you

eat less than three slices you insult Ma Whipple."

"Sufferin' catfish! I already feel cheered considerable."

They cheered up considerably more when Ma spread her food on the little table in the trailer. Steaks, whisked from the broiler and served on warm plates piled high with brown fried potatoes, sent forth such appetizing odors that Tod even forgot for the moment that there was chocolate cake for dessert. Ben Whipple reached over and turned up the oil lamp. Outside, the shadows deepened.

On the edge of the clearing a cottontail crept out from the underbrush and sat up, his ears pointed, his nostrils quivering. Laughter floated toward him from the trailer. Yellow light slanted across the turf. Overhead, in the luminous blue of the sky, stars came out one by one. Suddenly an automobile roared down the highway and passed with gleaming headlights. Startled, the cottontail scampered back into the brush.

No one in the trailer, however, noticed the car or the speed at which it passed. For they were no longer in a hurry. Only the broad highway lay before them—and what promised to be a leisurely trip home.